SECRET OF Souls

THE AGE OF ENDINGS BOOK 1

AUBRIE NIXON

Shadow Wolf Press
Las Vegas, Nevada

CONNECT WITH AUBRIE

Social Media handle: Aubriewrites

Website: aubrienixon.com

SECRET OF SOULS

THE AGE OF ENDINGS BOOK 1

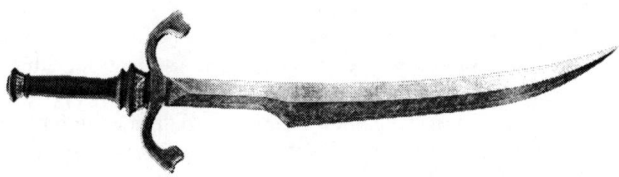

AUBRIE NIXON

First Edition

Library of Congress Control Number: 2017946009

ISBN: 978-0-9885851-5-7

Books may be purchased by contacting the publisher and author at:

Shadow Wolf Press
8635 West Sahara Avenue, #425
Las Vegas, NV 89117
www.ShadowWolfPress.com
Info@ShadowWolfPress.com

Cover art by Andreea Vraciu
Interior formatting by Clark Kenyon

Cover design © 2017 by Shadow Wolf Press
Cover art and Chapter art © 2017 by Shadow Wolf Press

For my fellow black-hearted minions of darkness: you are not alone.
We are many.

CHAPER 1

The light from the moon was unnervingly full and bright, with a strange blue tint that kissed the air around it. There were no stars to be seen. The creature Zephera hunted bowed its head to drink from the lake, unaware that anyone watched it. It was a majestic black stag with antlers white enough to rival freshly fallen snow. She took in her surroundings from the trees where she lurked, narrowing her eyes at the large clearing her prey occupied. She was reminded again of how impersonal the weapon was as she unsheathed an arrow, holding it steady on her bow. Truthfully, she wasn't good at ranged combat, but what she lacked in skill with the bow, she made up for tenfold with her hands and her blades. She sighed, frustrated with the weapon in her hands. Hunting a special stag? She had been irritated with her master when he had assigned her this mission. She was an assassin, not a huntress. Zephera inhaled deeply, whispering a quick prayer to Taeon, the god of the hunt, that she wouldn't miss. The prayer wasn't uttered in loyalty to the deity; instead, she used it to steady her breath and still her hands. She held the arrow steady on the bow, then fired.

The stag let out an unearthly sound as the arrow grazed its powerful leg, wounding it slightly. Zephera cursed under her breath. The beautiful creature began to shake violently. It screamed and swayed. Its once-pristine black fur tore apart and another creature emerged, ripping apart its host and discarding the remnants like a husk. This new beast's sleek, dark fur glistened in the moonlight. As it reared onto its hind legs, it stood twelve-feet tall, stretching claws the size of daggers into the night sky. Its new lupine face growled, sharp teeth clenched, baring black gums, red eyes searching the direction from where the shot had come. Terror seized Zephera. She couldn't get her legs to move. She could only stare at the newly transformed beast, her eyes wide with horror. What was this creature? She had never seen anything like it. The animal moved with dark grace—a predator on the hunt for its prey. Like a fly caught in a web, she could do nothing but breathe. The bow slipped from her hand. She cringed at the incriminating sound it made as it hit the ground.

The monster was a few feet from her hiding spot. Glancing around the brush, she assessed her surroundings. In thirty seconds the beast would be upon her. Zephera had to take it by surprise to get the upper hand.

She jumped out from behind the Mygylo bush, directly in front of her target. The monster growled in surprise and in that second she dragged her blade across the ground, sending handfuls of dirt into the beast's face and eyes. It thrashed, temporarily blinded from the dirt. The beast swiped at Zephera with its massive paw, narrowly missing her face and giving her the opening she had been waiting for. She lunged at its side, as high as she could reach, leaving a shallow cut just below its rib cage. A paw came crashing down as she parried, catching her blade. The force would've broken her arm, but she let go just in time. The creature rested its paw on the weapon, using its other paw to cover the freshly exposed flesh on its side. The wound was superficial, but it had served its purpose. The creature's head was now within reach.

Zephera darted away, but quickly doubled back and charged straight at the beast. Using a log for leverage, she vaulted, landing on the beast's shoulders. It immediately tried to buck her off, but before it could reach up and grab her, she unsheathed a second blade and drove it directly into the beast's eye—the one spot vulnerable enough to deliver the killing blow. The curve of the weapon guided the blade directly into the brain: blood sprayed from the wound into Zephera's face. She choked back a scream as it coated the inside of her mouth. She spit the blood onto the ground, gagging at the taste of rotten milk and coppery death. The beast howled, its back arching violently and tossing her high into the air. Then it came crashing and tumbling to a halt against the very same log she had used just moments ago.

Zephera laughed as she stood up, sheathing her weapons. It was a hollow sort of laugh, one originating from fear and adrenaline rather than amusement. She let out a breath as the echo faded, sitting down near the dead beast. The air smelled of fresh death. The moon shone down on her long, raven hair and porcelain face, both of which were covered in black blood, making her look like a dangerous and deadly monster herself. Closing her dark eyes, which were filled with flecks of blue and gold, she leaned against the slain beast.

"I shall call you Latiff, gentle giant," she said playfully to the corpse beside her. She laughed again. Her voice was hoarse, her legs ached, and her arms were worn out. She had been hunting the stag for a fortnight. Her mission was to kill it and bring it back to Baleem, her master. The creature's organs were to be harvested and were said to have wondrous powers. This creature, however, was no stag. Had her master known that?

A light wisp of air teased her. She brushed her stinging face with her fingertips and stared as red blood stained them. She hadn't even noticed she had been injured. As she examined the gash with her index finger, she peeled the skin apart, causing more blood to pour from the wound. It was deep enough it would probably leave a scar.

"Ugh," she groaned, cringing at the pain. Now she needed stitches, along with a bath and a proper meal.

Getting up slowly, Zephera stretched her arms high above her head and rolled her neck in a slow circle. Breathing deeply, she began to make a large fire in which to burn the body after she harvested what she needed. She felt a pang of excitement as she watched the fire grow. Would the creature have familiar anatomy? She smiled as she prepared the cloth dressings and bags she would need. The feel of her fingers between her prey's flesh was exhilarating and she welcomed the opportunity to learn more of the mysterious creature she had just killed.

Not having the time or the energy to clean the body the proper way, she opted for the quicker, messier route. She grabbed her dagger and curved blade and then began cutting into the fresh carcass. The tough flesh was difficult to pierce, but eventually she was able to cut it away enough to pry apart the skin and muscle, revealing a cave of dark blood, organs, and bone. Zephera stifled a gag at the smell. Her eyes widened with excitement as she cut out its heart, followed by the liver and other essential organs. She lifted them carefully onto a cloth, wrapping each in layers of protective dressings. After she was finished with the organs, she sawed through the neck, spraying herself and everything around her in a thick layer of black blood. She grinned as she continued cutting through the thick flesh and muscle. The sound of fraying tendons filled the air.

She ripped the head, along with its remaining tendons, from the body and threw it onto a linen cloth, letting the rest of the blood empty. Then she coated the body of the creature with a green, flammable liquid known as Inarcate. Grabbing a large stick from the fire, she threw it onto the body of the beast. Flames instantly engulfed it, rapidly filling the air with the stench of burning flesh. The dark rot from the mysterious creature combined with the tangible scent of singed fur was almost too much to bear.

Looking down at her ruined leathers, she hissed and undressed, tossing them into the fire. She walked in the moonlight towards the lake and got in. Blood and dirt flaked off as she scrubbed. Floating on her back, she let the water take her. It felt cool and wonderful against her skin. Her thoughts began to wander, something she rarely allowed. It was a small reward she gave herself after a kill. It made her feel more human, more vulnerable. Losing mental focus could be fatal in her line of work. For now, she needed this small piece of humanity. She needed to feel normal. She let her mind go numb and bob lightly along with her body. Before long, her mind grew dark and turned to thoughts of death and the strange, burnt corpse lying on the shore.

Death was easy, peaceful. Living was the cruel joke. It was a hard game, one she had played for many years. Yet death still frightened her. She was reminded of her own mortality every time she killed.

CHAPTER 1

Groaning deeply, she forced herself out of the cleansing water and made her way to the shore. She dressed in clean clothes from her bag and headed down the trail to the nearby town. She would find an inn and get some sleep. From there, she would catch a ride with a traveling merchant back to Illuminas. Her curiosity about the strange creature was stronger than her fear. She needed answers. In order for her to get those answers, she had to return to the Keep.

CHAPER 2

For three days, she rode in the back of a silk merchant's cart. Merchants normally paid her no mind, but the silk merchant wanted to talk, to get to know her. Vexed, she had almost cut his tongue from his mouth one night as he slept, just to shut him up. Instead, she used her swift fingers to flick the back of his head every time he spoke. Zephera smiled to herself as the merchant kept looking behind him in astonishment, not knowing the origin. Eventually, he stopped talking to avoid the sensation. Perhaps the merchant wouldn't speak again, even after they parted ways, due to his fear of the pain.

When they approached Illuminas' gates, she stopped to take in the exquisite sight of the city. The buildings were carved from the purest stone, but none of the architecture could compare to Mirrador Palace at its very center. It was ancient, designed by the King of Light in centuries past, and was made of the world's finest white marble and diamonds. A beacon of hope and of great power, the palace symbolized the city's dedication to the Light.

Shaking her head, Zephera changed her focus back and trudged towards the first part of the city: the Outer Ring. She smiled politely at the Servants of the Dead. Although the city was boisterous, the Outer Ring was filled with mausoleums and stone coffins. The city's poorest people lived inside the mausoleums with dead they had never known. In times past, there was limited room within the city walls, and the poorest of the rabble had lived like wild animals, with no roof over their heads.

But years ago, an agreement had been made: in exchange for the upkeep of the strange cemetery, the people were allowed to take up residence there as they pleased. Thus began the people's nickname of Servants of the Dead.

The entire economy of the Outer Ring thrived in the business of death. While Zephera specialized in ending life, the people here specialized in what happened after. The Outer Ring was full of mourners for hire. Zephera thought the position rather humorous and pointless. Funerals were often a grand affair, a celebration of one's life and status. Typically, the wealthier the deceased, the larger the coffin, and the need for more coffers. The wealthy were buried in the mausoleums. The coffins of the poor were chained to the cliffside to keep them out of the reach of wild dogs.

Zephera bowed her head to a woman crying and shrieking with grief. She stood to watch the woman's performance with a mix of awe and annoyance. She was a professional mourner charged to the funerals of the wealthy who couldn't spare tears on their dead. This woman's very livelihood was based on the Elite and their need to always remain composed. The woman, whose eyes were red and tired, stood from her performance and bowed. She was met with applause and cheers. The woman winked at Zephera, giving her a knowing wave.

Despite the smell of decaying bodies, the feral animals who wandered among the shacks and the hungry eyes of the people who lived there, this was Zephera's favorite part of the city. Most wished her a blessed day. It always amazed her that these people who had so little still took the time for such mundane pleasantries.

As she reached the wall that separated the outer city from the inner one, she fixed her leathers and pursed her lips. This part of the city called for poise and perfection. She passed women donning the latest fashions in boutiques with the finest cloths. Though the market here was lavish and beautiful, the people were not. These were the Elites—the wealthy residents of the city whose riches came from the slave trade and the lands they owned and rented to the farmers. Their colossal homes and horse-drawn carriages lined the cobblestone paths. The residents wore stern faces and scowls. It seemed a curse to Zephera; the Elites had all, but always desired more, never satisfied.

Beyond the shops and parks of the Elite, in the furthest corner of the city, lay a large tract of land. A secretive compound stood there, walled off from the prying eyes of the public. Known as The Keep, it was home of the Guild of the Great Warrior Baleem, Master of Arms. The existence of The Keep was famous throughout the kingdom. It was where their soldiers trained and their assassins lived. The people of the city were well acquainted with Baleem as he was the right hand of the King. He over-saw the darker matters that come with running a kingdom.

The hair on the back of her neck rose as she sensed someone following her. Not altering her stride, she took several wrong turns to see if the shadow, which trailed a few paces behind her, would disappear.

It did not.

She turned down a mostly-deserted street near the Keep and grabbed a dagger from the harness around her leg. Closing her eyes, she pictured the figure in her mind and honed in on its position. Whipping around, she threw the dagger to the place where the shadow should've been.

She opened her eyes as the dagger sailed through the air. She sucked in a breath as the figure caught the dagger and laughed. A long, gloved hand threw the dagger to the ground and swept off the hood which con-cealed its face.

"Welcome back, Zephera," said a young man with gorgeous gray-blue eyes and a lopsided grin. "I followed you for a mile before you noticed me. You're too distracted after a mission. It'll be your undoing, love." He chuckled as he ran his fingers through his shaggy blonde hair, and tight-ened the strap on his blue tunic.

"Zad!" Zephera snapped. She glared at the man in front of her. She had known Zad for six years. Though he was like family, the thought of actually killing him ran through her mind.

"You know, you're still the only one who calls me Zad. Everyone else just calls me Zadkiel."

"Zadkiel is such a ridiculous mouthful. It doesn't roll off the tongue quite as easily as Zad. Plus, what kind of name is Zadkiel anyway? Who names a child such a thing?" She laughed mockingly as she held her hand out for her dagger.

"A woman mad out of her mind, that's who." Zad chuckled, placing a gloved hand on her shoulder and giving it a squeeze.

She cocked her head and flashed a smile. "I'm sorry about the dagger, I thought—"

"—that I was going to kill you?" Zad interrupted. "Kidnap you? Sell you to the slavers?" He raised a mischievous eyebrow.

"I would've gutted you before you even laid a hand on me." She smiled wickedly.

"Always so violent, Beasty," he said, suppressing a laugh. She shot him a glare. She hated that nickname.

She threw the pack containing the severed head and wrapped organs at him. "I need to eat."

Grabbing the bag of organs from her he wrinkled his nose. "No antlers?"

"There were… complications." She wasn't sure how much to tell Zad just yet. She continued walking toward the Keep. "Where's Baleem?"

"The Lady of Death had *complications*?" he teased.

Zephera ignored the jab, eager to speak with Baleem. She raised her eyebrows, pursing her lips impatiently.

Zad cleared his throat. "He's at the stables with Elis. She's giving birth to the pups as we speak. I'm sure he'll be eager to hear what happened on your journey. You might, however, want to take a bath first. You reek."

He smirked, scrunching up his nose. She punched him in the arm and headed to her rooms.

After bathing and grabbing a quick meal from the kitchens, she walked to the stables. Baleem was there with Elis, his prized hound. Elis breathed heavily and lay exhausted as six black-and-white pups tugged at her teats. Baleem looked up as Zephera arrived, his dark skin glistening with sweat.

He was dressed in a light cotton tunic with deep green pants and his brown leather boots were coated with dirt and grime.

Zephera studied him carefully. He looked much older. She noted the deep shadows under his eyes and the way his beard was growing at odd angles. His dark brown eyes filled with warmth as she approached. Holding back a frown, Zephera purposely kept her face blank. She knew that he was adept at hiding his emotions. But so was she, and she had been trained to read the face of even the oldest and best of spies at a young age. Something was wrong…

"My girl, my Zephera! You've returned. I feared you wouldn't." He stood, patting her head softly, like he used to do when she was a child.

Zephera raised an eyebrow. Though Baleem's gesture was small, it conveyed his worry. She bit her lip. "Yes, but sir, there's something I need to tell you, about the stag…" She looked at her master. His face warped into confusion and something else she couldn't quite place—fear perhaps.

"I know. I sent a message with Jameson. He left a few days after you did, tracking your route, but he hasn't returned yet. He was supposed to send word when he had reached you. I assume from the look on your face that he never found you?"

"I haven't seen Jameson since before I left. What was he supposed to tell me?" She chose her words carefully, trying to assess the situation.

"I think you know, girl, and again, I apologize. There's much we need to discuss. Follow me," he said, as he picked a bit of straw from his tunic.

He led her across the grounds and into the Great Room. The room was a study in light and shadow. Stone ceilings towered overhead in pointed arches, supported by pillars ensconced in the walls. Stained glass windows shaped like teardrops pointed at the ceiling's apex, bleeding sunlight into the space by day and painting the floor with moonlight by night. The east wall was lined with books filled with tales of heroes and mythical creatures. Opposite, images embroidered in gold thread danced gleefully across a black velvet tapestry which shrouded the entire west wall. It told the story of the War of Sorrows and the battle between the Lands of Somber and the Empire of Lucent. All knew the legend; mothers told it to their children at bedtime as a cautionary tale.

Long ago, two kings ruled the realm: Erro Sorrowhand of the western Lands of Somber and Gregour Lucent of the eastern Lucent Empire. Though the two kingdoms differed greatly, they managed to coexist and maintain the delicate balance between the righteous light of the east and sinful darkness of the west. Despite the realm's social renaissance, Erro Sorrowhand craved more power. He sent his lover, the Dark Priestess Malina, to infiltrate the Empire of Lucent. Her mission was to gain the trust of King Gregour and kill him. Instead, the two fell in love. Malina became pregnant with his child, and Gregour asked her to marry him.

When news of their marriage reached Erro, he erupted in dark fury. He sent his Warriors of Darkness to seize Gregour's lands in a brash attack on the Empire of Lucent. The armies of Erro ravaged the country of Nostorra, murdering and pillaging without mercy. They burned cities and villages until they reached the nation's capital, Illuminas. During the siege, Malina went into labor and died in childbirth.

Crushed by grief and confounded by the enemy at his beloved city's gates, Gregour reached deep into his heart. He flung aside all the layers of decency he had covered himself with and grabbed hold of an emotion locked away and festering at the core of his very soul: hatred. Using forbidden magic, he cast a spell that uprooted the Lands of Somber and sent them to another realm, forever severing the kingdom of darkness from the rest of the world.

Zephera loved the dark and daunting tale. As a child, she had begged Baleem to tell it to her again and again. Deep in the night, she would steal down to the Great Room and run her finger along the tapestry's gold threads, repeating the story to herself and filling in details with her imagination. She was sure there was more to the tale than what Baleem and the tapestry told. Now she shivered, staring at the tapestry and recalling the monstrous creature she had killed. She dragged her gaze from the images and turned her attention to the room.

Two lions carved out of marble stood as sentinels on each side of the fireplace. The heads of deer, bears, and leopards were mounted on the front wall. The chairs and furniture were made of the finest leathers, polished weekly to maintain their supple sheen. Her favorite piece was the large bear skin rug that covered the floor in front of the fireplace. On cold nights, when she was too restless to sleep, she would venture down to the room and lie on the rug and watch as the fire devoured the logs from within, making them glow with red scales.

She sighed and returned her attention to Baleem. He lowered himself into the chair closest to the fire and motioned for her to sit. He smiled at her, but it didn't quite reach his eyes. He let out a deep breath and looked at her intently.

"There are strange tales from beyond the city and throughout our world. The stories I've heard are troublesome and frightening, even for me." His voice held a raspy edge, and he paused, deep in thought.

"There are things in this world that are very powerful and very old," he continued. "Things that are coming. The world needs to be ready when they return. It's important that you trust no one—not even yourself, my darling girl. I've done things to get you here, to make you what you are. I feared I had lost you to one of the creatures of darkness this past week. Yet here you are, standing in front of me. You are truly remarkable. There are things I must tell you, things you must know. I'm sorry it's taken me this long." He closed his dark eyes and rubbed his temples.

"When I found you, you had been left out to die, and I knew I had been led to you. I'd had a dream, you see, of a child, thrown out and abandoned to perish in the cold of winter."

She knew this story well. Baleem reminded her often of her roots. She was from a city in the north called Rindow. Her parents had been disciples of the Light, zealots who followed their own interpretation of the Book of Clarity. They were cultists—superstitious and wary of anything different. She had been born with a small, dark mark on her forearm. Her parents took it as a sign that she was of the darkness. When she was only a few hours old, she had been taken to the woods and left to succumb to the elements.

CHAPTER 2

"You were such a small babe, quiet and lovely. Your eyes were bright and filled with life. I knew I had been led to you for a reason. An abandoned child raised into the life of a warrior—you've always been destined for greatness."

His eyes locked with hers. Suddenly, she felt a small sensation entirely foreign to her.

The monster she had killed—what was it? She thought back to her lessons on the people known as the Dark Ones. They hadn't been seen since King Amous had defeated them five hundred years ago. They had brought from their land creatures known as the Rot. These creatures spread sickness and pain throughout their world. Although it had been five hundred years since the end of the war, people still whispered about them, superstition making people afraid to say their names aloud. The gods had abandoned the world in those years and had yet to return. People still prayed to them, out of habit perhaps—or fear. Zephera prayed to them only out of curiosity. She had never received an answer. She knew they were gone. She had more faith in the Dark Ones than she did in the gods; they at least had power, even in their defeat. Their name alone could silence a room. Perhaps she should pray to the Dark Ones. Maybe then she would get an answer.

Her master's voice interrupted her thoughts. "You fought a creature from the darkness called a Shasakar." The word rolled off his tongue like a writhing snake.

Her eyes widened. "A shapeshifter? But those are creatures of legend. They're long dead and gone. The last known sighting of one was right before King Amous disappeared. He hunted them to extinction after one of them killed his wife and child."

He tilted his head, and a crooked smile crossed his face. "So you do remember your lessons." He cleared his throat and clasped his hands, looking into the fire. The flame's flickering light caressed his features, making him look much older and warier.

"A Shasakar is one of many creatures that dwell in the darkness, long thought to be extinct. Recent reports have provided me with the whereabouts of some of the creatures—reports which, unfortunately, I received too late. For that, I'm sorry. Had you died..." He bowed his head in shame. "There are few who believe that the Rot were ever truly gone. I've dedicated much of my life to the research and study of the creatures. I believe the Rot are returning. There will be a resurgence of the sickness which plagued our land so long ago, and the creatures who now roam the world are just the beginning."

Zephera exhaled deeply and steadied her hands on the arms of the chair.

"You think that there will be another Dark Age?" she asked. "But how? We don't even know how it was stopped last time. King Amous disappeared after they were defeated." She struggled to keep her voice steady.

Her master and mentor turned to look at her, his face unreadable.

"I've heard tales of a way to eradicate the Darkness from this land. I need to consult an old friend before we pursue the matter further. But something is coming, Zephera my girl, and we must prepare ourselves to face it."

A knock at the door made her jump. A servant hurried in, trembling with fear, and whispered in Baleem's ear. His brow furrowed. He didn't tolerate cowards.

"Leave us, you daft fool," he spat at the servant. The poor man rushed out of the room.

Zephera sighed. Baleem's kindness only seemed to extend to her and Zadkiel. The rest of the assassins and warriors employed at The Keep hated her for that. They never spoke to her if they could help it. She preferred it that way.

Baleem placed a hand on her shoulder, pulling her back to the present. "There are matters I must attend to. Please get some rest and don't speak of this to anyone." He bowed his head slightly and rushed out of the room.

Zephera watched as Baleem left her to sit in silence. She leaned back in her chair and gave a tired laugh. If this really was the return of the Dark Ones and the Rot, life as she knew it was about to drastically change. What would become of her? Of Zad? Of the grand city of Illuminas? She let her hair out of its braid and twisted the ends between her fingers absentmindedly. She always did this when she was thinking. If what Baleem said was true, war was inevitable. A small part of her longed for the excitement of war. All of the death, destruction, panic—it was what people like her thrived on. Shaking back the dark thoughts, she groaned. The other part of her was frightened at what might come…

"Could just be a coincidence Zephera, calm down. Nothing has been confirmed yet," her shaky words echoed in the empty room.

Taking a deep breath, she walked the deserted gray stone corridors to her rooms on the furthest wing of The Keep. Baleem had housed her in the dorms years earlier but she had started too many fights and arguments among the other assassins and soldiers. They had filed so many complaints against her that Baleem had moved her to her own set of rooms. Zephera smiled when she opened the drab oaken door.

She looked around the dimly lit chamber she called her own. Her closet was ajar, giving a tantalizing glimpse of the furs, leathers, and velvet and silk dresses that hung inside. Ah, her closet. Her clothes were the thing she missed the most when she was gone. She walked over to her shelf, which was filled with books and other trinkets from her travels. Her favorite was a lovely bottle of perfume that smelled of rose water which she had bought while journeying to the Rose Fields of Sarilo.

She ran her fingers over her writing desk, leaving a clear path through the dust. Then she touched her unopened, dusty writing books. She hadn't felt the urge to write in years, ever since her tutor, Morwynn, had left the Keep. As awful as Morwynn was, she had inspired Zephera to write. Morwynn put her through hell and back again, but her harsh methods had taught Zephera to speak and write dozens of different languages. She loved to dream up stories of people of different races who were free and normal. She wrote of adventures similar to her own, epic stories of men and women who fell in love and spent all the rest of their days together. She wrote because it was a fantasy, something she would never have—an experience she got to share through the characters in her stories. Dwelling in fantasy for a time was all the therapy she needed to face the harsh reality that was her life.

Zephera stripped down and pulled the covers back from her bed. She smiled as she laid down, eager for her dreams to take her away from her dark and frightening thoughts.

CHAPER 3

Zephera slept restlessly, her dreams filled with the Shasakar and other monstrous creatures that existed before the Light Age. She dreamt of immense power and horror, a great evil that spread throughout the kingdom of Nostorra like a plague and devoured her whole until all that was left were the creatures.

She woke suddenly to a knock at her door.

"Zephera, wake up!" Zad's optimistic voice called through the door. "I haven't seen you in ages, and I need a visit to the bakery. C'mon. Get dressed. I'll be in the courtyard. And hurry up!"

"UGHH," she grumbled. Zephera hadn't slept well at all. Nightmares had plagued her dreamscape. She had slept better on the road—at least there were no interruptions in a bumpy carriage.

She stretched her arms above her head and yawned, then pulled her black hair out of her face into a single braid. She dressed in her favorite linen pants and cotton tunic, the latter of which had gold embellishments on the sleeves. After picking lint from the sleeve, she put on her walking boots and headed to the courtyard.

Zad was standing with a guard near the gardens, his eyes wide and his jaw clenched tightly. As the guard continued to speak in a hushed whisper, Zad's features scrunched into a scowl. They were talking too quietly for her to hear any of it, but she could sense that whatever it was, it wasn't good. Zad looked up as she approached, his face softening when he saw her. The guard bowed his head to her and uttered a quick farewell.

"What was that about?" she asked curiously.

"Jameson. He was found alive, but only barely. They brought him in late last night. It's unlike anything Baleem's ever seen." He bit his lip nervously.

"I'm sure if there is anything to hear, Baleem will tell us."

"Maybe, but even he seemed worried. He left for the castle at dawn. Apparently, Jameson was screaming about—" He turned his head to look around and dropped his voice to barely a whisper. "He was screaming about the Rot. He was covered in his own vomit, along with some kind of dark, murky substance."

Her heart fell and her eyes widened. "You saw him then?"

"Just a glance before they ushered him down into the under chambers. It was a terrible sight. He smelled of death, and the look in his eyes—I've never seen any man or creature possessed with such a look, even the ones I've killed. It was terrifying."

She sucked in her breath. "Even if the world is ending, we still need to eat. Let's go. I'm dying for a cinnacake." Her voice sounded a lot braver than she felt.

Zad chuckled, his smile lightening the dark shadows that danced on his face. "Food! That's all you ever think about, isn't it? You have a stronger stomach than I do. What was it you wanted after your first assassination? Honey-glazed pork and mashed potatoes? Honestly woman, you are a twisted little thing." He pushed her playfully.

She smiled. "Glazed carrots. Don't forget, I also had glazed carrots." They both laughed and headed on foot to the city shops.

Baleem left the Keep in a hurry. He watched over his shoulder to make sure he wasn't being followed. He took side streets and avoided the main crowds to avoid being seen. He shuffled into the nearly deserted alleyway. A hooded figure stepped out of the shadows and addressed him.

CHAPTER 3

Baleem smiled. Even hooded, the figure couldn't hide its feminine curves.

"You're aware that the time is drawing near. Is she ready?" the figure asked Baleem warily.

"She will be. I've spent years going over how I would tell her, but when I finally had my chance to tell her everything about where she actually came from, I stumbled. She looked frightened and overwhelmed from her journey. It just didn't feel right," Baleem muttered, frowning at the noise from the nearby market place.

"It would've been better coming from you. She will be angry when she finds out you knew," the figure replied, adjusting her hood.

"So be it," Baleem whispered, staring directly at the figure. "The things the boy said—the blood, the fear in his eyes—the plagues are returning. It won't be long before the window opens for The Rot to return. It feels the same as before, even after all of this time. I can feel the darkness in my bones. It aches, and I fear for this world."

"We must gather the others. Have you a sense of their whereabouts, Baleem?"

The warrior's eyes darkened and he stroked his graying beard thoughtfully. "I have an idea of their last known locations. The mage will be easier to find. Her magic has steadily been getting easier for me to sense. Zephera can be of use to us to find her, but she must not be aware of the true cause of her mission. She's loyal, but even this would shake her faith in me."

"You taught her well, Baleem. She will be our greatest weapon against them."

"Or our greatest downfall," Baleem said, fear glazing his eyes.

"The others won't let that happen, Baleem. Bringing them back will set things into motion quickly. We must be sure this is the right path."

"There is no right path here. You of all people should know that, my friend."

"All too well," the figure replied, sounding sorrowful. "We must locate the First. Only then can we stop the Plague. The blood of the pure is the only way, and this time, we will find her before it is too late."

"She'll be hard to pin down. Her story is old, and there is very little written about her, hardly even a mention. I think I know a way, however. It'll be dangerous, perhaps even a fool's quest, for I'm not sure if it'll even work." He furrowed his brow, thinking deeply.

Nodding, the figure took out a small scroll and handed it to Baleem. "Give this to your king. It's the name and location of the Other. Summon him, and he will come. It's been many years since I spoke to him. I would avoid telling him much of anything for now. I'm not sure he can still be trusted."

"Thank you, my friend," Baleem whispered sadly and pocketed the letter. He looked from the alley to the bustling market place. "After we go down this path, we may never meet again."

"I would think not," she replied, pulling the hood back. Smiling fondly at one another, the pair bowed their heads and parted ways. Baleem headed out into the crowded market square walking through the crowd of busy shoppers, merchants, and boisterous children, his pathway taking him back to the Keep.

CHAPER 4

Zad and Zephera left the bakery with sticky fingers and full bellies. The air was light and full of the scents of nearby shops and stalls. It was near the harbor, where people from all over the world came to buy and sell their goods. The bustle of the shoppers was something Zephera always found comforting. They had such easy, carefree lives. As a child, she had longed for the normalcy of their lives, but as she grew older she knew it was something she would never have. Even if she had the choice to live as they did, it wasn't something she even remotely deserved. She had done too much. She was too full of hate and disdain.

Her thoughts were interrupted by Zad's light chatter. He told her the most mundane things. He recounted his reconnaissance mission to the West and spoke of a wondrous, sugary fruit known as a Famoca berry, brought to the market last week by a dark-skinned merchant. He told her of the prank they pulled on the new recruits by putting itching powder in their undergarments and about the new weapons shipments. Zephera loved to listen to Zad talk. He was good and pure. He had a light soul, and he was everything she wasn't. He only killed because he had to, only taking the lives of those who had to be punished. He never enjoyed it. It broke him every time. For days after a mission, he was always withdrawn and hard to reach. She never understood why he stayed at the Keep. Baleem was willing to let him go. But he didn't want to leave. He said he longed to make a difference in the world and had the connections and means to do so working under Baleem. Truthfully, she would've been broken if he left. She hated her selfish need for him.

By the time they returned to the Keep, the sun was blistering hot despite the shade from the towering buildings. They arrived at the gates, sweaty and tired. The Keep was eerily quiet. The normally bustling noises from troops training and bands of soldiers and assassins coming and going had been silenced. Instead, a gleaming ivory carriage stood at the entrance.

"That's the king's carriage," she said in alarm, looking at Zad. His left brow arched slightly, telling her he shared in her curiosity. A man dressed in white and crimson silks approached them. He was short and stout and reminded her of a toad. Zephera smirked at his clothing. He must have felt the need to overcompensate for his short stature with gaudy drapery.

"Pardon me, are you Zephera and Zadkiel?" he inquired, his voice full of forced pleasantry.

"We are. Can I help you, sir?" Zad asked with polite concern, always the gentleman.

"I'm to bring you both to the Palace, straight away," he said, eyeing their sweaty clothes. Then, before he could stop himself, he blurted out, "Such a pity that you won't have time to change."

The strange man must have realized his mistake because his brown eyes widened slightly and he scratched his balding head. He cleared his throat, motioning for them to get into the carriage.

Zephera sat in the seat opposite Zad, and the man joined them, taking a deep, calming breath.

The ride to the Palace stretched on for what felt like an eternity, with nothing but awkward silence and the sounds of the carriage wheels bumping over the cobblestone streets. The courier's face was frozen into an uncomfortable smile, and every time they made eye contact, he bowed his head. Zephera looked at Zad and saw he wore the same forced smile. She couldn't help but laugh.

Mirrador Palace was at the center of the city. It was the tallest building in the land and was graced with glistening white marble and diamond pillars. Ivory taken from a long-extinct, large animal accented the colorful gem embellishments. Zephera hated the idea that an animal had been hunted to extinction for its tusks just to satisfy the greed of a king who lived five thousand years ago. But such was the way of the world. Old magic preserved the Palace's pristine, white gleam. The spell used for such a marvel had probably cost the crown a great deal. While the Tower of Light was technically under the control of the crown, spells for vanity cost the royals a pretty penny.

When they arrived at the courtyard, the little toad man ushered them inside without a word. He led them through an oaken door at the servants' entrance and down several long, chilly hallways. They came to a room that was the size of her bedroom back at the Keep. Inside was a table made of blackened wood from the rare ember tree. It was placed near a broad window. A small fire crackled in the fireplace grate, and a few large, shiny dark red leather chairs were scattered throughout the space. It was a rather disappointing room, given that it was inside such a gorgeous castle. Baleem sat at one end of the table, so Zephera sat down across from Zad. Now that she was closer, she could now see the table was polished and engraved with intricate designs. She thought it was an odd place for such a beautiful table.

Zephera and Zad both exchanged curious, nervous glances as they waited for Baleem to speak.

"I apologize for the short notice." Baleem addressed the two assassins. "I would have contacted you before you came to the palace if we had more time. There are dangers emerging which must be dealt with immediately."

"Is this about Jameson? Is he all right?" asked Zad, his voice filled with worry.

"I'm afraid Jameson was infected with an ancient sickness known as the Decay. He died shortly after he was brought to us." Baleem looked forlorn. "The Decay comes from the Rot, from the infected blood of a creature of the Darkness. The disease spread quickly. Four of our men who came in contact with the substance on Jameson's body have been stricken and are in quarantine now. I fear that they won't make it. I can't let anyone tend to them. I can't risk an outbreak." His sorrowful voice rattled tightly.

"You mean to tell us that you are leaving those men to die without even trying to help them?" Zad asked, outraged.

"Once you come in contact with even the smallest amount of the blood, you risk being infected with the Decay. Those who contract it die a slow and painful death, replete with visions of darkness. They become mad and hunger for flesh. We can't risk it. The sickness travels fast and kills all who are unfortunate enough to have it. These men understand the necessity and have been given Avio to end their suffering if they so choose."

Zephera raised a single eyebrow. "Onyx Petal? Interesting. I was under the assumption that the herb was reserved for only those at risk of being captured. Why waste it on men who are going to die anyway?"

Zad glared at Zephera. "It's a mercy, Zephera. Darkness needs to be eradicated by any means necessary. Even if it means ending a life."

Zephera clicked her tongue, appalled at Zad's attitude. She opened her mouth to answer when they were interrupted by the toad-like servant, who nearly tripped as he escorted a large man with ginger hair into the room. The large man wore elegant clothes that rivaled the best of Zephera's wardrobe back at the Keep. Her eyes widened as she took in this regal man. It was the King.

"Five hundred years ago"—the king's deep voiced boomed throughout the room—"as thousands of people fought the Rot, the Decay spread like wildfire, sending many good, brave people to their deaths. Some chose to be taken by the Dark Ones rather than succumb to the sickness. Weaker souls took their own lives out of fear. It was chaos. I won't see our lands share that same fate."

Zephera eyed the king, squinting slightly and wondering how his beard could look so unkempt. It was brown, and nearly down to his waistband, with large patches of ginger and white. It snarled in places, sloping gently with the curve of his rotund belly. She imagined it must've been uncomfortable to have such a tangled mess strapped to your face.

"You are young and able, which is why I requested you for this mis-

sion, Zephera. You have encountered a dark creature before, correct?"
He raised an eyebrow.

She felt a pain in her shin and looked from the king's beard to Zad,
whose eyes bulged out of his head as he stared at her intently. She would've
laughed and told him he looked like a scared goldfish if it hadn't been for
Baleem clearing his throat loudly on her right. She smiled gently at the
king, struggling mightily to keep her eyes focused on his deep, brown
eyes. She noted that they weren't an attractive, soft glowing sort of brown.
Instead, they were like mud mixed with decaying seaweed. She fought to
keep her features neutral as she answered him.

"Yes, Your Majesty. My mission was to kill a black stag. I tracked it for
a fortnight and grazed it with an arrow before it changed into something
monstrous. It was unlike anything I've ever seen. After a struggle, I killed
it," she told the king matter-of-factly.

The king raised his bushy eyebrows in shock. "You're very skilled, or
perhaps lucky. Few men could slay a dark creature and live. Even less
were skillful enough to avoid getting the blood from their kill on their
bare skin."

She opened her mouth to speak, but Baleem interrupted her. "I've
taught her well. Her armor has been designed to cover her skin but still
remain light enough for battle." He cleared his throat and looked up, his
eyes boring into hers. She looked down at her hands. They were shaking.
Was she infected? Why didn't her master want her to say anything? She
had no such armor, and she had been covered in the creature's blood.
Some had even gotten in her mouth. She cringed at the memory of the
revolting tang of sticky iron and rot. She could still taste it when her
mouth got too dry.

They sat in uncomfortable silence for what felt like an eternity until the king spoke again. "I'm glad you are so strong and skillful. You'll
need it on this mission. I need you to seek out and eradicate the creatures invading our world. They've invaded before when the veil between
our world and theirs grew thin. We must stop them before the sickness

spreads." The king looked at the pair of them as though they were his last hope.

Zephera couldn't believe what she was hearing. In an instant, she forgot her fear of the king and instead felt a burning anger.

"I'm sorry, but you want us to travel all over Nostorra to kill these creatures? All of them?" She laughed in desperation and disbelief. "That could take years. We could search our entire lives and still not find all of them." She shook her head. "You are out of your mind, old man. And Baleem! Why would you think this could be the slightest bit possible?" Her hands batted the air in front of her. She started to stand up from the table, not caring that she was putting herself above the king by doing so. This was absolute madness.

"Zephera Travelle, sit down NOW!" Baleem yelled furiously.

She glared at her master. His face had turned dark with anger, and his hands were shaking.

Baleem turned to the King. "I apologize, Your Majesty. I take full responsibility for her behavior. She's young and hasn't yet learned to check her temper."

"Sit, old friend. She has spirit, and these are trying times indeed." The king looked at her. She couldn't tell for sure, but she thought she saw the ghost of a smile in his eyes. "Zephera, please, sit. I wouldn't send you on this mission if I thought you would fail." She pursed her lips and sat down, not daring to look at her master.

"Now, on their own, these creatures are strong," the king conceded. "However, it's their blood that stops us from ever being able to truly defeat them. We need to find a way to eradicate the poison in their blood that causes the plague. There is one person who could perhaps help develop a cure. The only trouble will be finding her. She hasn't been seen for many, many years. It may seem like an impossible task, but I assure you, it isn't. It'll be difficult and rather trying, but not impossible."

"Zephera, you are the only one who can do this, the only one who has fought these creatures," Baleem murmured.

She looked at Zad, whose eyes were filled with questions and determination. The image of an old crone bobbed before her mind's eye. "How are we supposed to find her? Just ask around for any sign of a mad, old woman who might have a cure for the plague?" she added, her sarcasm the only tool keeping her from exploding.

"Not quite." Baleem smiled darkly. "She's very good at using spells to cover her tracks. She's been evading us for years, but recent reports have brought to my attention three items of hers that I need you to acquire. Once we have those, we can use a simple summoning spell to locate her."

Zephera let out a harsh laugh. "That's all? Three items, a summoning spell, and a batty old hermit? Sounds fun, maybe for the Royal Guard or hirelings. But not for me. I don't fetch items. I kill things."

"Ah! Glad you pointed that out, Zephera!" the king exclaimed. "Those items aren't just lying around, waiting for just any common guard or hireling to find. No, that old woman, Reina, is too careful for that. They'll be well-hidden and guarded. I believe *that* would fit your particular talent for killing things." He smiled darkly.

She glared down at her hands. Then she closed her eyes and took a deep breath before answering.

"Fine," she breathed out. "But you can't expect Zad and me to do this alone."

"Of course not. I've selected people from my own personal guard as well as the Tower of Light to assist you on your journey."

She looked at the king in surprise. "The Tower of Light? You are sending a light mage with us?" Her voice was full of curiosity.

The king smiled, his thin lips tight and harsh. "As I've said, this is a matter of utmost importance, and I'll send only the best." He stood up, his large stomach pressing against the edge of the table. "I think I've explained your mission well enough. Every moment we spend talking here wastes precious time. I'll leave you. Good luck." The two men turned from the room and began immediately discussing plans.

She sat in silent disbelief, staring intently at the table, her lips curved in a snarl.

"What do you say, Beasty? A journey to the ends of the earth, darkness all around, and death at every turn. Let us save the world, eh?" Zad quipped, kicking her playfully.

She peeled her eyes from the ember wood table and looked at Zad. His face was full of nervous excitement. He smiled at her, moving his shoulders in a little jig. "UGHHHH," she scoffed, trying not to smile at his ridiculous enthusiasm.

"If you are so excited to run to your death, let's duel." She smirked.

"Tsk, tsk," he clucked, shaking his head with laughter.

"I suppose if we wish to live, we must save the world. We can't exactly continue living here with a plague consuming everything. It would be quite dreary," she said dryly. "And, after all, we are the best. I wouldn't trust our fates to anyone else."

"No, we couldn't have that. What if they poured milk in their bowl *before* the puffed sweet oats in the morning?"

"The horror," she mocked. She wasn't in as jovial of a mood as she seemed, but putting on a show for Zad helped calm her nerves.

They both laughed. Baleem came back into the room, his face creased with stress.

"Have you decided?" he questioned.

Zephera stifled a laugh. She hadn't gotten the impression they had much of a choice.

"When do we leave?" Zad asked. Baleem's face lightened.

"You'll stay here tonight and leave at first light tomorrow. I'll send someone to the Keep to fetch your things." He turned and scuffed out of the room, running into the toadish servant.

"Sorry m'Lord," the toadish servant squeaked.

The servant, his squashed face now red from embarrassment, motioned for them to follow him. "Come. I'll show you to your rooms. Dinner will be brought to you later."

CHAPER 5

Zephera paced back and forth in her room, waiting for the sun to go down. She was confused, angry and afraid. Was she going to be sick with the plague? Why hadn't Baleem had her quarantined like Jameson? What was he playing at, hiding it from the king and Zadkiel? Zephera leaned against a cool wall, and slid to the ground. Should she sneak out of her rooms and find Baleem? This was eating her alive. She had to know what to expect from the blood she had encountered.

She was about to stand when a paper slid under the door. She stood quickly, flinging open the door. To her disappointment no one was there. She looked out into the hall, hoping to catch a glimpse of whoever had left the note, but it was empty. She reached down and picked up the small parchment from the stone floor.

In Baleem's handwriting it read: *You are immune to the effects of the blood. Burn this note, and tell no one. -Baleem*

Zephera turned the parchment over, hoping to find more explanation on the back, but it was blank. She growled, feeling annoyed with her master's vague explanation. She threw the note into the fire, scowling as the flames devoured the parchment, turning it to ash.

She lumbered to her bed and laid down. She put her pillow over her face and screamed into it. She closed her eyes, calming her fast beating heart and slowing her breathing. She forced herself to sleep. After all, she would need it.

The sun blazed through the stained-glass window, showering the room in rivers of color. Zephera stared up at the ceiling, her eyes bloodshot from exhaustion. She hadn't slept a wink. Her body ached from the lack of rest and she groaned as she sat up and walked across the cool stone floor. She dressed in yesterday's clothes and pulled her raven hair into something more presentable than the mangled bird's nest it had become.

Once again, her thoughts turned to the king's impossible quest. She was an assassin, a Lady of Death, and though she was trained in many things, stopping a plague wasn't one of them. It pained her to admit she was frightened. Frightened for what would become of their world if they failed. She shook her head as she opened the heavy oak door and walked down the long, dimly lit hall to Zad's room. She needed someone with whom to share this unsettling feeling—dread, was it? It was so foreign. She rapped three times on Zad's door—two long, one short—a simple knock, really, but one that she always used. She waited, but there was no answer, so she knocked again. Annoyed with Zad's ability to sleep like the dead, she opened the door. The room was empty, the bed stripped of sheets. It looked like he had already left. Footsteps sounded in the hallway behind her. Zephera peeked her head out and saw a tall, plain-looking woman dressed in servant's clothes.

"Excuse me, miss. I was looking for you," the servant squeaked, not daring to look her in the eyes. "Your master and friend are down in the Great Hall. You are to join them." Zephera nodded and, without saying a word, set off to find Baleem, Zad, and whatever or whoever else waited for her.

New voices greeted her as she arrived in the Great Hall. She walked into the room and saw Baleem, Zad, and two other people dressed in traveling clothes. The female was tall with golden hair and pale skin. She stood next to Zad with her hand on his shoulder, laughing at something he was saying. Zad was smiling from ear to ear; she felt a small flicker of jealousy.

Zephera walked over to Baleem, who was hovering over the table, looking at maps and speaking with the tallest man she had ever seen. The tall man had short blonde hair and kept his back hunched, as if trying to blend in, not that it helped. Even hunched over, he was still a great deal taller than Baleem.

"Ah! Zephera, come here, my dear," Baleem said, motioning for her to join them.

He clasped a hand on her shoulder, almost making her knees buckle.

"This is Brenner. He's a mage from the Tower of Light. He'll be joining you on your journey. His specialty is Mendicarius. His training is both in healing and fighting." Baleem said this with pride and excitement in his eyes.

She nodded politely and stuck out her hand. "Zephera," she said.

The mage returned her nod and engulfed her hand in both of his. His large hands were surprisingly soft, which she speculated probably came from a life in the tower studying potions and practicing spells. Hers were calloused and rough in comparison, and she quickly pulled her hand away.

"Have you spent all your life in the Tower?" she asked with intense curiosity.

Brenner nodded and smiled, although his smile didn't quite reach his eyes.

She was impressed with the mage. She had never met one before, and his presence was exciting. Though she had heard the mages were mute, she hadn't expected them to communicate so easily. She smiled warmly at Brenner. "I've never actually met a light mage. It's quite an honor. I'm pleased you'll be joining us."

The mage bowed his head in quiet thanks.

"What's the plan, Baleem?" she asked.

"Plan? I thought you had one," Baleem blurted out.

She exhaled and looked up at the ceiling impatiently.

"Gods above, Zephera," Baleem said. "I'm only joking. You need to lighten up."

Suddenly, a familiar hand gripped Zephera's shoulder. "I'm always telling her that Baleem, but you know our Zephera. Strictly business," Zad said with laughter in his voice. She shrugged his hand off, annoyed.

"We are waiting on another member of our little troop. He should be here soon," a soft voice said from Zad's right.

Zephera looked up to see the thin, disturbingly gorgeous blonde she had noticed earlier. She had an irritatingly large smile on her face.

"I'm Oriana. You must be Zephera Travelle. Zad has told me so much about you," she said enthusiastically without taking a breath.

Zephera raised an eyebrow, suddenly miffed. "Zadkiel, I hope you told her good things," she cooed, mimicking the girl in front of her, eyes narrowing protectively.

"Of course!" the girl exclaimed. "I'm just so pleased to meet you, Lady of Death. Your reputation amongst the guards... well, I was expecting someone taller, maybe. And scarier." The girl laughed, her golden eyes filled with excitement and warmth, unaware that she had awakened a beast.

Zephera's eye began to twitch, something she couldn't help when she was feeling particularly angry. She balled her fists, trying to keep from exploding at the girl. She must've looked like a crazed animal because Zad interjected, "Looks are deceiving. I wouldn't want to be on Zephera's bad side. She can be terrifying, and she's tough. There's a reason they call her the Lady of Death."

The trio was interrupted by the entrance of a tall, muscular ox of a man. He had tan skin and hollow eyes, and his dark hair was pulled back from his face with a black velvet ribbon. He wore dark-colored leather armor with three—no, four—daggers strapped to his legs. Zephera's eyes darted over the rest of him, looking for any other weapons. The steel toes of his boots were sharpened to a point. There was a bit of dried blood on one of them. She pursed her lips. Impractical, yet effective.

A hushed silence fell upon them. He was only a few years older than she was. He obviously commanded a lot of attention and respect wherever he went. She glared up at the beast of a man. *I could take him*, she thought, annoyed at the looks of awe everyone in the room was giving him. Even Baleem was looking at him with wide eyes and an expression of wonder.

CHAPTER 5

"I assume we're almost ready to leave?" the man asked, his sonorous voice uncaring.

Baleem came to his senses first. "Yes, yes, we were just waiting for—" he stopped mid-sentence. The man stared down at Baleem with an expression that would've made anyone run for the hills.

She fought back a laugh. Her own master was scared of this man? Please.

"We were just waiting for you to grace us with your presence, Sir Knight," she said sarcastically.

She heard Zad suck in his breath. The man looked at her with such a dark stare that even she felt small. But she stood her ground and didn't look away from his piercing gaze.

"Is that so?" he spat.

"Indeed."

"Daegan," he introduced himself coolly, not bothering to offer his hand.

"Zephera," she replied, still not breaking eye contact.

"We were supposed to head to the stables once you arrived, Daegan," Baleem interrupted.

"Then let's go. We have a world to save, do we not?" Zephera snapped, walking out of the room and leaving the stunned party behind her, along with the brooding Daegan.

Reaching the stables first, she quickly changed into her favorite armor, keeping her tunic and pants on underneath for warmth. The stable hands had been busy. The horses were already loaded with their travel supplies and map. She sheathed her weapons and grabbed an apple from her pack, feeding it to the white horse she always rode. She was excited to see her horse. It had been a few weeks since she had been able to ride her. Winter had been infected with equine influenza and had only just gotten over it. "Winter, you silly thing. What have we gotten ourselves into?" she asked the horse as the others shuffled in.

The group surrounded Baleem, waiting for him to speak.

"You'll head north out of the city to the small village of Darley, near our borders," Baleem was saying. "There, you'll go through the Mountains of Dreer. I've marked on the map the path you'll need to follow through the pass. Somewhere near the pass is an ancient stone altar. I'm not sure what item you'll find. All I know is that it's there. Look for something out of place, something that feels old and full of magic. Reina's impossibly difficult, but she isn't cruel. She knew there would be a time when she was needed again.

"The next item you need is one of Reina's personal items. She's rumored to have grown up in Watford, the village on the north side of The Mountains of Dreer. I have a suspicion that something of hers will be there."

Zephera glared at Baleem. "A suspicion?" she glowered at her master. "We are risking our lives for a SUSPICION?! You don't even know for sure?"

"Zephera..." Zad whispered to her.

"You judge too hastily, foolish girl. For once, shut that mouth of yours and listen." Baleem eyed her dangerously.

She folded her arms like a pouting child and leaned against the armor stand. She felt her cheeks grow hot as Baleem continued.

"Now, we've narrowed down the location of the third item to two different places. Until we are certain of where it is, I won't burden you with the information. It'll only cause more stress and confusion. An associate of mine will meet you in Reina's old village and update you with any progress we have made. So please, wait there at the inn after you've acquired the first two items." Baleem looked around at the group wearily. "It's a lot, and we are short on time. Asking anyone else to make such sacrifices... well, we are very grateful for you all. We must keep the reason for your mission secret so we don't cause mass panic. So please, be wary of whom you speak to and what you tell them."

He looked around at the sturdy group of warriors and smiled. "Any questions?"

"No. Thank you, Baleem. I've gone over the maps, and I believe we'll find the items. We will stop this," Zad said with authority.

Everyone nodded in silent agreement. Zephera watched as Daegan finished packing his bag and mounted his horse. As if sensing her stare, he turned to face her. She narrowed her eyes, meeting his glare. He didn't react. She busied herself by tightening Winter's saddle. She felt tired, angry, and scared. She hated it. She contemplated saying something to Baleem. She still had questions about so many things. Before she had time to reconsider, she found herself walking across the barn to him. He was busy saddling a gray mare for Oriana, who was readying her bow and arrows for travel. As if she needed one more reason to dislike the girl, she used those sorry excuses for weapons. She held back a scoff.

"Jealousy is very unbecoming of you, Zephera," Baleem smirked.

"What? I'm not jealous," she said, the last word tasting like bitter milk.

"I would be concerned if I were you, Zephera," Baleem joked. "You pride yourself on being cool and calculated. We wouldn't want you to start having feelings now, would we?"

She turned to walk away, irritated with Baleem's assumptions.

"Honestly, stop this horrendous act of entitlement and loosen up. I'm only teasing, Zephera."

Arms folded across her chest, she turned on her heel to face the man who had raised her. She quickly glanced around the stables, making sure the others were occupied. "Fine, I will, but only if you tell me why I'm immune to—"

"Hush. Not here. There are too many ears," Baleem whispered, looking across the stable to where the others were saddling their horses. Daegan was watching her intently. Zephera shot him a crude gesture with her finger and he looked away.

Baleem patted her shoulder gently. "As I've said before, there's much I need to tell you. I've just never found the right time or place. When you return from your journey, I promise I'll answer every question. For now, this will have to suffice." He handed her a thick envelope. "Burn it when you are done reading it. Do you understand?"

Nodding, she took it and placed it in her satchel.

"Don't show it to anyone, not even Zadkiel. You'll understand in time." The old man reached out and hugged her. She tensed at the sudden burst of affection from her master. They hadn't shared this kind of affection since she was a young girl.

She pulled away and looked up at the man she had come to think of as her father. His face was harsh and full of worries she would never know. She felt a sudden, sad need to hug the old man one last time. She squeezed him tightly and breathed in his musky oak and pine needle scent. He was what kept her going. He was her family.

"Zephera, it'll be all right. I need you to know that I love you and always will, no matter what. Read the letter, complete your task, and return home."

"Okay," she whispered.

He smiled and kissed her forehead. The gesture, though small, felt so final. She walked to her horse and put the satchel in her saddle bag. The others were already on their horses, ready to take leave. She mounted Winter, took one last look at Baleem, and rode out of the stables.

CHAPER 6

Zad led them out of the city gates and through the nearby villages. They rode for days, stopping only to sleep and eat. The roadside villages were small and their inns and taverns were drab and mediocre in comparison to the trading villages Zephera was used to stopping at. She had hardly recovered from her last mission before being sent on this one, and her body ached from their hard, brisk pace. She at least had the scenery of forest, plains, and farms which were beautiful this time of year.

Her companions were infuriating. Oriana's insatiable need to be friends took all Zephera possessed to not disappear and leave this doomed world to its fate. She wasn't a team player and preferred to work alone, something she was reminded of every time Oriana opened her mouth to speak. Her voice, while smooth and sweet, was like salt in an open wound. Zephera cringed, her eye twitching madly as Oriana led her horse to walk next to Zephera.

"Zephera, darling, you look positively mad! There's far too much testosterone on our little team. We girls need to stick together." She giggled.

Zephera crossed her eyes and pulled a face, trying her best to match Oriana's insufferable giggle. "Tell me, Oriana, why are you here?"

"To help save the world, of course! When I was recruited for our quest, I jumped at the opportunity! To rub shoulders with you, well, it's quite the honor. And there's the whole world-saving part."

Zephera grimaced. She hated the girl's seemingly fake attitude. "So, fame? That's your motive? Figures... the most useless people want glory without actually having to work for it. What exactly is your skill set, Oriana? Are you going to flash that perfect smile of yours at our enemies and hope you can seduce them into stopping them from slaughtering our people? Because so far it seems like that's all you are good at." She glanced at the girl.

Oriana was quiet for a few seconds before responding. "Well, you are far more likely to gain allies with a smile than an ugly scowl. What's the saying? You catch more bees with honey?"

Zephera glared at the girl as Oriana rode ahead, seemingly unfazed.

Quiet laughter sounded beside her. She glared at Zad. "What?" she spat.

"Nothing… nothing at all." He smirked. "I just don't think I've ever seen someone stand up to you before. It's rather refreshing."

She shot Zad her meanest glare.

He shuddered mockingly. "Whoooohooo. You are scary when you get like this, Beasty."

She reached into her bag and grabbed an apple and threw it at him.

Zad caught the apple before it hit him in the chest, smirking as he took a bite.

The next few days melded together in a blur of riding, eating, and sleeping. The views had begun to melt together. They rode through farmland and forest. It was all infuriatingly similar. Zephera normally enjoyed her rides with Winter. She craved the time she had alone with the horse on missions. Though she was alone, she was able to think; to get lost in her own head, and the vast fantasies she created there. This mission, however, was filled with Zad and Daegan's constant bickering. Though she had to admit it was rather entertaining. While Zephera didn't necessarily like Daegan, it was amusing to watch the two men squabble over the most ridiculous things. Well, Zad squabbled. Daegan purposely did things to annoy him.

A few days into their journey, they stopped to rest and eat at a roadside tavern. Zephera knew it well and frequently stopped there on her missions. The food was divine, which was rather ironic given that the place was called "Hell's Tavern." It lived up to its name in every other way, however. Several broken windows had been boarded over rather than replaced, blocking out the sun. The roof had a few obvious holes in it, and the wood siding was faded and buckling with age. It was a gloomy cesspit that catered to thieves, murderers, and the kind of folk that would kill you if you looked at them wrong. It was exactly the kind of place Zephera loved to haunt.

She smirked at Oriana's dainty gasp as they approached the tavern. The girl tried her best to hide her horrified expression, much to Zephera's delight. Zephera tossed her hair over her shoulder and opened the old wooden door to the decaying building.

"Welcome to Hell," Zephera jeered, sweeping her arm out and offering a mocking bow to her companions.

She smiled with contentment as she took in the dim, stuffy atmosphere. The interior walls were dingy with smoke, soot, and grease. The familiar fragrances of roasted pig with a tang of mildew and sweaty bodies assaulted her senses, and she breathed in rapturously.

She winked at the others and walked to the bar, which was covered with such a thick layer of sticky filth that even her dagger couldn't scrape through. She motioned with her hand and whistled at the bartender.

The bronze-skinned man, who had been scrubbing a crimson stain on the floor, looked up. His black eyes narrowed at the interruption. He reluctantly got to his feet, glaring at her.

"What?" he snapped.

"Some ale for my friends, and whatever that heavenly smell is."

The man snarled, revealing a row of perfectly straight teeth. "Are you going to pay me this time?"

Zephera laughed. "Oh, my dear Aldon, when have I not paid you? Last time you said a night with me was all you would ever need."

"It was. Until you drugged me, took my money, and stole my favorite horse."

"You mean the money you owed me, and you said I could have Winter if we continued our... relationship," she purred, leaning over the counter and grabbing the man's chin with her finger and thumb.

Aldon growled and grabbed Zephera's head, crushing her mouth furiously with his. He pulled her up on the grimy counter, and her legs wrapped around him. The noise of the room faded as she lost herself to passion. She didn't pull away until Zad coughed uncomfortably. She smiled at Aldon and tapped his face with her hand.

She caught Zad's eye. He looked like he was going to be sick. She felt a strong sense of satisfaction at his reaction. She loved making those around her uncomfortable with her sexuality.

"Don't be such a prude, dear Zad," she chided.

Aldon pushed her off the counter. "Take the table in the corner, you dreadful woman!" he said, dismissing her.

"Thank you, Aldon. Winter's tied up out front, if you want to see her. I promise to pay this time—with gold. And if gold doesn't suit you, I believe I have a few extra minutes..." She winked, her hand trailing down her body.

"Be gone, she-devil. Eat and drink. Then we can talk about payment." Aldon shooed her off before heading into the kitchens.

Zephera smiled and gave Zad a toothy grin before leading them to the cleanest table and sitting down.

"Do you do things just to spite me, Zephera?" Zad asked.

Zephera raised an eyebrow. "To spite you?"

"That rather disturbing display back there..."

She let out a sound of disgust. "Disturbing? How so? I was just kissing an old friend of mine."

Zad shook his head. "This place is revolting. Look at the riffraff that infests it. The building's falling apart and is crawling with disease. It's no place for a lady, or anyone of respect for that matter."

Zephera laughed. "Respect? Zadkiel, we kill people for a living. We're no better than common thieves. You judge too harshly those who you don't know, my friend. This place," she gestured around her, "accepts any manner of folk without question, even those of us with tainted souls."

Zad shook his head and reached for her hand. "Your soul isn't tainted, Zephera. If you would just quit hanging around these types of people, you would see the potential that you have to do good."

Before Zephera could respond, Daegan scoffed loudly. "Do you think yourself above the common criminal, Zadkiel? You seem to enjoy over-compensating for your dull personality and mediocre skills by looking down on others. It's rather tiresome."

Zephera looked at Daegan, her eyes wide, trying her hardest not to smile. She bit her lip, excitement filling her soul with hope of what Zad might do to Daegan.

Zad stared at Daegan, his jaw clenched.

They were interrupted by a commotion near the bar. An intoxicated man swayed on his bar stool and then crashed to the floor. The glass holding his ale shattered on the ground and splattered amber liquid everywhere. Angered at losing his drink, he spewed a series of curses as he lunged to his feet, stumbling into the dark-haired man seated next to him. Zephera's face lit with eagerness. It was time for the night's entertainment.

The drunken man, a scruffy regular called Gunter, clumsily staggered to his feet, words slurring together. "What choo sitting there for? Yer in my way!"

The other man, bearded and bald, stood, pushing Gunter against the bar, his arm at Gunter's throat.

The man grimaced as Gunter's knee caught him between the legs. He let go of Gunter, bending over to try and catch his breath. Gunter kicked him in the gut and then lost his balance and fell to the ground again. The two men wrestled, fists and limbs flying through the air. The rest of the tavern's patrons had gathered around the two men to cheer and bet, but as the fight grew more vicious, the atmosphere went from frenzied to deadly. Zephera stood excitedly, hands on her blades and poised to fight. She surveyed the room, daring the other patrons to test her. Just as she was about to launch herself at the two grappling men, a bright blue light flared through the room.

Zephera raised her arm to shield her eyes. As suddenly as it had come, the light disappeared. The discomfort in the tavern was evident in the groans and scoffs that filled the air. Brenner stood in the middle of the room near the two men, his hands glowing brightly. Both men were passed out.

Zephera laughed at the indifferent look on Brenner's face as he glided back over to the corner and sat down at their table. She hadn't even noticed he had gotten up. He smelled of copper and fresh magic. She patted him on the back, feeling a sense of admiration for the mage.

"Beautiful," she said to him, raising her eyebrows playfully. He smiled back and busied himself in a notebook. Zephera laughed at her companions' expressions. Zad looked taken aback. Daegan's usual mask of cool indifference was firmly in place. Oriana, however, seemed just as enthralled as Zephera, eyes as wide as saucers and a large grin plastered on her face. She clapped excitedly.

They were interrupted by Aldon, who brought a tray full of plates to their table. "Roasted pig with glazed onions and garlic stuffed potatoes," he said as he placed the plates on the greasy table. Zephera smiled as Oriana's eyes glistened with excitement at the meal in front of them.

"This looks amazing!" Oriana exclaimed. She held a fork in front of her eyes, inspecting it. "The silverware's surprisingly clean."

"Of course it is, you daft girl," Aldon barked at her. "Is the rest of my establishment not up to your standards, little princess?"

Zephera sat up straighter in her chair, curious as to where this conversation was headed.

Oriana shrugged. "No, it's actually quite abominable, though I suppose that's part of its charm." She smiled.

Zad sucked in his breath. "I apologize, sir. She meant no offense. She—"

Aldon's roar of laughter cut him off. "I like this one, Zephera. She has iron balls. 'Part of the charm.' HA! What's your name, girl?" he asked.

"Oriana," she replied, offering him her hand.

Aldon took it graciously and kissed it. "Well, Oriana, perhaps I'll get two for one tonight. Would you like to join Zephera and me after dinner?"

Zephera cocked an eyebrow at the thought.

Oriana smiled widely. "Oh, Aldon, that's sweet of you, but I must decline. I prefer those of the fairer sex. I'm sure you would be quite generous, but I'm afraid I wouldn't be the best of company in a man's bed."

Ale spewed out of Zad's mouth, spraying the side of Zephera's face. "Sorry, Zephera," he choked, handing her a cloth.

Daegan laughed. "Did you really suppose she would think of you in that way, Zadkiel? I don't believe even your lack of manhood would entice Oriana."

Zephera rolled her eyes and wiped the side of her face. "Why is it that men find it so difficult to believe that some women aren't interested in them? Some of us have standards, you know."

Aldon laughed. "Some people do, yes. You… not so much." Zephera's mouth fell open. She stood and brought her dagger to Aldon's throat.

"That wasn't very nice. I would bleed you dry right here if your food wasn't so damned nectarous." She kissed his cheek and sat back down, taking a bite of the savory meat.

They finished their meal in silence, which Zephera was grateful for. She leaned back in her chair, patting her full stomach.

"I do believe I should give Aldon a proper thanks for that meal. I'll be right back." She stood and glanced around the table at her companions, daring them to question her. Oriana looked delighted and gave Zephera a flirtatious wink. Zad glared at her, his eyes narrowed. He shook his head in disgust.

"Awww, Zad. You'll be okay. Just give me a few minutes. I promise I won't be too long."

Daegan laughed quietly under his breath. "Zadkiel seems to be— what's the word? Jealous. Take as long as you need, Zephera. I enjoy watching him squirm."

Zad growled angrily, slamming his fist on the table. "I'll be outside."

Rolling her eyes, Zephera went to the bar where Aldon was serving a dangerous-looking man. Their hushed tones cut off abruptly when she arrived. "Don't stop on my account, gentlemen," she said, sitting down next to the man. She stifled a gag. The stench emanating from him made her eyes water. It was so putrid that she was afraid she was going to lose her dinner. She grimaced at the man who glowered at her with dark, dead eyes.

"Ye are one of them aren't ye?" the man growled at her.

"One of whom?" Zephera asked.

"I can smell it on ye. Evil, darkness. Ye bring death."

Zephera clenched her jaw. "The only smell here, sir, is you. And yes, I do bring death. I crave it, and if you aren't careful, you'll meet yours at my hand." She glared at the man, who glared back. Then she peeled her eyes from his and smiled at Aldon. "Where are your manners? Introduce me to your friend, Aldon."

"Zephera, this is an old acquaintance of mine. He was just leaving."

She clucked her tongue. "Such a pity."

The strange man stood up and held out his hand. It was covered in filth and was tied with a bloodied rag. Aldon took it and bowed his head slightly to the man. Zephera watched the man leave, suspicion in her eyes.

"You keep interesting company, Aldon. Care to tell me what that was about?"

"No. And if you know what's good for you, you'll stay out of it. It's business, and you should mind your own."

Zephera folded her arms over her chest. "Rather curious, but I won't pry. Now that I'm full, I have other needs that you should see to. Shall we?"

Aldon held his hand out to her. She glanced over her shoulder and gave Daegan a sly wink before following Aldon to the back room.

On the last night before they reached the mountain village, Zephera sat against an old cedar tree on the edge of a clearing and watched Zad and Oriana sparring. Oriana seemed to take to the dance of death quicker than most. She blocked Zad's blow with her right arm. Surprising. The girl favored her left arm with the wooden broadsword. The way she moved with such light grace was intriguing. When Oriana brought the faux blade to Zad's neck, Zephera laughed. A look of shock crossed Zad's features, but it vanished as quickly as it had appeared. He fell to the ground in mock death, grabbing the fake wound at his neck and choking unconvincingly. He kicked his legs in a final, desperate bid for life, finishing the show by rolling his eyes back in his head and sticking out his tongue.

Oriana threw her beautiful golden head back in laughter, and Zephera rolled her eyes. *He's not even that funny*, she thought to herself.

She grumbled and watched as Brenner set up the camp. He was bent over a pile of kindling and wood. With a snap of his fingers, he lit the fire. Magic. It was so strange to see it being used for such a mundane task. After setting up the fire, Brenner worked on establishing a perimeter line around the camp, using some sort of thin, nearly invisible wire she had never seen before. Why the silent mage always insisted on a bloody perimeter was anyone's guess. They were still within the limits of safety. Perhaps he was the paranoid type. She didn't say anything about it, though. His caution wasn't hurting anyone. Besides, who was she to judge? She was relaxing against a tree, doing nothing to help set up the camp.

She felt Daegan approach despite not being able to see or hear him. Out of habit she put her hand on the sheath of her weapon. His dark figure emerged from the shadows and sat down next to her.

"You know, for someone your size, you sure are quiet," she said, wincing as she realized she had just inadvertently paid him a compliment. She was feeling unusually generous that evening.

He said nothing, instead staring ahead to where Zad and Oriana were now unloading their supplies and preparing dinner for the night.

"Perimeter's secure," he said abruptly, breaking the silence.

"Oh, good! Such a relief to know you and the mage can secure a safe campsite. You do realize we are still within the confines of the kingdom, right? There's nothing out here but farmers and trading villages. Unless of course, you are trying to protect us from some cows, Sir Knight."

Daegan looked at her, his eyes dark and piercing. She met his gaze. The look in his eyes was still menacing. Yet, even though she felt small and afraid, she was also curious. Such anger and hatred were behind his gaze. What horrors had this man known? What had he lost to hold such darkness in his eyes?

"No task is wasteful, regardless of where we are. We will always be in danger. It isn't my job to babysit a spoiled and mediocre assassin. It's my job to make sure at least some of us get out of this alive." His voice was full of disdain and mockery.

She would've been angry at the asinine man if she hadn't been so exhausted. She had nothing to prove to him. She was the Lady of Death. She could gut him with her eyes closed. Well, perhaps not with her eyes closed. He was rather tall, muscular, and dangerous. Maybe she could do it when he was sleeping. She laughed at the thought.

"You should be careful, Sir Knight. You're using too many words. I might actually learn something about you," she said softly.

He raised an eyebrow. "I don't wish to make friends. I'm here for one thing. There's no reason to grow familiar with any of you. There's work to be done."

"Yes, sir!" Zephera snickered. She arose and left the sullen knight underneath the shade of the cedar tree.

Everyone seemed absorbed in their tasks, so she grabbed her bag and yelled out a hurried "going to wash up" as she headed into the forest. She was familiar enough with the area to know that within a few minutes' walk through the trees and brush was a small creek deep enough to swim and bathe in. It ran west to Lake Eyleen. In the morning, they would pass through the last village near the lake and follow the sun until they arrived at the Mountains of Dreer. This would be their last night spent within the confines of the kingdom. Safety was an insubstantial thing—a state of mind more than anything. Zephera let her thoughts wander. Was anyone or anything truly ever safe? What were people even trying to protect themselves from? Death? Sickness? Injury?

Death claimed all in the end. Why prolong the inevitable? Why seek the "safety" of walls? And the beings people sought protection from, were they simply seeking safety, too? She thought of the dark stag. It had been so peaceful until she injured it. Its attack had been a sort of self-defense. Yet its blood held a deadly plague. Kill or be killed. What was the point of it all? Perhaps she should stop trying to help the world. Allow death to take her whenever it came, leaving the world to its fate. Let death reap this world and save it from itself.

Such dark thoughts for someone so young, said a familiar voice inside of her head.

Zephera stopped dead in her tracks. She had been so caught up in her own thoughts that she hadn't been paying attention to her surroundings.

"Get out of my head!" she screamed.

Zephera, my dear, you let me in. Your thoughts have been elsewhere. So distracted. I know Baleem taught you better than that.

"Show yourself, woman!" she demanded. She scanned the dark woods, looking for any sign of movement. She unsheathed her weapons and stood ready for a fight. Then her body was seized by a sudden pressure. She couldn't move. It had been four years since she had heard that voice and felt this magic. Four years since she had seen her.

My dear, are we not past this sort of introduction? Tsk, tsk.

Zephera fought as her lungs emptied of air. Finally, she succumbed and fell to the ground. The last thing she saw before her world turned black was a tall figure wearing a crimson dress.

CHAPER 7

Zephera was taken back to her childhood. She was a young girl—short for her age but able to compensate for it with her wit and skill. Baleem was much harder on her then, working her to the bone with training exercises, pointless chores, and lessons. Even then, she never saw it as punishment or cruelty, just life. When other children outside the walls of the Keep were playing and going home to loving mothers and fathers, she had been learning to dissect animals to get the best parts of the meat and marrow. She had learned how to keep the skins intact for leathers, and had also learned the best ways to disable a man with her bare hands. Zephera could make a weapon out of just about anything.

By the age of twelve, Zephera had suffered eighteen broken bones, ten fractures, and countless stitches. She could speak several languages and could describe any of Nostorra's plants and list all of their properties. She was smart, spirited, and lethal. She was given her first mission when she was fifteen: track and follow a fellow assassin who had retired from the Keep the previous year.

Baleem had assigned someone to follow the man the day he had left the Keep. Baleem was a kind, patient man, but one thing he wouldn't tolerate was betrayal. It was difficult to fathom why anyone would betray the old master. Perhaps it was money, power, the promise of protection, blackmail. Whatever the reason, they always got caught, and they always died… eventually. Baleem took pride in his work. When a mark needed to be punished, he didn't give them a quick death. Baleem didn't believe in granting mercy to those who had wronged him.

To say she was excited about the mission was an understatement. She was young, naïve, and unaware of what the taking of a life would do to her. She was excited to use her skills and earn Baleem's respect. He was the closest thing she had to family, and she wanted to please him.

She had been tracking the mark for two weeks. He had been in the Illuminas, not far from her home. He was living such a commonplace life now. He had walked from the inn he was staying at in the Heights to a bookstore a few streets away. Then he had gone for tea at a cafe on the corner and walked back. For two weeks, he had kept this same schedule, doing nothing out of the ordinary. Zephera had begun to wonder if the man had done anything wrong at all.

She followed the man to the cafe and sat at a table at the bakery across the street. She munched on her cinnacake and sighed as the man ordered the same thing he always did. He was dreadfully boring, and though she trusted Baleem fully, a flicker of doubt crossed her mind. Either this man was incredibly good at hiding his betrayal or he was innocent. She was about to go sit next to him and gut him right there when a woman with a tall neck and huge nose sat down at the table next to the man. She subtly passed him something and he pocketed it. He took another sip of his tea, tossed some coins on the table, and left.

She moved to follow him, but the tall woman turned and stared at her. Zephera felt her body go completely still. She couldn't move. She tried to breathe, but it was like sucking in water. She began to get dizzy, and her vision blurred. She could barely make out the pale figure of the woman sitting across the street from her.

The woman arose and approached her. "In thirty seconds you will pass out from lack of oxygen. I'm going to release you from this hold because I need you conscious and alive. I don't wish to kill you, but if you attempt to run or kill me, I won't hesitate to do so."

She felt her lungs fill with air and she gasped in relief. She was embarrassed at her weakness. Her limbs felt heavy as the feeling in them began to return. Her vision cleared until she could see the woman again. Her long neck and nose made her look a bit like a crane. Her red hair was drawn into a tight bun, pulling back the skin over her cheekbones and hollowing out her face. Yet she had a strange sort of beauty about her, full of power and mystery.

"Every day you come to this bakery for a cake and follow that man. For one of Baleem's people, you're very sloppy."

Zephera hunched down, taking on the identity of a scared teenager. "I'm not sure what you are talking about. I'm very frightened. Please, madam. I need to get home to my mum. She'll be worried!" Zephera hoped the woman would believe her.

"Do not insult me by lying, Zephera. I have known who you are for quite some time."

"I—I don't know what you are talking about," she choked.

"Of course not. Just let me do the talking," the woman said tightly. "I'm Valessa, Keeper of the Light Tower. Baleem is an old friend of mine, and I assume from your shoddy job at following that man that this is your first mission." She paused. "That man is not the traitor Baleem is looking for. I know with certainty that you could have killed him. I do not doubt your skill in dealing death. But I do know that your first kill is one you will always remember. It changes you. The murder of an innocent man is not one you want to have on your hands."

"Baleem is never wrong. He wouldn't kill one of his own if there wasn't a good reason."

"You are correct. Baleem doesn't kill innocents. But the information he received was incorrect. There is a traitor in his midst. Unfortunately for him, it's someone still under his employ."

"So, this traitor gave him bad information? Why?" she asked the woman in disbelief.

"You are young, not stupid. There are a million reasons why they might have done this. The reason does not matter. What does matter is that the man has been falsely accused. I warned him to get out of the city and disappear. You can tell Baleem you were successful and that your mark was killed. Or, you can tell him you failed and that there is a traitor in his midst. Pray tell, which one do you think he will believe?"

"Why should I trust you?"

"You shouldn't. You should, however, trust your gut. Trust what you know and feel to be true." The woman looked at her intently.

"Who betrayed him?" she asked quietly.

The woman smirked. "That my dear, is my secret to keep. for I deal in information and secrets. Giving away my power to you does not seem very wise. If Baleem wishes to know who betrayed him, he will come to me with a trade. If not, that's his prerogative. Just pass on the message."

Zephera looked into the woman's eyes. She had always felt drawn to people's eyes. Feelings could be easily hidden from the face. But the eyes told Zephera what she needed to know. The woman's emerald eyes were filled with desperate urgency. The soul behind those eyes was far older than her chronological age. They told a story of triumph but also pain and sadness. Somehow, she knew the woman was telling the truth.

"How do you know Baleem?" she asked suddenly.

The woman shifted uncomfortably and smiled sadly. "He is a very old friend of mine. I have not seen him in many years. But I try to look out for him when I can."

"Or when it suits your needs?" she retorted.

Valessa smirked. "Clever girl. Can't they go hand in hand?"

Zephera shrugged. "I suppose so. Doesn't anyone ever do anything out of the goodness of their hearts?"

"If they did, we'd all be poor or dead."

They stared at each other for a few moments, silent.

"There are many things you are ignorant of. I know you want to please your master, to prove yourself. And you will. But today is not that day. Things will be set into motion soon enough, and when they are, you will long for the days of simplicity."

She stood and extended a hand to the young assassin.

"We will meet again, Zephera, but not for some time." Zephera stared in shock at the outstretched hand. She didn't take it. Valessa raised an eyebrow and bowed her head in silent farewell. Then she walked down the street and disappeared into the crowd of shoppers at the market.

When that day comes, you need to be ready. You will understand in time, dear. Valessa's voice echoed in her head.

The memory faded into darkness and another one started. As Valessa's voice filled her head once more, she realized it wasn't a memory. It was a message.

Things are falling into place, dear one. I told you to prepare. These next few weeks will be the hardest you have ever endured. But, if you persevere, if you live through this, everything will begin to make sense. I know you have questions, and I have answers. But first, I need you to stop this plague. I need you to cure this land. You're the only one who can. I'm sorry I can't be of more help right now. Please, you must not give up. Trust in yourself and no one else. If you don't stop this, death and darkness will overtake everything. We will all die. You can't fail.

Zephera awoke with a start. Looking around, she realized she was still in the forest. It was dark. She hugged her knees to her chest and closed her eyes tight. She was terrified—of their mission, of the confusing message from Valessa. She feared the plague was just the start of their troubles. She curled her lip into a snarl at the thought of Valessa, how she had waited until Zephera was out of the perimeter to attack her. Valessa's magic must not be able to reach through Brenner's perimeter fence. She made a mental note to ask the mage later.

Then she laughed. It was a choked sort of sound. the kind of noise a madwoman would make. She stood up, putting her hands on her sides to try to dull the ache she felt. Then her head began to spin. She cried out and collapsed back down.

"Darkness, death. It's impossible, all of it."

Zephera sat there a good five minutes, laughing. She was acting like a child. She continued to sit, head in her hands, her dark hair forming a fortress that shielded her from the outside world.

As she rocked back and forth, she breathed in and out slowly, thinking of the lake, how wonderful it would be to swim right now. She closed her eyes and willed herself to believe she was there, floating on her back, calm and peaceful. It wasn't until she felt a hand on her shoulder that she looked up.

"Zephera, are you all right?" Zad whispered quietly. She nodded, staring up at Zad. She was frightened, yes, but she had to do something. She hated the look of fear and concern in his eyes and would do anything to never see it there again.

"What happened, Zephera? You've been gone for a few hours. After you didn't return to camp, we got worried. We've been searching for you for over an hour." We? She looked around and noticed Daegan leaning on a nearby tree, staring at them with an inscrutable expression. Zad held out his hand to her. She took it, not wanting to talk yet. She just wanted to get back to camp.

"I need sleep. We can talk tomorrow," she croaked, walking past them and through the woods towards camp.

She heard Zad start to protest, but as much as she wanted to give him the answers he sought, she was too tired to even know where to start. She ignored him and kept walking, though he stayed on her tail.

"Let her go. She's been through enough," Daegan said quietly to Zad.

She arched her eyebrow, surprised by his uncharacteristic kindness. She wasn't sure what to make of it and was too tired to care.

CHAPER 8

The sun began to kiss the sky, slowly peaking over the mountain top. Zephera breathed in the cool air around her, keeping her eyes closed and focusing on the sounds of the world arising from its slumber. The warmth of the sun grazed her face, and she felt someone's eyes upon her. She smiled softly, embracing her last few seconds of weightless freedom before she opened her eyes to face reality. She stretched her arms above her head and groaned. Her body ached with emotional exhaustion. Glancing over to the fire, she saw Zad watching her intently. He smiled when he saw that she had awoken, and he motioned for her to join him.

Biting her lip, Zephera stood up, ready to face the music. Sitting next to him, she laid her head on his shoulder.

"I'm sorry I scared you," she whispered, taking his hand in hers.

"You really did. You just left, and when you didn't return... Zephera, I've never been that worried in my life. When we found you... I—I've never seen you act like that. What happened, Zephera?" he asked fearfully.

"I believe the *Lady of Death* has finally realized that our mission won't be as easy as she first thought, or maybe she just realized she isn't as good as she pretends to be," Daegan said dryly.

Zad's hand tightened around Zephera's protectively. She shook him off and spun around to face Daegan, for once annoyed at him instead of angry.

"I was attacked," she said narrowing her eyes into the best glare she could muster. "The last thing I remember was a voice, and then I felt cold, and, well, now we're all here."

She couldn't tell them everything, not until she had more answers. She had a feeling some of her questions could be answered by Baleem's letter. She gasped. His letter!

"My bag! Where is it?" she asked, looking around frantically. "Did either of you retrieve it from the woods?"

"Bag? No. I'm sorry, Zephera, I haven't seen your bag," Zad said quickly. "I promise we'll look for it, but can we focus on the fact that you were attacked in the woods?" He shook his head in disbelief, wondering how she could possibly be worried about a bag.

Her eyes flared, and she stood up angrily. "I need my bag."

Zad growled in frustration and walked away, trying to busy himself before Zephera hit him with the tantrum she was about to throw. She turned to face Daegan, whose eyes were full of amusement.

"You look like shit," he said casually, peeling an apple with a small dagger and popping a piece of it into his mouth.

She fought off a sudden feeling of embarrassment, knowing he was probably right. She could feel that her eyes were swollen and her face was caked with dirt.

"Where's my bag?" she bellowed.

He stared at her with an astute smirk on his face. Then his eyes narrowed.

"From what you described, there's a mage somewhere in those woods— one who left you for dead—and you want your bag?"

She glared at him, her lips pursed. Their gazes locked.

"I haven't seen it. Sorry," he said dryly.

She felt her heart stop. Her vision clouded, and she felt the world start to spin. Daegan stood up and steadied her, gripping her shoulders tightly.

"Easy now," he whispered, his voice unusually gentle.

Zephera looked at him, her face pale.

"Did you need something in that bag, Zephera?"

The sound of her name on his lips should've thrown her off, but she was too worried about finding Baleem's letter. She closed her eyes and steadied her breath. She shrugged his hands off, perturbed that he was still touching her.

"Yes. It's important. Essential. We need to go look for it. Now!"

He just nodded and walked towards Zad to pass on the importance of finding her bag. She knew how ridiculous it all seemed to them but she needed that letter.

When it was time to leave, Zad agreed to take the small detour to search for her bag. It would only cost them an hour and they were getting an early start anyway. After readying the horses, she helped Brenner with the perimeter line and watched as he slowly wound up the wiring.

"Brenner, I have a question," she said quietly.

The mage nodded, not looking up from his task. She wondered how much she could trust him but she knew if anyone could help her understand what had happened in the woods, he could.

"You were raised in the Tower. Did you ever meet the Keeper?"

He kept his eyes down, acting as if he hadn't heard her.

"Valessa, the Keeper of the Tower of Light—do you know her?"

The mage nodded his head slightly.

"She can get inside your thoughts, right? Project her voice into your head?"

The mage's fingers tightened but he didn't look up.

"Brenner, I realize that you don't know me, and you have no reason to trust me. But there are bigger things at play here than you and me. I need someone on my side. Someone who understands."

Finally, he looked up at her, his face unreadable, his eyes full of determination.

"Can you do what she did, Brenner? Did she teach you?"

The mage stood up and walked away.

"Dammit," she swore.

They finished packing up their campsite. Zephera began to feel anxious as they headed in the direction of where she hoped her bag would be. She felt Zad's eyes on her as she hopped off Winter and walked to where she had encountered Valessa.

"Wait, Zephera. Whatever attacked you could still be out there," he said, jumping off of his horse and tying it up next to Winter. "I sent the others ahead. They'll meet us at the next village."

"Good. I could use a break from them."

"They aren't that bad, you know. Daegan's different but seems to have a good head on his shoulders. And Brenner—It's kind of hard to get to know the guy when he can't speak."

"And Oriana? What do you think of the little goddess?" Zephera asked begrudgingly.

Zad eyed his friend nervously. "Goddess? Oh, Beasty, don't let her hear you say that." He laughed.

"Why not? She knows she's beautiful."

"You would like her. Just talk to her and give her a chance."

"No, thank you."

Before Zad could reply they heard a rustle in the trees ahead. Zephera froze. She closed her eyes and listened intently. A branch snapped. Her eyes flew open and she unsheathed her weapon, ready for a fight. She glanced at Zad, who had his shield and sword raised. The trees were thick here. If there was more than one enemy, they wouldn't stand a chance. The bush ahead rustled and a small figure limped out.

It was a hound. Zephera let out a breath of relief and sheathed her weapon.

"Just a pup," she breathed.

"He's wounded." Zad approached the creature. "You should know better than to sneak up on hunters in the woods, little one," Zad whispered gently as the hound whimpered and laid down at Zad's feet. Zephera watched as Zad bent down and softly petted the poor creature's matted and bloodied fur.

"Look at his markings. He's one of those warrior dog breeds."

Zephera gasped. "A Gurzay?" She walked over to the poor, mangled pup. He must've been the runt left for dead.

"Get him to the village. I'm sure Brenner can help. I'll finish up here and meet you once I find my bag."

Zad looked at her incredulously.

"I'm not leaving you here."

"Zad, that hound is going to die if you don't get him help. I can handle this on my own. I promise."

"Zephera, I'm not leaving you." The look in his eyes told her not to argue.

She reached into her tunic pocket and pulled out a vial of ointment, thanking the gods that some odd instinct had caused her to take it from her saddlebag earlier. Though the rare and expensive healing ointment wouldn't completely seal such a serious wound, it would do until they could get the pup to Brenner. She rubbed it on the hound's wounds and gently set him down. Then she took her cloak off and put it over him. He whimpered in gratitude before falling into a deep sleep. "Satisfied?" she asked Zad.

"Immensely," he replied.

They continued the search for a few minutes. Finally, they came to the spot where she had been attacked. Her leather satchel was there, at the base of a tree.

"Thank the gods," she whispered and bent to retrieve it.

She looked through the contents. Everything was there—her extra clothing, food, a bag of coins, extra supplies—everything but the letter. She felt her heart drop. She dumped the contents of the bag out, her hands shaking. No... No... No! There was no way a thief would've taken it and left the other contents of the bag. It had to be Valessa. That stupid, stupid woman!

She packed the contents of her bag and quietly walked to where the pup was sleeping. He opened his small eyes when she bent down to pick him up.

"Zad! I found it! Let's get going," she said, climbing onto her horse.

"Ah! Good!" He appeared from behind a few trees.

She did her best to keep her face neutral as she waited for Zad to mount his horse. She held the bundle in her cloak and waited for Zad to follow her.

"Zephera?" he called out.

"Yes?"

Her friend smiled his quirky half-smile and tilted his head. "We'll get through this. I won't let anything happen to us. If you need to talk, I'm here, okay?"

"Okay, Zad," she agreed.

"And Zephera? There's no one on this earth that will ever replace you."

She rode Winter off through the woods, clinging to the small bundle. She furrowed her brow. He had looked so sincere, so concerned.

CHAPER 9

They reached the small fishing village around noon and met up with their companions near the edge of Lake Eyleen. Zephera's arms were exhausted from carrying the pup for so long. After dismounting, she promptly handed him to Zad. Then she peeled off her boots and went to sit at the water's edge. She put her feet in. She loved how the sunlit water illuminated her toes. The refracted splotches of light danced over her pale skin, making it seem like a thousand fireflies danced over her.

She glanced at the shore. Brenner and Zad stood over the Gurzay hound they had rescued. They seemed to be deep in their work, mixing herbs and poultices as Oriana softly stroked the pup's head. She hoped they could save him. He was so small and deserved a fighting chance. If he lived she would call him Dorjan.

The Hounds of Gurzay were said to be strong and deadly. Warriors used them in battle. They were flesh-hungry creatures who killed for sport. Feared by many and used exclusively by only the greatest warriors of Nostorra, they were bred for their cruelty and size. Now she had one of her very own. He was too young to have received the training that he was bred for. Like her, he was broken, scared, and small.

She stood, breathing in the brisk mountain air, and started up the path. She was met at the shoreline by Daegan, who held three dead rabbits in a trap. He obstructed her path. She glared, trying to go around him, but he cut her off, forcing her to bump into him.

She growled angrily. "Can I help you?"

"Did you find everything you were looking for, buttercup?" he asked dryly.

"Did the leather satchel next to my boots give it away?" she retorted.

She saw a ghost of a smile dance across his face.

"Move."

He raised an eyebrow and smirked. "As you wish." He bowed and extended his arm, directing her up the path.

She stomped past, grumbling under her breath. She couldn't understand Daegan. He was hot and cold, his moods troubling and mysterious. Perhaps he was used to commanding respect and compliance, something she didn't intend to give him. He had done nothing to earn her trust, so she wouldn't bend to his will. She was Zephera, prodigy of Baleem, the greatest warrior who had ever lived. She was equal in skill to Daegan and just as intelligent. Perhaps he just wasn't used to having another person match him, let alone a female younger than he was. She vowed not to let him get under her skin.

She sat next to Brenner. The hound was sleeping soundly in his lap while he busily worked on what appeared to be a small pack.

"How's he doing? Do you think he'll live?" she asked Brenner.

He nodded and continued working.

"What's that?" she asked, pointing to the pack.

The mage pointed to the dog and then back at her.

"A pack for the hound?" she asked excitedly.

"Just until he gets better," said Oriana. "He really is something, isn't he? Fate was on your side, little one."

"We'll need to leave here soon. We need to reach the village of Darley by nightfall. We can leave the horses in the village and trade for supplies; the path up the mountain is too strenuous for them," Zad said.

"I hate leaving Winter. She's been so good to me," Zephera lamented.

Zad put his arm around her. "She'll be there when we get back to the city. We *will* go back, Zephera."

Daegan boiled rabbit meat and they all feasted on stew and potatoes before they started their journey into the Mountains of Dreer. From there, they would trek through the mountain pass to the mysterious altar and, if they were lucky, emerge on the other side in a few days' time.

When they arrived in Darley they found it strangely empty. The market was closed, and the shutters were drawn on the houses. The few villagers who walked the roads avoided their eyes and hurried about their business. They came to the trading post and tied up their horses. The shopkeeper inside seemed surprised to see them.

"We haven't gotten many visitors in these parts lately," he said.

Zephera eyed him warily. She had a sinking feeling that something wasn't quite right in this village. She peered out the shop window while Zad spoke to the shopkeeper.

"What can I do for you?" the shopkeeper asked sternly.

"We need a place to leave our horses and trade for a few supplies," Zad said. "We are about to head through the mountain pass, so any cloaks and gear would be appreciated."

Zephera brought her head closer to the window, noting once again the barren streets. Out of the corner of her eye, she saw a dark shadow gliding into an alleyway just outside of the shop. She watched carefully, waiting for the shadow to return. She was about to turn away, cursing her paranoia, when she heard screaming. She was aching for a fight. Not pausing for even a heartbeat, she ran out of the shop into the street. Her hand gripped her dagger as she sprinted toward the commotion. A group of people rushed towards her, fear in their eyes. She pushed past them, running as fast as she could, the others at her heels. She felt the familiar adrenaline rush that came before a battle against an unknown enemy.

A crazed man ran towards them, screaming uncontrollably. Black liquid oozed from his eyes and ears.

"It's the blood. He's infected! Don't let him touch you," Zad yelled from behind her.

Zephera watched as the man ran towards the town square where a few villagers were standing near a large fountain, unaware of the impending danger. "We have to stop him!" she yelled at Zad. Then she screamed at the villagers, "Run! You need to run! Don't let him touch you!"

Fortunately, she didn't have to tell them twice. They seemed to have been through this before. They ran into the nearest home and slammed the door shut. Bolts slid into place as they locked the door. The crazed man screamed, clawing at the door. She sucked in her breath and motioned with a slight nod of her head for Zad to take the path to the man's left. She took the path to the right. She watched the man pound on the door, growing increasingly frenzied. She crept up slowly near the fountain, the water's passage from one tier to another just loud enough to mask their footsteps on the gravel.

She felt something flash past her left cheek. She stopped in surprise and watched as an arrow buried itself in the man's back. He snarled and switched his attention to Zephera, staring at her for a moment before he charged, oblivious to the arrow in his back. She swore under her breath as another arrow zoomed past, grazing her cheek and missing the diseased man completely. She reminded herself to kill Oriana later for not knowing how to aim and once again wondering what exactly her use was within the group.

She raced toward the man, trying her best to mirror his angry, distorted face. Then she darted back towards the fountain's edge. She smirked as the man approached her. He stopped just short of Zephera and suddenly changed directions, heading straight for Zad. She swore under her breath. "RUN! ZAD, RUN!" she yelled frantically, throwing her arms in the air. He hurtled down a nearby street, the man close behind. Following them, she called out, trying to yank the man's attention away from Zad, but he was relentless. Out of options, she threw her dagger at the man. It missed, bouncing off his heel unnoticed. She swore, cursing the gods. She scrambled to keep up with the pair. Then Zad suddenly came to a stop.

They had reached a dead end. Zad rounded on his target. His gray-blue eyes gleamed with adrenaline and his brow was furrowed in deep concentration, making his features dark and oddly wild. He didn't seem to notice her.

The man lunged at Zad, baring his grimy teeth and growling like an enraged bear. Zad parried, his shield and sword swaying, ready for blood.

The man charged. Zad grimaced as the man threw him backwards with unearthly strength. Zad tried to regain his balance, but tripped, knocking his head on a nearby cart. His eyes rolled back and he fell, sword and shield clattering to the ground next to him. He was out cold.

Zephera swore. "Idiot." She lunged at the man before he could step closer to Zad.

She straddled his back and wrapped her arms around his neck. He screeched, clawing at her arms and lurching around the narrow alley. He knocked her into an old, rusted cart. It snagged her tunic. Releasing her grasp, she fell to the ground, ripping her sleeve and flesh in the process. She rolled and unsheathed her scimitar. Before she could spring to her feet, the man barreled into her. She landed on her back. As he jumped on top of her, she raised her weapon to hold him at bay, one hand on the hilt and the other wrapped around the blade. The man howled, gnashing his teeth like a rabid animal. She tried to grab her other dagger, but the man's inhuman strength prevented her from freeing one of her hands from the blade.

Her arms began to shake, and the blade sliced into her palm. She cried out as the blade sunk deeper into her skin. She struggled to hold it steady, but the weight of the man was beginning to crush her. He snarled at her, his rotten teeth close to her face, aching for a bite of her flesh. She turned her head and closed her eyes, her arms about to give out. Suddenly, the man stopped, and she felt the weight of his body slump against hers. Warm blood poured onto her face as the man's head rolled onto the street next to her, his face frozen in a permanent snarl. She wiggled her way out from under the body.

Sitting up slowly, she threw her blade to the side. "Don't touch me!" she yelled as Daegan offered her a hand. But she saw he was already covered in blood and black sludge. She stared at him in horror.

"The plague passes through the blood! Are you trying to kill me?" she screamed.

"Relax. Do you think Baleem would just let you go off on a journey without informing someone of your immunity?" he asked grabbing her under her shoulder and helping her to her feet.

She shrugged him off, furious. "You didn't think that information might've been useful? Why didn't you tell me you knew?"

"I could ask you the same thing," he countered gruffly.

Staring at him in disbelief, she gestured to his armor, which, like her, was covered in black blood. He smirked.

"Your immunity is unique, but it doesn't make you special. I've been studying these creatures my entire life. There are few who share this ability. I am one of them."

She raised an eyebrow, catching her breath.

"Who are you?" she asked warily.

"Who I am and where I come from is irrelevant. All you need to know is that my people sent me to the king to search for a cure."

"Are there others who are immune?" she asked.

"Yes. It's rare, but there are a few."

Zad thankfully chose that moment to sit up, grumbling and rubbing his head. Daegan turned to glare at him. "Useless," he muttered under his breath. Zad got to his feet and hazily walked toward them. Sweat and dirt had matted his golden hair to his forehead, making him look disheveled. His face drained of its remaining color as he caught sight of the blood covering Zephera and Daegan.

Zad opened his mouth to speak but was cut off by the others' arrival. They looked equally horrified at Zephera and Daegan's appearance.

"We need to wash off, and this body needs to be burned," Daegan said to the shopkeeper.

"What's going on? Explain, please," Oriana demanded, running after him as he shuffled past the group.

Snarling, he whipped around to face her. "There are few in this world who are immune to the effects of the plague. Zephera and I happen to be two of them." Turning on his heel, he stalked past her.

"What do you mean? This is... this is insane!" Oriana choked, close to tears.

Zephera looked up at Zad. He looked like he was going to be sick.

"I'll tell you everything I know, all right? But I need to get this filth off of me. I'm going to be okay. Everything will be okay," she said more for herself than anyone else.

She turned away from them all and marched after Daegan.

CHAPER 10

When she arrived at the lake, Daegan was nowhere in sight. She looked at the water longingly. Almost getting mauled by a diseased man had severely shaken her confidence. She needed a boost. A swim in the lake would be a welcome distraction. She stripped, removing even her undergarments, and jumped in. The water chilled her tired skin. She dove under the surface of the water and stayed there, looking at the hidden world beneath the surface. It was eerie, dark, and full of mystery. The light from the evening sun shone down from the surface of the lake, making the water dance like fireflies in the night sky. She wished she could stay beneath the surface forever. She didn't want to face her companions, who would probably look at her with disdain. She was the Lady of Death—cold, calculating, murderous. She wasn't someone who fell apart and wept.

Zad had looked at her as if she was broken. The pity and fear in his eyes had been infuriating. Nothing was going right lately—her uncharacteristic breakdown, the blood, the immunity, Daegan and his dark presence, the letter from Baleem. Everything. The knot in her stomach seemed to grow more tangled and tight with each passing day. She was overwhelmed and scared.

But floating naked in the lake, she felt light. Her anxiety melted away with the blood and grime. For this small moment, she was free.

She returned to the surface and breathed in the cool mountain air, looking again for Daegan. He was on his back several yards away, humming a strange, and eerie tune. It was one she thought she recognized. He looked peaceful. The sunlight made him glow at first and then disappear from view as the sun dropped down toward the horizon. She watched him swim to the shore and dry off. His wet hair touched his shoulders, accenting his muscular, chiseled chest. He had done the smart thing and kept his undergarments on. She closed her eyes, floating on her back. When she looked up, Daegan was walking back towards the village without so much as a backward glance, for which she was very grateful. What had she been thinking, stripping down completely naked? She panicked as she realized she had forgotten to grab her bag with her extra clothes. *Oh gods*, she thought. *What am I going to do?*

She treaded water, waiting to see if he would come back.

"Daegan?" she yelled hopefully.

No answer. *Damn. Damn. Damn.* She swam closer to shore and stood there, in waist-deep water, watching as the setting sun painted the sky in oranges and pinks. The moon peeked out from behind the clouds where it had been hiding, lighting the lake around her. It was starting to get cold. She would just have to put on her dirty clothes and bathe again later. She swore as she tiptoed to her clothes, covering herself as best as she could. But her clothes weren't there. Instead, there was a small dagger, one she recognized. Daegan had been using it to peel an apple earlier. She imagined the smirk on his stupid face, and her eye began to twitch. She wouldn't give him the satisfaction of waiting helplessly in the moonlight for someone to find her. She would just have to walk back to the village naked. She just hoped the roads were empty of people. She crept up the path, shivering and hugging herself tightly, one hand gripping the dagger tightly, the other pulsing with pain from where the blade had sliced it earlier. Grimacing, she concentrated on the weight of the dagger. She was going to throw it at Daegan's head. She smiled at the thought of bursting into the inn, naked and swinging a dagger.

"They'll think I've gone mad." She laughed.

The crunch of cart wheels on the road made her stop dead in her tracks. She instinctively grabbed for her weapons, knowing she didn't have them on hand. She sucked in her breath and swore. Holding her head high, she looked straight ahead and did her best to cover what she could as the cart approached. She smiled awkwardly, struggling not to make eye contact with the couple and their two children. The woman gasped, trying to shield her children's eyes, and her husband stared straight ahead, his eyes wide in disbelief. She heard the children giggling. She sighed as they rode past, and cursed Daegan's name, shaking her fist at the night sky.

After walking for what seemed like ages, another figure appeared on the road. Squinting, she tried to see who it was. She could make out a tall, girlish figure with golden locks glistening in the moonlight. Oriana. The young woman held up her bag, along with a fresh set of clothes and undergarments.

"Errr, Zephera? Daegan said you might need a change of clothes," she said carefully, as if testing her mood. Relief flooded through Zephera, followed by a sudden burst of annoyance.

"That's because HE TOOK MY CLOTHES!" she yelled, stamping her foot. She felt herself tumbling as her foot caught under a branch. She fell right into a pile of what smelled like horse dung.

Oriana stifled a laugh.

"Are you laughing? Seriously? I just bathed in a lake and am walking NAKED back to the village, and now… well, I just fell into shit."

Oriana laughed harder.

"Stop! It isn't funny! Gods, give me the clothes so I can get dressed."

Zephera grabbed the bag and clothes and stomped over to the trees, using leaves to brush off what filth she could. She dressed quickly and returned to the road. Oriana was still laughing uncontrollably, clutching her sides and trying to catch her breath.

Zephera glared at her, walking past without so much as a thank you.

"Wait! Zephera, wait! I'm sorry for laughing."

Oriana ran to catch up, trying to stifle a giggle as she ran.

"I'm not going to wait for you if you keep laughing," Zephera said coldly.

"All right, sorry. But, you have to admit, it was kind of funny. I mean, if it was anyone else, wouldn't you have laughed, even a little bit?" she asked.

"With everything that's happened, he just left me there, defenseless and NAKED! He's a pompous, self-righteous ASS!" she said hatefully.

"Well, he did send me to fetch you, so he can't be that hateful, can he? And besides, what on earth possessed you to think it was a good idea to swim naked with that gorgeous specimen?"

"I've gone mad. That's the only explanation I've got. I've literally gone mad."

"Do you think he saw anything? I mean—you, naked?" Oriana's eyes were wide with excitement.

"Oh, gods. I don't know. He would be a lucky bastard if he did," Zephera joked.

"There's that confidence. Perhaps you aren't as mad as you thought."

"Do mad people know they are mad?" Zephera thought aloud.

"I don't think so," Oriana answered. "It's the mad ones who tend to think the rest of the world's lost it while they are the sane ones, but I'm not the one walking naked in the moonlight."

Zephera threw the girl a dangerous look. Oriana smiled slightly, shrugging. They walked in silence, Zephera too angry to do anything but breathe. Thinking Oriana wouldn't dare bother her further, Zephera began to relax.

"Zad is worried about you, Zephera. You really frightened him."

"I know," she whispered back.

Oriana gave her a small smile as they approached the inn. It was a cozy little roadside cottage. Quaint, with a homey feel.

"We'll stay here tonight and head out at dawn. We've lost a day, but it'll give us a chance to try and understand the plague a bit more," Oriana said quietly, the door closing behind her.

Zephera nodded in agreement, surveying the room. It was small, with a bar and a few wooden tables. A large fire was roaring in the corner of the room, and Zad sat in an oversized armchair, talking with the shopkeeper and Brenner. Daegan was nowhere to be seen, which was smart, because if she had seen him, not much would've stopped her from stabbing him through the heart.

"So, you've returned in one piece," Zad said, looking a bit worse for wear as they sat down. "Are you ready to tell us what exactly has been going on? Because a lot of things have been strange lately, and it started with that mission you went on, hunting that stag. What happened, Zephera? You haven't been yourself, and with everything that's going on with these dark creatures—you being attacked… I don't know what to think."

Zephera glared at him, seething. "Oh, so we're going to do this *now*? I was just attacked by a mad man, covered in plague blood, and left naked in the woods. You aren't even going to ask me if I'm all right before you start questioning me?" She winced. Her tone was harsher than she intended.

Zad choked. "Naked in the woods?"

She threw her hands in the air, "Is that all you got out of that? Really? You are such a pig!" she yelled, throwing herself down onto the armchair next to Zad.

Someone cleared their throat. She had forgotten about the shopkeeper. "If you'll excuse me, I have some things I need to attend to," he said quietly, dismissing himself.

They watched him hobble off before turning their gazes to the fire, neither of them speaking. Finally, Zad sighed, breaking the silence first. "I'm sorry," he whispered. "As much as I would love to hear about your naked adventure in the woods, I need to hear about you, this mission, and your blood immunity."

Zephera turned to look at him. He seemed exhausted and worried. Always worried. There was no use in keeping any of this secret any longer, so she told him and the others about her mission—the Shasakar, her conversation with Baleem, and her encounter with Valessa. At the mention of the Keeper's name Brenner's face went white. He gave a slight bow to his companions, excusing himself for bed. Zad and Oriana listened intently, nodding and exchanging occasional glances. When she finally finished, the fire was nearly out. The small embers struggled to catch the remaining charred wood, leaving ghostly shadows on both the walls and their faces.

"So, you and Daegan are immune? Do you know why?" Oriana asked, her voice barely above a whisper.

"I don't, but I have a feeling the answer to that question was in that letter. We could ask Daegan, but he probably wouldn't help. It'd be better to try and see what was in that message."

"I suppose you are right. Maybe he'll open up more eventually. He definitely is a mystery," Oriana murmured, deep in thought. The fire made her golden eyes dance with light. She tore her gaze away from the dying embers. "There isn't much we can do tonight, and I'm exhausted. See you at dawn."

Zephera watched her walk away, wishing there was something more to hate about the girl. Oriana had accepted her story and seemed determined to help her get answers. She was maddeningly helpful.

Zad looked at her intently. "Why didn't you tell me earlier, Zephera? Why did you hold all of this in? You could've shared the burden. I told you I'm always here. I'm not going anywhere." His voice dropped off.

Shrugging, she put her head in her hands. "Honestly, this has all been incredibly overwhelming. I didn't know how to tell you, and I didn't want to worry you."

He clucked his tongue. "I know, I know. You like to suffer alone, brooding in the corner. I'm surprised you and Daegan don't get along better, you are so similar."

"We aren't! I'm nothing like him." She threw a pillow at him.

He tried to dodge the pillow, shooting awkwardly out of his chair, but his foot caught on the leg.

"OW!" he yelled as he fell.

Zephera laughed. At first, Zad looked annoyed, but then he started laughing, too. She went over and lay down on the floor next to him.

"I'm sorry I didn't tell you," she whispered.

"Me too."

She gazed into his warm, gray-blue eyes, eyes she had known for years, eyes that told her she was safe, that told her that with him, she was home. She felt the knot in her stomach release slightly. Zad reached over and tucked a strand of hair behind her ear. He rested his hand on her face. Then he brought his face closer to hers. The knot in her stomach returned instantly. She sucked in her breath as he parted his lips, moving closer to hers.

"And here I thought you two were just friends. Yet you desire her, even when she reeks of shit." Daegan stood at the door, looking amused.

Zephera's eye began to twitch. She jumped to her feet.

"YOU!" she yelled, launching herself at Daegan.

Daegan smirked as Zephera came at him. Zad quickly got up, grabbing Zephera by the arm, and pulling her into him. The wound on her hand reopened, causing Zephera to hiss. She tried to wriggle free, but Zad pulled her away. "Careful beasty, don't waste your energy. He isn't worth it."

Zephera growled. She glared at Daegan. "I will kill you; maybe not today, but I swear it. I'll cut out your lungs and make you wear them like wings."

Daegan whistled. "Delightful."

Zephera screamed as Zad held her tight. "Let me go Zadkiel!" she thrashed.

"Promise not to kill him?" Zad whispered in her ear.

Zephera closed her eyes and slowed her breathing. "I promise," she muttered.

Zad let her go. In an instant, Zephera turned on her heel and sauntered up the stairs, Zad close behind.

"Zephera, wait up, I want to talk to you."

Ignoring him, she ran up the stairs to her bedroom, not stopping until the door was locked behind her. She sank down, resting her head on the old wooden door, her eyes closed in angry confusion. She brought her knees to her chest. Oh gods, what was he thinking? He couldn't do this, not now, not ever! *He's my family, not... not...* She couldn't even finish her thought. She sat still for a few minutes. Footsteps sounded in the hallway. She sucked in a breath when they stopped outside her door. She knew Zad rested his hand against the other side. She sat quietly, listening to him breathe. She bowed her head in relief when he finally retreated to his room down the hall.

Zephera fumbled for her bag, pulling out fresh dressings and ointment to treat her wounded hand. The intensity of the pulsing pain had been increasing all night as the adrenaline wore off and was now nearly unbearable. *First cleanse, then stitch,* she reminded herself through the haze of pain.

Gritting her teeth, she pried the lid off the vial of gold ointment. The reek of the ointment assaulted her senses. It stank almost as much as she did.

Steadying her shaking grip, she poured the ointment into the wound. Stars littered her vision as the liquid frothed, burning away dirt and infection. She stumbled over to the basin, sloshing water from the nearby jug into the porcelain bowl. Using a moistened cloth, she dabbed gently at the wound, hissing as the fabric rubbed at the raw, tender skin. Her eyes narrowed as she peered at the wound. When she was certain it was clean, she lit a candle and threaded the needle.

Her stomach twisted as she pierced her skin with the needle. She always hated this part. Baleem never let anyone else stitch her up when she was wounded. She had to do it herself. She had several ugly scars, reminders of when her young, inexperienced hands had feebly tried to stitch her own wounds. Eventually, after much trial and error, she had learned how to fix a wound properly, though she never grew to hate it less. The mending of flesh always made her feel sick. Flesh was meant to be split apart, not fused back together. It was, however, a necessary evil. She finished the last stitch and brought her dagger to the string, cutting it. Then she used her teeth to help tie a knot before wrapping her hand in fresh dressings.

Exhausted, she dropped onto the straw bed next to Oriana, envisioning all the ways she could kill Daegan and make it seem like an accident.

CHAPER 11

She drifted into a restless sleep, dreaming of a shadowy abyss filled with gnashing teeth and black ichor. Shadow creatures stalked her, never getting too close, but always watching her. Diseased men and women chased her through forests to the edge of cliffs. Everyone she knew was piled up dead around her, black sludge encasing them. She tried to run, but she had nowhere to go.

"Zephera! Zephera, my dear, listen to me," Valessa called.

She opened her eyes with a start, trying to shut the woman out, but found herself on a grassy hill. Through the dense fog that surrounded her, she could make out a few figures creeping noiselessly around her.

"Hello? Valessa? Where are we?" she asked, searching the vast void.

"Your mind, dear girl. Your dreamscape."

"What? How is that—"

"Possible? Well, you called for me. An old magic that has not been seen on this earth for five hundred years is awakening, turning the impossible into the probable. I don't mean to frighten you, but I need to speak with you."

"I have nothing to say to you, Valessa. You've done nothing but toy with me and your vague answers make me question everything even more. Let me out of here!"

"It is your dream, Zephera. You can leave if you want to. I'm sorry for how I have handled our past meetings. I assure you, we won't meet like that again." Valessa said softly, reaching for Zephera's hand.

Zephera jerked her hand away, and a look of hurt flashed across Valessa's face. "No? You'll just show up in my head instead? Where's the letter from Baleem? I know you have it! What did he write that you didn't want me to know?"

The ground around them began to shake.

"We don't have much time, Zephera. Do not trust him!"

"Don't trust who?"

The world around her grew dark, the mist becoming so thick she could no longer see her own hand. The ground shook so violently that Zephera fell and tumbled down the hill.

"Zephera! Zephera! Wake up, damn it! Wake up!"

She opened her eyes to see Brenner and Oriana standing over her, looking frightened.

"What happened?" she asked.

"You were having some sort of fit, tossing and turning and moaning like you were in pain," Oriana said, eyes still widened in alarm. "I couldn't wake you, and then Brenner showed up. He helped pull you out of whatever nightmare you were lost in."

She sat up, her head heavy with fatigue. "I'm sorry for waking you. Oriana, Brenner, thank you." Brenner nodded and left the room.

Oriana held out a hand and helped her to her feet. "Don't mention it. We might as well get up now."

Zephera dressed quickly, brushing and braiding her hair. She packed her bags and headed downstairs to get some breakfast. Daegan was brooding over some maps with a disheveled Zad. Zephera's heart fell into her stomach. She didn't want to speak to Zad just yet, especially after last night.

They didn't look up when she entered, which was a blessing. Zephera didn't know if she could face Zad just yet, especially on an empty stomach. She ate her eggs and oats quickly and headed outside to get some air. Finding the perfect spot for the sunrise, she sat down near the town square. Brenner sat down next to her, offering her an apple. She took it gratefully, always happy for more food.

CHAPTER 11

"Good morning, and thanks again for helping me."

The mage nodded and gestured to her hand.

She held up her bandaged hand, "Oh, I'm fine. I cleaned it out and stitched it last night. It should heal nicely now." She smiled.

Brenner held his hands up against her arm and looked at her intently. "You want to heal me?"

He nodded.

"All right. I suppose you can, if you want to."

The mage removed the bandages. The skin beneath it was swollen and starting to scab. He took her small, calloused hand in his large smooth ones and she felt heat and pressure. It stung, but only a bit. When he removed his hands, the wound was gone. There was no trace that it had ever been there, not even a scar.

She raised her eyebrows and let out a small laugh, "Thank you," she said softly, looking up at the mage's face. It was soft and his smile was contagious. She flushed and smiled back. His eyes were kind. She hadn't noticed before, but they were the most gorgeous shade of blue that she had ever seen. They looked like heaven. She shook her head, mesmerized by him. Then a small bark interrupted them. A fluffy head poked out of a pack on Brenner's back. She couldn't help but laugh. Brenner smiled and reached for the hound.

"I'm pleased you made it through the night, Dorjan." She patted the pup on his massive, black head. "He looks much better today. Thank you for healing him."

The pup barked in agreement. She sat and played with the dog, laughing as it licked her face.

"Are you ready?" Zad interrupted. "We have a long day ahead of us." He still wouldn't meet Zephera's eyes. She handed the pup to Brenner who put him back into the pack.

The others joined them. Zephera followed behind the others out of the village to the base of the mountain. She gazed at the tall, majestic creations in front of them. They were beautiful and covered in brush, the trees green and pristine. She peered at the fog-shrouded mountaintops.

It was a long way up and a long way down. Once they started up the path, there would be no turning back. Zephera let out a deep breath and took a step forward.

CHAPTER 12

They climbed for hours until the sun reached its highest point in the sky. It was blistering hot and the air around them was dense. No one complained when Zad decided to stop and rest and get a bite to eat. The group sat in silence and watched as Dorjan jumped and played, chasing his tail and tripping over his gigantic paws. Zephera barely had time to rest her legs before they started their trek again. They stayed close together, the terrain harsh and hardly traveled. The dangers that lurked around them were unknown. There were rumors of the perils, death, and strange creatures that lurked about. Few had traveled the pass. Most who braved it were never heard from again, and the ones who did return came back changed, driven mad by unspoken horrors.

"Evil lurks in those mountains," the innkeeper had said. "It was once used by merchants as a trading route between the villages. But that was long before my time. The world has changed since the Dark Ages. It's too treacherous now."

Yet, such was the nature of their journey: deceptively difficult and delightfully dangerous.

Zephera normally enjoyed the silence but the tension in the air was maddening. She needed some form of distraction. She cleared her throat. "Do you honestly think that there are creatures up here that'll make us go mad?"

Daegan laughed. "You're already mad, Zephera. I don't think any sort of creature should be blamed for that."

Zephera shot him an icy glare. "Gods above, Daegan. Shut up."

Daegan clicked his tongue. "Touchy, touchy."

Zad slowed his pace to stand with Zephera. "I'm sure there are many unknown creatures and things up here. This journey wasn't meant to be easy." He gestured around at the rocky, steep terrain. "Though if it gets any more difficult than this slope, I doubt we'll live to tell the tale of the dreaded Mountains of Dreer."

Zephera laughed. "There's no way I'll admit defeat before we've even gotten started. However, I will agree that fighting an unknown enemy in this terrain would be rather… trying."

Zad smiled at her. "Always the optimist."

On they went, into the abyss of the unknown. Fear was one obvious reason for the group's silence. The other was utter exhaustion. They hiked for three days and made camp at the edge of a clearing. They took turns keeping watch while the others slept as soundly as they could. The noises in the surrounding forest were strange and distant, made by mysterious creatures they knew nothing of. The days were uneventful and long. The higher they climbed, the colder it got, and the harder it was to breathe. The trees grew further and further apart as the group ascended. There wasn't much said, just grunts and a lot of pointing. Eventually, even that was too tiring. Even Dorjan, who usually seemed to have so much energy, seemed exhausted. He stayed soundly in his pack, only coming out to cuddle with Brenner or to eat.

On the fourth day, the incline gradually began to even out, making the terrain flatter and easier to maneuver. The greenery slowly disappeared, and they came to a rocky cliffside. Zephera stopped and looked out at the world below. It was magnificent. Everything below her was so small, so beautiful. It was as if time stopped and she was its keeper. The sky was dark on the horizon as the sun began to set, indicating that a storm would soon be rolling in.

"We should make camp here, against these rocks. It'll help shelter us from the storm," Daegan asserted.

"No, we need to keep moving," Zad argued. "If we stop now, we may not be able to reach the top of the pass. That storm looks fierce and I would rather we get to the other side before setting up camp."

Daegan glared at him, running his hand through his dark hair. "That would be unwise. Look, the storm will probably hit us in the next few hours and we can use that time to prepare a stable shelter to wait it out."

"I disagree. We need to keep moving. We don't know what's out there, only that it's nothing good. I don't want to stop unless we have to." Zad's anger rose.

"Yet you want to continue up the pass and get stuck in the storm? We're all exhausted. We need to stay here, where it's open and we have a view of the land to fend off any incoming attack," Daegan said, standing up.

"No," Zad snarled, standing to face Daegan. "*I* have the maps. *I'm* the leader and *I* say we keep going."

"I will NOT take orders from some insolent child," Daegan growled.

Zad spat at him. Daegan leapt at him, knocking him onto the ground. Daegan's fist struck Zad's face repeatedly. Zad's eye immediately began to swell shut. Zad shoved Daegan off and rolled over, coughing and spitting blood. Zad got to his feet, unsheathing his sword, and readied it at his side.

The two of them circled each other, daring the other to strike first—Zad with his sword, and Daegan with his fists. Oriana screamed at the two of them to stop and Brenner held her back from trying to jump into the fray. Dorjan was whimpering from his pack, frightened by the sudden brawl. Brenner looked to Zephera with his expressive eyes.

DO SOMETHING! she heard in her head. Brenner motioned with a slight jerk of his head toward the pair. She looked wildly from him to the two fighting men. Their eyes were locked on each other, feral rage blinding them to everything else. Zephera jumped in the middle, her back to Zadkiel, just as he launched himself forward at Daegan. He plowed into her, knocking her off her feet. She landed face-first in the dirt. He fell on top of her, pinning her down.

She grumbled, flipping onto her back and sitting up. "What in the name of the gods do you two idiots think you are doing? Are you trying to get yourself killed, Zad?" She threw a handful of small pebbles in his direction.

Daegan laughed from behind her. "So you think I would win against your boyfriend? Interesting."

"Shut up, Daegan! Just go!" she screamed at him. She turned her attention back to her friend.

"Zadkiel, have you lost your mind? Fighting in unknown terrain? With *him*?"

He looked at her for a moment, his jaw clenched tight in anger. Then he sulked away.

"Zad! Zad! Where are you going?" she called after him, standing up.

Let him go. He needs to cool off, Brenner said in her head.

She whipped her head around to look at him, her eyes wide.

Don't. We can speak later, he thought to her coolly, not bothering to look at her.

She glanced at Oriana, who looked frightened. "We can set up camp here," she barked, not meaning to sound so harsh. "We're all tired, and everyone's a little on edge." Oriana nodded silently and began to unpack the tents and supplies.

Zephera stomped around the camp, fuming at Zad's stupidity. What was he thinking, attacking Daegan? What if he had killed the man? Not that she hadn't dreamt about killing him herself plenty of times. Zad may have been a trained assassin, but he didn't get into pointless pissing contests like this. It wasn't like him.

She busied herself by setting up a perimeter around the camp, unwinding the wire and wrapping it around the wooden stakes Brenner had driven into the ground. After finishing the perimeter fence, she helped Oriana with the tents. They worked in silence, not bothering to look up from their work.

"We are all exhausted. To be honest, I thought it would be you who broke first, not Zad," Oriana said quietly as they finished.

Zephera sat on a log and unsheathed her dagger, cleaning it with her tunic.

Taking a long sip from a canister of water, Oriana finally asked, "Is he going to be okay?"

Daegan appeared from behind them, putting a pointed boot on the log next to Zephera.

"Who cares?" he interjected. "If he doesn't get over it, my point will have been made. He's a cowardly child."

Standing suddenly, Zephera balled her fist and threw it into Daegan's smug face, sending him stumbling backwards. Surprise flashed over his dark features, making him look vulnerable for a moment.

"You are an ASS!" she huffed, reeling her fist to punch him again. He caught it mid-air and twisted her arm, pulling her against him. He held her tight against his chest. She tried to get free, kicking her legs and thrashing her body, but he was too strong.

"Let me go! Now!" she screamed.

"Calm down first," he whispered gently in her ear.

She thrashed harder, trying to loosen his grip, but he squeezed tighter.

"Zephera, calm down. I'll let go, just relax."

She stopped moving, willing her breathing to slow. She was shaking with anger. He held her until she calmed.

"I'm going to let go now. Don't punch me again, all right?" he whispered.

She nodded slowly. He released her, and she stalked away without looking at him, fearing one glance at his face would send her into another rage and she would punch him again.

She walked off in the direction Zad had fled. Her anger beginning to spark again as she thought of Daegan. She hated him. She hated his face, his pompous attitude, the way he mocked them. She found Zad staring out over the valley below. She sat next to him and took his hand. They watched the storm inch closer, covering the world below in rain.

"I'm sorry I said Daegan would win in a fight between you two," she said softly.

He looked at her sheepishly, his right eye swollen shut.

"I'm only sorry you let him hear you say it," he said dryly. "Just because you were right doesn't mean I want him knowing it."

"Zad, that's not—"

"It's true," he interrupted. "But only because he's huge and I lost my temper. Let him try and start a fight with me when we're back home; I could kick his ass." He laughed.

She smiled. "I punched him."

"You what?" Zad looked at her incredulously.

"I punched him, right on the lip. It's going to make eating rather strenuous the next few days."

"I'm not sure if I should be pleased or angry."

"I didn't punch him for you. He took my clothes."

They looked at each other and laughed.

"I'm sorry if I made you uncomfortable the other night," Zad murmured.

She willed herself to look at him. His expression was full of hope.

She bit her lip nervously. "You didn't. I just…" She paused, trying to find the right words.

She looked away as his hopeful expression disappeared. She hated hurting him. But he was her friend, and now wasn't the time to sift through her feelings for Zad. They were on a mission, one that held their very existence in its grasp. There was no time for distractions, especially ones of that sort, though she did wonder what it would be like, with Zad. She looked at his lips, full and soft. Her mind wandered to what it would be like having her mouth on his. She felt herself go red. No. Not Zad. But why not him? He knew her better than anyone else. He was always trying to lift her up, to get her to better herself. He knew her strengths and weaknesses. He knew her favorite foods, her likes, her dislikes. He knew her completely. She shook her head, banishing the dangerous thoughts from her mind.

"I… I…" Zephera didn't even know what to say. They sat in silence for what felt like forever.

He nodded, staring out at the approaching storm. It wasn't until the wind started to pick up that they returned to camp. Brenner and Oriana were adjusting the tents and the shelter. Daegan was readying leftover stew over a small fire. They ate in silence, hardly looking at one another.

"Well, this has been another bright and cheery day," Oriana said, standing up and rubbing her hands together. "I've thoroughly enjoyed it, but I'm exhausted. Wake me for my shift, will you, Zephera?"

She nodded, feeling exhausted herself, but was too angry to sleep. There wasn't much need for keeping watch. The storm was raging, and she could hardly see her own hand in front of her face, let alone any approaching threat. The perimeter fence would give them fair warning if anything came near their camp. She sat outside the tent, the wind and rain pouring down on her face, chilling her to the bone.

Do you want some company? Brenner's voice spoke inside her head.

She jumped, thinking she had dozed off.

Sorry, I did not mean to startle you. He sat down beside her and handed her a vial of a red liquid. *It is falahi—liquid heat. It will help keep you warm.*

"Thank you." She opened the bottle and downed the liquid. It was sweet and tasted like cinnamon. Instantly, she felt warmer.

I can teach you to project your thoughts into my head if you want. She threw him a look of surprise. He shrugged. *It is easy if you have a good teacher,* he smirked.

"Oh?" she laughed. "And who taught you?"

A good teacher.

She shook her head and smiled into her hands.

Just picture yourself talking to me, like we are now, only silently. It will take some practice, but you will learn. Pretend that it is your only way of communication. You cannot speak, you cannot write. The only way to communicate is through sheer will.

Zephera closed her eyes tightly, concentrating on speaking with her mind. She clenched her teeth so tightly she thought she was going to chip one.

Easy, there. I said it would take practice. Do not strain yourself. Besides, it is not like anyone can hear. They are all asleep, and the wind is too loud.

Shrugging her shoulders, she leaned back against the rock. The rain pelted down on the makeshift roof above her head.

"Tell me about yourself. What was life like in the tower?"

Quiet mostly. Mages do not do much speaking.

She laughed. "Ah, a joker, I see."

I can juggle, too. But I suppose that is not what you want to know.

"Juggle? That's an interesting skill. So, you are a healer, a joker, and a juggler? Is there anything you can't do?" They sat in silence and watched the rain.

I made a medicinal compound for you. You will need to take it every night to keep your mind guarded against Valessa.

She whipped her head to face him, surprised. "What? How did you know she's been speaking in my dreams?"

You forget, I am quite accustomed to the Keeper's ways. I know your mind is weaker when you sleep. She is able to enter when you do not have your guard up, though being up here makes it impossible for her to get through. He gestured to the air around them.

"Why is it different up here?" she asked curiously.

She needs to be close to you, at least within a few miles. Any further, and it takes a great deal out of her. She would not follow you up here. She is powerful and strong, but even she has her limits.

Pulling her dark hair out of her face, she stared into the darkness around them, her heart pounding. Things were complicated. She was changing. Fear had always been a fleeting thing to her. Now, it was taking over her life. She was losing her mind. Was Valessa responsible?

"I don't know what's happening to me. For the past few weeks I've been changing. I feel different. I'm not strong enough to lead this group, and I know you all see it. Even Zad sees it. That's why he's taken over from the start. What's wrong with me?" She felt Brenner gazing at her with what she knew must be pity but when she turned to face him she didn't see pity, but sadness.

I assume you are referring to your lack of control over your mind? She can get in anywhere, and with her last spell, she left you weak. She needed your barriers down. She needed you to question yourself. All of that fear and questioning chips away at the natural barriers already in place, making it easier for her to gain access to your mind.

"So having a complete breakdown like a child is just me losing my inhibitions. Right," she fumed, throwing her hands in the air. "And feeling like I'm completely going mad? What's that?"

Fear is powerful. Valessa can be stronger than fear. She is cruel and manipulative. She will stop at nothing to get what she needs and maintain control. He gestured to his mouth sadly.

"Did she do that to you? Make you unable to speak?"

Brenner nodded, closing his eyes, his hands tightening into fists. *When a mage reaches a certain age—it is different for everyone, but it is whenever we are in our prime, at our most powerful—we are given a talisman. It harnesses our power, helps us to control our magic and do powerful spells without depleting our energy levels. It is, in a sense, a mage's lifeline. Without it, we are missing a piece of ourselves. We are essentially empty. Once we are bonded with our talismans, she takes us under her wing. We train with her, dine with her, do everything with her. When she is done with us, we are stripped of our clothes, beaten, and tied down with iron chains. She takes our talismans—our souls—and we are rendered mute. Most die. Others are not so lucky and are forced to live life under her control, soulless and broken.*

She turned to look at him, concern filling in her eyes. She had an unusual urge to comfort him, so she placed her hand on his and squeezed it tightly. "Why did she let you leave the Tower and join us?"

Brenner smiled. *She took my soul, but she did not break me. As far she knows, I am under her control. She won't see it coming until it is too late.*

"You are a clever little devil, aren't you?" she quipped, smiling.

I will have my time, but first we need to focus on eradicating this pesky plague. It complicates matters and frustrates all plans of revenge, thoroughly making it useless to try until the cure has been found. His voice was filled with nonchalance.

"You seem certain we'll succeed," she said, unconvinced.

And you seem certain that we will fail.

She raised an eyebrow and pursed her lips.

Like I said, fear is a powerful tool, and Valessa knows how to use it. Doubtless, our mission may seem impossible, but having hope makes the outcome seem a little brighter.

"Hope or vengeance?" she asked quietly, running her hands through her hair.

Both. They are both powerful, driving forces. But though fear is strong, it is no match for hope. I can help you overcome your fear, Zephera. I can help you gain hope. I just ask that in return, you help me.

Just as she was about to answer, Oriana emerged from the tent. Her eyes widened in surprise at Brenner. He only nodded, giving Oriana a half smile and walked towards his tent. Sitting down next to Zephera, Oriana stretched her legs out and leaned against the cliff behind them, fluffing her blonde hair.

"I figured if I couldn't sleep I could at least do something useful," the blonde woman said quietly. "You can go. I'll take over from here."

"To be honest, I don't think I can sleep much, either. You can keep me company if you'd like," Zephera said, surprising herself with her offer. Oriana looked at her with wide eyes. She opened her mouth to speak, but thought better of it.

"Don't think that this means we are friends. We're not," Zephera blurted out. She threw her a look, and Oriana smiled silently.

They sat in silence for hours, watching as the storm dissipated, leaving the world a muddy, foggy mess. Zephera shut her eyes and listened to her surroundings. She let herself fall into a dark dreamland, covered in black blood and darkness. She wasn't afraid—just curious. Zephera studied the shadowy world around her, feeling content and peaceful in the eerie abyss. It was vibrant, its intentions clear, there were no feelings of confusion, no feelings of fear. There was only the rush of fresh possibilities in this new world. No hypocrisy, no secrets. Just the darkness and its graceful power. She looked around and came to a path, following it to a small pool of clear water. She bent down and touched the water, making a small ripple. She sat and observed the world around her. It seemed so normal, so right.

Suddenly a hand came out of the pool and dragged her in. Zephera struggled, flailing and kicking, trying to break free. But it was too strong. It pulled her underwater. She reached for her weapons only to find that her hands were gone. She looked around desperately, her vision hazy. The rest of her body started to disappear. Closing her eyes, she felt herself being shaken awake.

Zephera blinked, and looked up into the face of Oriana.

"Time to go," Oriana said, offering a hand. Heart still pounding from the strange dream, Zephera accepted and got to her feet, brushing dust from her pants. "We're almost done packing the supplies up. You fell asleep just before dawn. I figured I would let you rest a bit." Oriana handed her a piece of dried meat.

"Thank you. I'm sorry. I didn't mean to doze off," Zephera said gratefully, taking the meat and eating it quickly. It left an awful taste in her mouth. Too much pepper. She reached for her canteen and gulped down the rest of the water. Oriana nodded and walked toward camp. Zephera headed to the edge of the wood with her bag to change and relieve herself. She splashed a bucket of newly collected rain water onto her face and pulled her dark hair into a braid. She met the others just as they were going over the maps and planning their trek for the day.

"I've been thinking," she announced to the group. "I know I haven't been the best leader—or even companion—since the start of this journey, and I'm sorry. I haven't exactly been myself. There are many things at play here, and we all need to be at the top of our game if we are going to succeed. We can do this. We can find Reina and the cure. We can save our world, but we must be unified." She looked at Zad and Daegan. "We don't need to be friends, and we don't need to like each other, but we do need to work together. I know it'll take time for you guys to trust me, and that's okay, but we need to be able to put our differences aside. Otherwise, we won't get through this. To be completely honest with you, I'm scared, I'm tired, and I don't know what I'm doing. But I do know that if we don't succeed on this mission, we'll all die. We need to get to that altar, find that item, and get off this mountain." She looked to her companions. Their eyes flashed in silent agreement, and she nodded, motioning with her hands for Zad to lead the way.

CHAPTER 13

They hiked into the afternoon, stopping only for water and to share some dried fruit. They were running low on food and were a day's journey from the base of the mountain. Though Zephera had gone for longer periods of time without sustenance before, the thick air and strenuous path were rapidly depleting her energy stores. She could see that the others were tiring as well. They would need to hunt that evening and catch enough game to sustain them.

Dark woods surrounded them now, with vegetation so thick the light from the sun was almost completely eclipsed. Their journey was hampered by the old, overgrown path they followed.

In the densest part of the forest, they found a series of crumbling stone pillars. Strange symbols were carved into them, signaling that the group was near the path to the altar.

Zephera leaned against a pillar and watched as Daegan sketched the symbols onto a piece of parchment. His large hands moved gracefully across the paper and his dark eyes were wide with wonder. He looked relaxed, almost kind. As if realizing that someone was watching, he glanced up. His posture went from light to tall and strong. She met his eyes and quickly looked away. He stalked off. She closed her eyes and tried to listen to the world around her. The thick shrubbery made it impossible to hear anything but Zad and Oriana's short breaths and quiet conversation.

A branch snapped and her eyes flew open. She threw a look at Zad. He held up his hand to quiet the group. The only sound she could hear was her own breathing, which she slowed to almost non-existence. She waited in tense anticipation. Suddenly, the earth began to rumble. A loud roar issued forth from the woods in front of them and something crashed through the trees. The group reached for their weapons, readying themselves for battle. Zephera stole a glance at the others. They seemed calm, prepared to face whatever horror was headed for them. She didn't know if she hoped for one large creature or many smaller creatures. Whatever it was, she was ready.

Squinting into the black abyss, she noticed four tall, dark figures creeping towards them. Her heart began to race, and the familiar scent of death and decay filled her nose. The members of the group split off into the woods. Brenner shot a ball of blue light into the air. It illuminated the thick wood around them, showing her a break in the trees. If they were going to gain the upper hand on the monsters, they would need a clearing. She whispered a prayer to the gods, hoping the break would lead to a glade. She ran with the creatures at her heels. She saw another ball of light just a few yards ahead of her and followed it. She both cursed and praised Brenner for the help, for if she could see the light, so could the things behind her. She came to an open field and almost cheered. But remembering the monsters behind her, she put her joy away for later—if they survived what was about to come.

You are Zephera, Lady of Death, and you will defy all odds and win, Brenner spoke calmly to her mind. *Breathe, Zephera. Hope, fight, and win.*

She chanced a quick look over her shoulder at the creatures behind her. They moved from the dark wood into the light Brenner had conjured. She could now see their grotesque shapes. They were compiled of dozens of different animals. The smallest creature was the size of a grown man and had the face of a lion and the wings of a bat.

She stifled a scream. A creature with the head of a boar and the body of a tiger roared in challenge. It started towards Brenner. The mage's blue light shot out at the creature, shocking it. The monster's body fell to the ground with a thud, shaking violently. When the deadly convulsions stopped, black ooze seeped out around it, forming a pool of sludge.

CHAPTER 13

The other creatures circled the perimeter, growling and grunting as if trying to find another way to get to them. Zephera watched quietly, trying to decide what to do. Her best option was to charge directly at the smallest one. His disproportionate frame made his movements awkward, which made him the easiest prey. Just as she moved to attack, an arrow flew by, missing her head by inches. It landed in its intended victim, and the small creature yelled with rage, pawing at its body and trying to dig the arrow out.

Zephera took the opening and ran toward the ailing monster. She slid under its legs and sliced its heel with her dagger. Then she shot to her feet, stumbling slightly from the damp forest ground, bringing herself into position behind it. She bashed the creature's head with the hilt of her curved blade. It cried out, not knowing which wound to hold. Zephera smiled wickedly as the creature chose its sliced heel. She gripped her dagger tightly and jammed it into the creature's exposed neck. It bled out in seconds. Zephera fished her blackened knife out of the creature, a gleam in her eyes. She smirked as its body fell into the tangles of hanging vines, putting its corpse on display.

Her success was short-lived. She was knocked down by a powerful kick to the back of her legs. The air fled her lungs as she hit the ground, landing on an exposed tree root. Cursing, she rolled onto her back. As she struggled to catch her breath, another kick slammed against her head. The world grew blurry. She shook her head, trying to clear her vision, and sloppily got to her feet, drawing in great gasps of air. A man stood in front of her, he had yellow eyes and catlike teeth. He smiled, revealing his fangs and letting out a growl.

He had every characteristic of a human, yet he was no man; nor was he a creature. What was he? He drew his sword and motioned for her to grab her own. She bent down slowly and picked up her blade. Her heart pounded with uncertainty. She looked around at the others and saw that they were all facing the remaining creature.

Zephera and the man circled one another, their blades raised and their stances in sync. Their feet crossed in an intricate, deadly dance, and their bodies swayed to a tune that only she and the man-beast could hear. Zephera glared at her opponent, her eyes narrowed and her face a cruel mask. The man-beast snarled, spraying red flecks that looked like human blood into the air. She rushed at the man with a guttural scream and brought her blade to his chest. He blocked it easily, something Zephera had counted on. She brought her second blade down across his thigh, cutting through his dark flesh and leaving a thin line of charcoal-colored blood. The man-beast smiled.

She sucked in a breath. This warrior wasn't of this world. The black slime that oozed from his wound smelled of rotting flesh and mold. She lifted her eyes from the creature's gash and smiled back wickedly. The creature barked a laugh and lunged for her again. She parried, but he caught her curved blade with his own. They stared at each other, both daring the other to move first. Their blades kissed as they leapt into a dance of clashing metal and swooshing air. They continued on, striking and parrying, only able to scratch each other with their blades. It was an impossible fight. He was a skilled warrior and she was a trained assassin. They were too evenly matched.

There was a loud crash, followed by fire. Towering flames engulfed the woods around them. If they didn't move fast, they would both perish. Another ball of flame hurtled into the clearing. Zephera dove out of the way as a large tree fell to the ground where she had just been. She didn't waste any time looking back to see if the creature had survived. She just ran.

Back through the woods, Zephera, Brenner said in her head. *Hasten to the cliffs. We are close to the altar. Run.*

She fled to the woods. The screams of the dying creatures followed her. She didn't stop running until she made it to the cliffs. Spotting her companions, she finally fell to her knees. After calming her breath and her pounding heart, she walked over to the rest of the group. Something was wrong. Fear and anxiety permeated the air around them. Zad and Brenner were standing over a seated Oriana. She was covered in soot and blood, and she was holding her extended leg, her expression pained. Only Brenner looked up when Zephera arrived.

"I think it's broken," Oriana whimpered.

"Brenner, can you heal her?" Zad asked quietly.

Brenner examined the leg, his face a mask of composed peace, the crease in his brow the only sign of concern. The bone had snapped and was protruding out of her bloody, swollen leg. He shook his head slowly. Brenner motioned for Zephera to follow him and the two walked just out of earshot of Oriana and Zad.

"How exactly are we supposed to help her? Is she in any danger of dying?" she asked the mage.

At the moment, no. But if we do not get her to the nearest village soon, infection could set in. If she wants to keep her leg, we need to set the bone. My magic stores are nearly depleted, but I can use what energy I have left to heal her.

"How are we going to reset the bone?" Zephera asked quietly, a grim look on her face.

"We are going to have to hold her down," Daegan said coolly, emerging from the woods. Zephera must've looked horrified because Daegan quickly reached into his bag and pulled out a flask.

"Take a swig of this, buttercup. You are going to need it," he said lightly, taking a large swig himself.

He passed the flask to Zephera. She crinkled her nose at the smell of the alcohol and cleared her throat. "Bottoms up." She grimaced as she raised the flask into the air. The taste was atrocious. Some called it liquid courage. She called it liquid ass. She wondered how anyone could stomach the taste. She handed the bottle to Brenner, who refused.

"What if there are still creatures out there? Won't they hear her scream?" Zephera asked quietly, the warmth of the drink permeating her bones.

"I searched the area. They've retreated. I doubt they'll attack us again anytime soon. They are just as wounded as we are, if not more so." Daegan paused. "As much as it pains me to say, I believe you and I are the only ones who can continue on to the altar."

Zephera laughed at the irony.

He raised a bloodied eyebrow at her. "Brenner needs to stay with Oriana and will need what little energy he has left to get her to the village at the base of the mountain. They'll need Zad to help fend off any incoming threats. Unfortunately, that leaves you and me to finish off the first leg of our journey."

Before Zephera could protest, Brenner grabbed her shoulder softly and nodded. *There are bigger things at stake here, Zephera.*

"Fine," she grumbled. She motioned to where Oriana and Zad were sitting. Zad was whispering to her and stroking her hair. Oriana had a tight smile on her face. They looked up when the trio arrived.

"Oriana, are you in any pain?" Zephera asked her gently, sitting down next to the girl.

"Not much. I think the adrenaline's numbing the pain. Is it bad? I can't see with all the blood and dirt." Zephera caught a glimpse of her leg, her eyes widened in fascination. Her leg looked like shredded meat, and her bone was sticking out of the skin like an arrow protruding from the back of a stag.

She took a deep breath. "Oriana, I'm not going to lie to you. I need you to stay calm. Do you understand?" Zephera whispered with as much confidence as she could, giving her a stiff smile. Oriana's green eyes widened slightly and she nodded her head.

"Your leg is… well, Brenner's going to try to heal what he can. But your wound is very severe. If you want to keep your leg, we are going to need to set the bone. It's going to hurt badly. You'll need to be held down. Otherwise we risk the bone not setting correctly."

Oriana sat quietly, looking at all of their faces, her expression unreadable. "Okay," she finally whispered.

The group scurried into action, collecting two straight sticks for a makeshift splint and ripping apart bedding to bind the wound.

Oriana watched as they prepared for the horrific thing they were about to do. Zad never left her side. He whispered to her, explaining every detail of what was going to happen next. When they were ready,

Zephera pulled Zad aside to explain that she and Daegan would be leaving the main group. To her surprise, he didn't object. Zephera felt an odd sensation in her stomach. She shook her head, letting the feeling fade away as quickly as it came. She turned to walk back to the group. Zad frowned, grabbed her hand tightly, and pulled her towards him.

"I love you, Beasty. We will get through this." He smiled sadly at her and then planted a kiss on her forehead and held her a minute longer. She met his eyes, giving him a half smile, and let go of his hand.

Daegan was standing over Oriana. He held out his flask to her. "For your nerves."

Zephera laughed at Daegan's expression when Oriana guzzled down the whole flask without so much as breaking a sweat. An eerie, strange silence descended upon the group. Daegan and Zad lifted Oriana onto the cleanest cloth they had and placed a strap of leather in her mouth. Zephera sat at her side. Oriana's fear was palpable. It was the kind of fear that Zephera saw in her victims before she killed them. She had always been the one who caused that fear. Now she had to ease it. She had no idea where to begin. Oriana must've sensed her hesitation because she smiled weakly up at her, nodding slightly.

Zephera began to sing softly. It was a song she hummed to herself when she was sick or tired. Baleem used to sing her that melody when she was small. The melody was dark and strange yet peaceful and strong.

> *As the moon sleeps, day quenches the sky. Boasting its powerful might.*
> *It sings a proud song, but as quickly is gone, fearing the impending Night.*
> *For the dark awakens its nightmares.*
> *As the sun slumbers, the sky grows dim. The world recedes from sight.*
> *Though Darkness is strong, its true fear is come, a fiery fiend: the Light.*
> *For the day awakens its nightmares.*

Once forces of nature. Both calm, both chaos, neither of which knew shame.
Now mired in battle, warring for peace. Not nature, but Man is to blame.
For Man is the soul of nightmares.

Zephera closed her eyes. She was so engrossed in calming the girl that she didn't realize Daegan was watching her with his piercing stare. For he, too, knew that song.

Daegan tightened his hold on Oriana. Zephera held her down on the other side, continuing to hum the dark tune. Oriana looked up at Zad. He stroked her hair and smiled softly.

Brenner prepared the dressings and ointment. He didn't wait for the song to finish before he held up his fingers in a silent countdown. Three. Two. One. The quiet calm they had established was broken by Oriana's primal scream. The sound echoed off the cliffs and clawed through the air around them. Zephera closed her eyes and held Oriana down as tightly as she could. Brenner cut the mangled skin and poured boiling water onto the wound. Oriana thrashed and wailed. Zephera's hold on Oriana was slipping. Zad motioned for Zephera to switch positions with him.

She shook her head. She couldn't try to do what Zad had done for Oriana—to hold her hand and be her rock. It wasn't in Zephera's nature, especially not while Oriana's bone was being pushed back into her leg. She cursed her weakness. Finally, as Oriana's arm slipped from her grasp again, she let Zad take over. She scrambled to Zad's abandoned post at Oriana's shoulder. She cast around for ways to ease Oriana's suffering, but her mind was blank. She panicked. Her eyes darted from Zad to Daegan, begging for help. Zad didn't look at her. He was holding Oriana down and for some godforsaken reason was putting all of his energy into it. Daegan met her eye for a moment before looking down. A ghost of a smile drifted across his face.

Oriana continued to scream and thrash. Zephera was beginning to get a headache from the noise. Her panic turned into impatience. She clucked her tongue as Brenner carefully peeled the skin back and found no bone spurs.

Oriana screamed again. Zephera grabbed her dagger and brought the hilt down hard onto the girl's head. She went limp. Zad and Daegan looked at her incredulously.

"What?" she shrugged. "It was getting annoying. Knocking her out was a mercy for her and for us."

Zad couldn't hide his horror. Daegan laughed but quickly masked it with a cough.

Brenner never looked up from his work. His brow was furrowed in silent concentration. He placed his hands on Oriana's leg. With a quick movement, he used all of his weight to push the bone back into place. The crack of the bone filled the air. Zephera grimaced at the horrendous sound. Now that her role as comforter was made obsolete by Oriana's unconsciousness, she left her post to join Brenner. She glanced at the leg and gasped. The bone was almost completely healed. She gently touched Brenner's shoulder. He was burning up. He was using up too much of his energy.

"Brenner, the bone's healed. We can just close the wound with needle and thread. You need to stop. You're burning up." Brenner didn't seem to hear her. She shook him hard. "BRENNER! Stop!" Still the mage didn't seem to hear her, his mind entirely focused on healing the bone.

She closed her eyes and concentrated, clenching her jaw hard. *BRENNER! STOP!* The words screamed from her mind. Suddenly the mage dropped his hands, shaking. He looked at her with weary surprise.

You did it, he praised softly.

She smiled, relieved. "Daegan, the needle and thread please." She motioned for it with an open hand. "Zad, get Brenner some food and water. He can have what I have left in my pack." They followed her orders without question.

She looked at Oriana's leg, no longer mangled or broken. She held the needle carefully between her fingers and began to thread the skin back together as quickly and cleanly as she could, praying to the gods that it wouldn't scar horribly. What felt like an eternity passed before she was done.

When she was finished, she carefully poured what little ointment they had left onto the wound. Then she wrapped it carefully. Exhausted, she sat back and folded her arms across her chest.

Zephera addressed the group. "We can rest until dawn, which is in a few hours. But then we need to head out."

Even if any of them disagreed, they were all too exhausted to argue. Zephera unrolled her bedding next to Zad, her mood somber. She rested her head on his shoulder. His fingers entwined with hers. In that moment, even if it was for just a heartbeat, she felt peace.

CHAPER 14

Dawn came all too soon. Zephera awoke to a nuzzling at her side. Smiling, she opened her eyes. Dorjan gave a playful growl and pawed her face. She laughed, petting the hound softly behind his brown-striped ears. He gave a happy bark and ran towards Brenner, who was hard at work on a crutch for Oriana. Sitting up, she knocked Zad's arm away, which had been wrapped around her protectively. Her heart fluttered softly. She watched as he slept, the sunlight kissing his face and illuminating his soft features. His blonde hair was swept to the side, revealing the small scar on his eyebrow. She smiled, remembering how he had gotten it.

She was taken back to a few years ago at the Keep. Zephera glared at the assassin in front of her. The tall, gangly boy that stood there was the bane of her existence. He had tortured her since he had arrived. Jameson had been taunting her for days, boasting about his missions when she had yet to receive her first. He hung around her during archery lessons, doing everything he could to break her concentration. She never hit the target when he was around. Not that she ever hit it anyway, but she liked to blame it on Jameson.

Jameson had been strutting about the range when Zad was working with her on her aim. True to form, he started insulting her.

"Breathe, Zephera. Ignore him," Zad whispered gently in her ear, one hand on her shoulder, the other placed on her arm, holding it steady.

"I am, but he's making it diff-i-cult," she said through gritted teeth.

"ZEPPHHERRA!! Still working on that aim? Why don't you put those hands to good use and join me in my chambers tonight?" Jameson called.

She tensed and let the arrow fly. She missed.

She heard his boisterous laughter. He brushed past her, grabbing the bow from her hands. "Here love, let me show you how a *man* does it."

With barely a glance at the target, he drew the string and let go. The arrow struck the center of the target with a dull thud. Smirking, he turned to face her. "Now, why don't you make yourself useful and join me in the bath?"

Zad grabbed her shoulder before she could launch herself at Jameson. She screamed, throwing Zad's arm off and elbowing him in the face. She ran at Jameson, hitting him in the gut and knocking him to the ground. She straddled his stomach, and started pummeling his face, not stopping until she felt herself being pulled off of him. Zad had to use all of his strength to contain her rage. He was much taller than she was and he held her tightly. She thrashed, trying to break free to reach a laughing, blood-stained Jameson. From the looks of it, she had broken his nose.

"Yes, Zadkiel, hold her back. Control the stupid bitch," he said, spitting blood in her direction.

Zad growled. He let her go and punched Jameson in the eye. The blow sent Jameson stumbling back. He tripped over his own feet and fell to the ground.

"I really hate that word," Zad spat. Grabbing her hand, he led her out of the range without saying a word. His own face was swollen from her elbow, which had left a bloody wound just above his eye.

Watching Zad sleep had put Zephera in a strange mood. She frowned in confusion at the feeling in her gut. She closed her eyes, trying to shake it off. Separating from Zad when they were all in danger was a difficult notion to wrap her head around. They were all dancing with death and the thought of Zad meeting it first without her made her feel sick. He was a skilled warrior but his compassion was his biggest weakness. He would put the needs of Oriana and Brenner above his own and do whatever it took to get the others to safety, even if it meant sacrificing himself.

Stretching her arms above her head, she sighed. Feeling someone watching her, she looked over to see Zad smiling sheepishly at her. His gray-blue eyes filled with unspoken sadness and worry. Sitting up, Zad smiled softly, pulling Zephera into a hug.

"Beasty," he whispered, stroking her hair. "I'll see you in the village soon, all right? This isn't goodbye. You know if we had any other choice I would stay by your side."

She buried her face in his shoulder. "I know," she whispered.

Zephera got to her feet slowly, groaning while she stretched her sore muscles. She held out a hand to Zad, pulling him to his feet. She took her time rolling up their bedding and gathering up their supplies. She wasn't stalling. She just needed the precious last minutes she had with Zad to last as long as possible. With no food left in their supply, she skipped breakfast, stomach grumbling. Mumbling to herself, she wound up the last of the perimeter wire and handed it to Brenner. She watched Zad carefully from across the camp. He was standing tall, watching the sky.

He will be okay. We all will. Focus on the mission, and we will see you in the village soon. Brenner put a hand on her shoulder. Take these. He handed her three smooth stones.

Zephera looked at him curiously.

They are magicked stone. They glow. Just say Lux, and they will give you light.

She gave him a smile. "Thank you Brenner, really." She felt connected to Brenner. He made her feel normal.

He nodded his head, *Of course. Do be careful, will you? The creatures may be long gone, but Daegan can be just as dangerous and wild as any monster.*

Zephera laughed, winking. *Thank you, but I think I can handle him.*

After giving Brenner a hug, she went to help Oriana, who seemed to be struggling. Zephera helped her tighten the bandages around her leg.

Oriana never spoke, only watched as Zephera wrapped her leg in silent concentration. When she finished, she helped Oriana to her feet and Zad brought her the makeshift crutch Brenner had made her. It was formed from two sturdy sticks fastened together using torn cloth. It was simple and flimsy, but it would have to do for the hike down the mountain.

Oriana rested her weight on the crutch and smiled grimly. Her blonde hair was dirtied with blood and soot. "Thank you all for helping me last night. It couldn't have been easy," she said to the team, which stood in an awkward circle around her. Everyone looked grim except Daegan, who just scowled.

"You all look positively horrible," Oriana croaked. "Wasn't I the one who had to have my leg pushed back together by a group of bloody killers? You must admit I'm the best-looking one here, though none of you are able to pull off broody and tortured as well as Daegan." That quip earned a small laugh from Zad and a grunt from Daegan.

"She's right, I suppose," Zephera said, brushing dirt off her shoulder. "Perhaps we should get started. We do have a world to save after all." She gave a small nod to Oriana and Brenner before turning to Zad. "Get them to safety, okay? And by the Light, if you die without me and leave me to fix this mess by myself, I will never forgive you." She stared at him, taking in every detail of his face. His gray eyes were so full of determination. His soft features shone brilliantly in the sunlight. And his lips… his perfectly round lips. She parted her mouth slightly, licking her bottom lip.

"My eyes are up here, Zephera," Zad said softly, a hint of laughter in his voice.

She shuddered, embarrassed by his keen observation, and felt her cheeks redden. Before she could turn away, he grabbed her with his toned, strong arms. He held her in his embrace as she laid her head against his cool leathers. Kissing the top of her head, he whispered, "I love you, Zephera Travelle".

"Enough. We need to move out." Daegan's cool voice cut through the air.

Breathing heavily, she looked up at Zad. She fought the nagging urge deep within her telling him that she loved him too. Instead, she just smiled and gave him a small nod.

"Try not to kill him, will you?" Zad raised his voice as his head motioned in Daegan's direction.

"He would only be so lucky." Zephera laughed darkly.

Zad gave her one final squeeze before letting her go. "Careful, Beasty."

She watched as three silhouettes made their way carefully down the rocky mountainside. Daegan huffed behind her impatiently.

Once they disappeared from view she finally turned to him, looking straight into his cold eyes. "Lead the way, Sir Knight."

CHAPER 15

They walked in silence back through the woods to the incinerated field they had only just battled in. The air was filled with the remnants of burnt wood and the charred flesh of dead creatures. She wrinkled her nose at the stench. Smoke billowed around them, dissipating into the sky and leaving behind ash and embers. She followed after Daegan, her hands resting on her weapons. Although Daegan had said the creatures were long gone, she didn't want to risk another attack.

Daegan paused suddenly. "We need to stop here," he said abruptly.

Zephera took in their surroundings. They had arrived back at the stone path where the creatures had attacked them the day before. There were mysterious stone pillars with the faded carvings.

Recognizing the path, Zephera asked, "How can you be sure this is the path we need to take?"

Daegan glanced at her. "It feels different, doesn't it? There's a strange magic here."

She stared at him, unconvinced.

Daegan laughed. "It's marked on the map."

Zephera scoffed. "Very funny." She tried to reach out to Brenner with her mind to tell him that they had made it back to the path, but she wasn't sure if he would respond. He had said it was more difficult the further away you were, especially for someone untrained in the art, though it did help to calm her rapidly beating heart. She hoped they were doing all right.

Stopping near one of the pillars, Daegan pulled off a glove and gently touched the old carvings.

"Is fingering an old pillar going to give you the answers you need?" Zephera quipped. "I mean, I'm sure it's lonely being up here, far from civilization, but buy a girl a drink first." She chuckled to herself. Maybe if she caught him off guard he would annoy her less.

"Yes, I'm sure you could figure out a better use for an old pillar, Zephera," he mused.

She laughed loudly, throwing her head back. "I'm sure I could, if you ever finished with it."

"As motivating as that thought is, my dear, some things simply take time. Especially things that require the use of one's mental faculties. I'm aware that you don't have much experience in that regard, but for the sake of the mission, please do your best to reign in your perverse desires." With a sly grin he added, "I'm sure we can find a good use for them later."

She blushed and glared at him. Then she sat down and took her dark hair out of its braid and ran her fingers through it. She finished by pulling it back tightly from her face. She grunted in annoyance as he continued to work.

"Patience, Zephera. I'm deciphering the markings."

"Deciphering? How could you possibly understand it?" She rose and joined him.

He raised an eyebrow at her. "There are ways to understand ancient languages, though the process can be long and tedious. One must look for patterns and repeated characters. This appears to be a hieroglyphic language—one made with pictures and symbols. I think it's a message. Do you see how this one resembles the full moon?" He walked to the next pillar, "And this one, the waning moon."

"I suppose the next would be the new moon and the one after that the waxing?" she asked, embarrassed at her lack of knowledge of simple cryptography.

"You would be correct. But beyond that, I have no idea what any of it means," he said, his hand on his chin. "We need to keep moving. The altar shouldn't be more than a few hours' walk up the path."

"Lunch first," Zephera demanded.

Daegan shook his head. "Is that all you can honestly think about? Food? You are maddening."

Zephera shrugged her shoulders, sitting down against one of the pillars. She opened her bag, pulling out the rest of the dried meats and a few shriveled carrots. "Yummy," she said sadly, looking down at her pitiful meal.

Daegan sat down next to her, pulling out a rabbit leg and a baked potato.

Zephera's mouth fell open. "How? Where did you get that?"

Daegan raised an eyebrow. "I know how to ration my food to save the better parts for later." He took a bite of the rabbit leg, winking at Zephera. "Mmmm, delicious," he teased.

"I hate you," she mumbled, taking a bite of her dry meat.

They sat in silence for a half hour, relaxing as they nibbled on their food. Zephera searched her bag for more, but she was out. "We'll need to hunt soon, unless you have anything else in that bag of yours."

Daegan nodded. "With the amount of food you eat, we'll have to hunt more than once before our journey in these mountains is through."

"How long do you expect us to be up here?" Zephera asked, standing.

"As long as it takes, but no more than a day or two. We should reach the village of Watford by overmorrow. That is if we find the relic."

He shrugged his bag onto his back and stalked up the path without another word. Rolling her eyes, Zephera followed him. The path they took was surprisingly free from debris and wear. It was as if time itself had stopped, leaving the stones untouched by the elements. They followed the path until the sun had long since set. They arrived in a copse of trees, in the center of which lay a group of large stones arranged in a circular pattern around an obsidian block marred with etchings and divots. Zephera imagined they had been made when sacrifices were offered up to appease the gods.

Daegan stretched his arms above his head, groaning. "We'll have to sleep here. We can't do much searching in the dark. I'll take first watch."

Zephera nodded. "Sounds good to me." Unrolling her bedding, she claimed the spot furthest away from her companion.

Since they were no longer moving, Zephera began to feel the chill of the mountain air around her. Her teeth began to chatter and her arms were covered in goosebumps. Shivering, she began to gather firewood from the edge of the clearing, hauling it to where her bed was. Zephera crunched a handful of dry leaves and small sticks between her hands, creating a small nest of kindling. Unsheathing her dagger she carved a small notch in a large piece of bark, placing the kindling on top. Zephera let out a deep breath. She hated starting fires by such primitive means, but they were low on supplies, so she had no choice. She cursed under her breath, reminding herself to thank Brenner for all those chilly nights he had so easily lit the fire with the snap of his fingers.

Placing a tall pointed stick into the notch, she began to twist it between her palms. She did this for five minutes, arms quickly getting tired. The cold made her shiver; anticipation coursed through her as a small plume of smoke rose up from the friction. Zephera smiled as a spark lit below, gently illuminating the tinder. Grimacing at her sore body she got onto her stomach to gently blow the spark. Breathing out softly, the spark began to flicker, lighting the nest around it. Within minutes, the fire was roaring. Zephera eagerly warmed her hands. She searched for Daegan, who had just finished setting up the perimeter fence.

He wore a dark scowl as he stormed over to her. "A fire, Zephera?" he roared. "Those creatures could be anywhere. If they see the smoke they'll be drawn to us."

Zephera stuck out her tongue. "It's freezing, Daegan. We need a fire."

Daegan eyed her dangerously. "Put it out," he demanded.

Zephera shook her head. "Make me," she replied with a dark edge to her voice.

"Don't be stupid, Zephera." He spat.

Rolling her eyes heavily, she realized he was probably right. Not wanting to admit defeat, she stared at him defiantly.

Daegan growled and stomped his foot into the fire, extinguishing it.

Zephera sighed, lying down on her bedding and staring up into the night sky. The world was clearer here, and though she enjoyed the view of the stars, she missed home. She concentrated on the sounds around her. It was almost silent, save for the chirping of the crickets and the occasional howl of a wolf. She pictured herself snug in her bedroom back at the palace as she drifted off to sleep and into a dream.

Zephera stared at a hooded woman chanting over the obsidian altar. She heard a baby crying as the woman chanted. There was another bundle, however it wasn't moving. It was completely still. Zephera felt sick as she watched the woman dip her fingers into a bowl and smear a luminescent substance onto the crying child. She repeated the ritual on the other, breathing life into the child as she worked. Her face shone with a strange ecstasy as both children began to cry. A branch snapped behind her, and the woman looked up suddenly, eyes wide.

"You!" she yelled. Zephera was reaching for her weapons when a tall man with sleek blonde hair, wearing dark armor, stepped past her as if she wasn't there. His blue eyes bore a wicked unnerving gleam.

"You can't expect to win this, Malina. It's too late. You've already lost," the man said. "Give me the children."

The woman, who Zephera supposed was Malina, stood tall. "No, Gregour. It's you who are too late. The spell has been set. You will never win." She laughed triumphantly and said one final word before the man could reach her. "*Statera!*" She howled in delight as the children disappeared.

The man whispered a single word under his breath and an orb, light in color, shot out of his hands. It hit Malina directly in the chest. Light left her eyes as she fell to her side. The man, face as cold as stone, turned to Zephera and smiled wickedly.

Zephera sat up, covered in cold sweat. She blinked in the afternoon sky and sat up. "Why didn't you wake me earlier? It's got to be past noon!" she asked Daegan, whose dark eyes were fraught with exhaustion.

"Get up, we must search the clearing. There's magic here. I can feel it," he said, ignoring her questions.

"Daegan… I just had a strange dream, a vision."

Daegan eyed her suspiciously. "Tell me."

Zephera recanted her dream, staring pointedly at Daegan, who remained unmoved.

He paced around the edge of the clearing, his brow knit in thought. "There are legends of a powerful priestess who served the King of Somber. She sacrificed thousands to gain his praise. Yet nothing she did could appease his appetite for death and suffering. She longed to be with her master for all eternity, so she devised a plan: she would kill the King of Light, effectively rendering her dark master King of their world. For years, she tried to get close to the King of Light, infiltrating the ranks of his court until he asked for her hand in marriage.

"Yet, when the time came for them to marry, she couldn't bring herself to kill him, for she had fallen in love with him. She no longer wished to be a part of the darkness. She married the King of Light and devoted her life to serving their people and cleansing her soul of darkness. For a time, they were happy.

"She was pregnant with his twins when the palace was seized by her old lover and his dark forces. The King of Lucent delivered one living child as his wife lay dying. Furious, Gregour Lucent used forbidden magic to sever his kingdom from the Lands of Sorrow, cursing the world to be forever unbalanced. Unfortunately for him, he ended up cursing both realms. Every five hundred years, the veil between the realms grows weak, and the Rot are able to seep through into this realm, spreading their plague."

"Why are you telling me this?" Zephera asked him quietly.

"I think that's who you saw in your dream. A memory of some sort."

Zephera shook her head. "That doesn't make any sense."

Daegan shrugged. "Dreams usually don't. Come on, we need to find this item."

Daegan searched the brush around the altar, his brow furrowed.

"What is it that we are looking for, exactly?" Zephera asked.

"The Priestess was said to favor stags. She was also said to have died during the New Moon." He stopped at the base of a cedar tree and bent down to examine the plants at the base. "She was also a skilled botanist. Ah! Rosemary!" He laughed and snatched something from the ground. "Really Reina? That's it? A carved pine stag." He smirked, holding it up for Zephera to see.

She laughed. "Well, it seems you didn't need me after all."

Shrugging, he began to move away, "We should set up camp. We can hunt in the woods and leave at dawn. We should reach the village by tomorrow evening."

She shook her head. The thought of spending another evening with Daegan was repulsive. Perhaps she would just walk down the mountainside by herself, leaving Daegan to hunt. Her stomach growled as if in answer to her question.

"Excellent," she said, clapping her hands together. "I'll set up camp. Do try to get us something other than rabbit, will you darling Daegan?" she asked dryly.

"As you wish," Daegan replied, unsheathing his axe as he stalked off into the thick wood.

CHAPER 16

It had taken Zad, Brenner and Oriana the entirety of a day and half a night to hike down the mountain. They had arrived at the base in the middle of the night, exhausted and hungry. They stumbled upon a wooden shack within steps of the end of the mountain path.

The farmer, an older man who was kind and trusting, treated them to a meal in his little lean-to and insisted on showing them the path to Watford. He loaned them a mule, and gave them coin to leave it at the stables in the village. "I'll pick her up next time I'm in town," the farmer said with a smile.

Zad offered to pay the man for his kindness, but he had refused, stating that it was his life's duty to care for those in need. They thanked the man and watched him as he made his way down the path, back to his farm.

Zad held Oriana's waist as he helped her onto the mule. "There you go, easy does it," he said as she situated herself on the mule's back.

"Well, we all made it in one piece," he said, giving her a small smile.

"Not all of us," Oriana whispered sadly.

"Don't talk like that. The others will be fine." Zad looked at her, concerned.

"I know, but I feel responsible. We had to split up because of me. If anything happens…" Her voice trailed off. Zad took her chin in his hands.

"Oriana, we can't afford to think like that. We knew when we started this journey that there would be many things that could go wrong. As

Zephera says, 'It's an impossible quest.'" His voice jumped up to his falsetto range as he tried to mimic Zephera's feminine gruffness.

Oriana threw back her head in laughter. "That's NOT what she sounds like!" She sat up taller and furrowed her brow. "It's more like, 'I like killing. You guys are annoying. Daegan is the worst. Stab, stab, stabby stab. Quests are dumb!'"

Zad choked out a laugh. "Gods, she would gut us if she was here." Smiling, he looked up at the majestic dark peak that stood before them. "She's up there somewhere, eye twitching, trying not to kill Daegan." He let out a long breath. "It isn't your fault that we had to split up, Oriana. Things happen. That's just how it is. Don't beat yourself up, all right? You need to focus on getting better. We still have quite the journey ahead of us."

Oriana smiled. "I guess you are right. Thanks, Zad."

"Anytime m'lady. That's what I'm here for: professional impressionist, friend, and giver of useful advice." He puffed out his chest and flexed his muscles.

Brenner untied the reins from the fence post the mule had been tied to and motioned for Zad to follow. They walked sleepily through the outskirts of the village of Watford.

Zad stood tall, taking charge. "We can wait at an inn until the others arrive. I'll send word to Baleem that we are here. I wouldn't expect it to take more than a few days for our contact to meet us. Daegan and Zephera should be back before then." Brenner nodded in silent agreement.

When they arrived at the inn, they paid for two rooms for the week and Zad slipped the innkeeper a few extra coppers to enlist the help of his daughter for Oriana's bathing and changing needs. The inn was rather large for such a remote village. It was a trading stop, however, so the decor and food were better than anything in the smaller villages. They feasted on roasted goose with potatoes and honey-glazed carrots. Zad smiled as he bit into the steaming vegetables, wishing Zephera was there to enjoy the golden, sweet taste.

They all retired to their beds, exhausted from their journey. Zad found himself unable to sleep despite his tiredness. His thoughts were full of

Zephera and the way she had looked at him when he had tried to kiss her. She had seemed so repulsed. He was angry at himself for crossing that line. She was his friend, his family, and she meant the world to him.

When he held her as she slept, she hadn't pushed him off. She had nestled into his arms, warm and beautiful—his dark and dangerous Zephera. Yet, she walled herself off from the world, but he had scaled those walls over and over again. She wore the mask of a cold, fractured heart well, but to Zad she wasn't broken. She was life, she was warmth, and she was home. He worried for her, worried that she would shut him out one day. He had to keep breaking down her walls, had to keep showing her he would protect her. She didn't need to hide her heart, because he would protect it and never let it break. If she would only let him.

The knot in his stomach hadn't loosened since Zephera had been attacked in the woods. Seeing her broken and crying had shattered him. This mission was impossible, she had said. Yet he had pushed her to accept it, to risk her life to defeat a seemingly unconquerable threat. She had accepted the risk. Zephera, cold-hearted Lady of Death, had put the needs of the world before her own, and it was going to destroy her. He knew she wasn't telling him everything. How was he supposed to help her, to protect her, if she wouldn't talk to him? Daegan also knew more than he was letting on. Zad clenched his hands. If that man hurt her, Zad would lose it. He hated killing, but if Daegan let anything happen to Zephera, there would be no hesitation. Daegan would die by Zad's own hands.

He slept restlessly, every sound causing him to startle awake just as he finally drifted off. When sunlight started to peek through the small window of his room, he couldn't wait any longer. He dressed quietly, trying not to wake Brenner or the pup who was sleeping soundly at the foot of his bed. He made his way to the tavern that served as a dining hall for the inn. He hastily ate his bowl of oats as he wrote a letter to Baleem explaining the situation at hand. He handed it to the innkeeper, who said the message should arrive in the Capital within two days. Zad thanked the man and set out to explore the village.

CHAPER 17

Zephera unrolled her bedding and placed it far from where Daegan was sitting. He was skinning a snake and preparing it for their dinner. Her lips curled in disgust as he strung the revolting meat on a couple of sticks and placed them over the fire. As if sensing her gaze, he stated without looking away from the fire, "What? You said you didn't want rabbit."

"So, a fire is fine tonight?" Zephera asked.

She heard him laugh as she laid her head down on the cool ground. She didn't understand him. He seemed to enjoy tormenting her, and she let him. No one had ever gotten under her skin the way he did. She hated him. But he did have his uses. She watched him turn the meat over the fire.

Rolling her eyes, she decided to join him by the fire. "You said your people sent you here for a cure?" she questioned.

"I did," he said, tearing his eyes from the glowing fire to meet hers.

"Well, where is it that you hail from, Sir Daegan?"

Eyes narrowing slightly, he replied, "Nowhere of importance."

"Is that so?" she asked, eyebrow raised. "For the amount of arrogance you display, one would think that you came from somewhere of great importance."

A ghost of a smile crossed his dark features. "Well, one would be wrong."

"Are you ever going to tell me anything about yourself? How about we play a game? A question for a question."

He let out a loud laugh. "The Lady of Death wishes to play a game with the likes of me? How could I refuse such an intriguing offer? Very well, Zephera. I'll go first." He cocked his head and gave her a sly smile. He brought his index finger up to his chin and tapped it, pretending to be deep in thought.

"What possessed you to strip down naked at the lake?" he asked with amusement in his eyes.

She clenched her jaw, knowing he was baiting her. Refusing to be caught, she said, "I like being naked. Clothes are so... constricting." She met his eyes and smiled as his eyes widened slightly in astonishment.

"Have I shocked your delicate sensibilities, Sir Knight?"

"You never cease to amaze me, Zephera."

She shook her head. "My turn..."

"It's not, actually. It's mine."

Before she could argue, he clarified, "You asked if I was shocked by you, and I answered, making it my turn yet again. This is your game, Zephera. Don't you know the rules?" He poked at the fire with a stick, forcing the embers to drift upwards, illuminating the dark air around them. "Do you trust me?" he asked.

She was taken aback. Pondering her answer, she bit her lip as she recalled Valessa's warning, *don't trust him,* and wondered if she'd been talking about Daegan.

"I believe you're here to stop this plague like the rest of us. But I don't think that your motives are as pure as you say they are. Nor do I think that you are telling me everything you know about our immunity. You're hiding something, which could either be wise or devious. Whatever the motivation, it endangers us. Withholding useful information could lead to our downfall. So, to answer your question, Daegan, no, I don't trust you."

"A decision both wise and foolish. You are right not to trust someone you know to be lying. But at the same time, if you don't trust me, then we can never truly know one another, which it seems to me is something that you very much want. I would advise against it, however. I don't think you'll particularly like what you find."

Zephera stared at him in confusion. "You said you didn't want to get close to any of us, that you had no interest in making friends. So why the sudden change of heart?"

His dark eyes flashed dangerously. "Is that the question you are choosing to ask? Or would you care to ask another?"

"You've done nothing but belittle us. You taunt Zad and harass me, and yet you want us to trust you? To come to know you? It's rather curious."

He let out a cool laugh. "You are a trained assassin—one of the best— and Zadkiel is a mediocre warrior. Yet you both let the words and taunts of a stranger get under your skin so easily. It amuses me. You also intrigue me. Your presence has grown on me like a fungus."

She guffawed and punched him in the arm. "You are an ass. You act cold and distant, yet I think that you are quite the opposite. You crave acceptance and want others to recognize your skill and worth. Deep down somewhere in that dark soul of yours, I think you may actually want a friend." She folded her arms across her chest, pleased with herself.

"You imply that I have a soul." He clucked his tongue. "Very well, I'll admit a small part of me wonders what it would be like to have you as a friend."

She clutched her heart in mock surprise. "Ah, and here I thought I was but a mere mortal. I'm overwhelmed with delight that His Holiness, the Dark and Handsome Daegan, wants to be friends with me. Whatever shall I do?"

Laughing, Daegan pulled the meat sticks out of the fire and handed one to Zephera. The heat had cooked the meat to a crisp, producing curled, dry strips of what used to be a living creature.

"It tastes better burnt." Daegan said as he bit into the blackened meat. Wincing, she did the same. They sat together in silence as they both struggled to chew. Daegan took a sip from his canteen before offering it to Zephera, who used the cool water to swallow the last bit of tough meat.

"You think I'm handsome?" he asked when she had finished.

Her shoulders stiffened as she turned to glare at him. "I think I'd rather we didn't speak to one another."

Daegan snorted, leaning back on his muscular arms. They sat quietly, listening to the fire spit and crackle.

Daegan's voice finally broke the silence. "I was sent here many years ago by my people to observe the City of Light. There were whispers of another Dark War. My people have devoted their lives to studying the remaining text on the Dark Ages. We felt that if the need arose, we could lend our knowledge and help put an end to another Dark Age before it began. When the whispers grew louder and all evidence pointed to the start of another plague, I had to offer my services to your king. It's been many years since I became an advisor. In that time, I've learned a great deal about the history they teach here. While it isn't entirely truthful, there's enough to it that even your king is worried enough to listen to my advice and assemble a team to stop the plague."

Zephera was speechless. When she didn't say anything, Daegan continued, "I chose four skilled killers who I knew would be useful. I had heard of a strong and beautiful assassin, one who was trained by the great Baleem himself. I knew I had to have you with me. I also knew that you wouldn't go without Zadkiel, however useless he might be. His presence had to be tolerated in order for me to have you." He shrugged, looking down at his feet. "I want you to trust me, but you've shown me through sheer stubbornness that in order for you to do so, I must tell you everything you wish to know." He looked at her intently, searching for any sign of protest. She bowed her head, signaling for him to continue.

"I've known the Keeper of Light, Valessa, for many years. She offered me her greatest pupil—Brenner. And Oriana, though not as skilled as you and I, is adept at uniting us. She's an intelligent woman, and her knowledge of traps and burglary are impressive."

Zephera snorted. "Burglary? You've got to be joking. Oriana?"

Daegan shrugged. "She was masquerading as a palace guard when I came to the city. She was adequately skilled with a bow, but even more skilled at picking locks, thievery, and setting traps. She's quite the scoundrel." He sounded impressed.

"Not good enough to evade your attention, though?" she asked.

"While she is good, I'm better. I'm trained in the art of sabotage. Picking out those who don't wish to be seen is a game for me, though I'll admit, finding her took longer than I'm accustomed to." He chuckled and ran his fingers through his dark hair.

"You said our history of the Dark Age isn't quite truthful. How so?"

Standing up, Daegan turned to face her grimly. Staring at her, a small glimpse of darkness shone in his eyes. He blinked, and it was gone. Taking a deep breath, as if pondering whether to speak, he said, "This is the tenth cycle of the Dark Age, not the second."

"What did you say?" Zephera breathed, her voice barely audible.

"Every five hundred years, a new cycle begins. The dream you had was something that the woman who started all of this wanted you to see."

Zephera stood, shaking her head in disbelief. "No, that can't be right. You must have been misinformed. Tenth cycle? That's impossible."

Daegan stared into her eyes intensely. "I know this because the last time there was a Dark Age, I was there."

CHAPER 18

Zephera felt like she had been punched in the gut. For a moment, she forgot how to breathe. She could do nothing but stare at the man in front of her, his eyes lit with anticipation. She tried to steady her breath. He had to be lying, or mad. There could be no other possible explanation.

"Say something, Zephera," Daegan spoke softly, stepping towards her.

She shook her head, holding her hands up. Daegan's words, though seemingly crazy, struck her strangely. Almost like some memory that unstuck itself from some long ago time, a slow certainty, frail as a bird, flew upwards in her mind. She knew he was telling the truth. How she knew was another question.

He watched her carefully, contemplating what he would do if she decided to run. "How old are you? You can't be much older than me," she asked in a hoarse whisper.

He narrowed his eyes. "That's a rather complicated question."

"Answer it," she seethed.

Daegan let out a deep breath, taking a seat. "When I was twenty-five, I was sent to your realm. That was 525 years ago. Every time a cycle begins, one of my people is sent here"—he gestured around them—"to the Empire of Lucent. When we cross over, some sort of magic stops our aging. We are effectively frozen in time. Our bodies cease to age, and we are more or less immortal. It's our curse, our sacrifice, to be forced to watch as the cycle repeats itself time and time again. We're sent here to stop it, to try to find a way to cure our Realm, but none have succeeded. We are forced to live out our existence in exile, never to return." He looked at her intently before starting again.

"The magic that forced our realms apart was strong, and the one who cast the spell doesn't want it to be broken. You've been raised to believe that the Darkness is evil. I can tell you beyond doubt that it isn't. When the King of Lucent cast the spell that broke our world in two, he exiled not just the King of Somber but all those who had the misfortune to live in his land. Most were good, innocent people who continued on in their new realm. But living in darkness for so long changed my people. We began to grow cold and cruel. Each new cycle chisels away at the humanity of my world. We've sent so many of our people over to try to make our realms whole again, restore balance, and free my people from the darkness that is slowly suffocating them. I fear, however, that with this latest cycle, it may be too late. That man you fought in the forest, he's the tenth and latest to be sent. He's also my brother, or was. I killed him many, many years ago. I'm not entirely sure how he still lives, but it can't be good. I fear whatever he was isn't entirely human. My father must be dealing with dark magic if my brother still roams the earth. He's a warped version of what my people were, what I hope some of them still are. We may come from Darkness, but we all have a choice. Just like you, born into the Light, have a choice as to what you will become." He stared at his feet, toeing with the dirt.

She stared at him in stunned silence. "I don't know why, but I believe you," she said quietly, her eyes meeting his.

Daegan stepped back, surprised. "You do?" He laughed shakily. "It's been so long since anyone has known my secret. It feels… freeing."

"You killed your brother, that sounds like an interesting tale."

"Perhaps…would you like to hear it?"

Zephera nodded. "Was he your first kill?"

Daegan smiled sadly. "Listen to the story, Zephera."

Daegan rubbed his hands together. "I had just left the honoring ceremony of my brother Tomic. He was to be the ninth Dark One to step through the portal and come to this realm. I argued with my father that

Tomic was far too ruthless to come to this realm, that he would do far more harm than good. But my father wouldn't listen. He favored Tomic for this ruthless and cruel behavior. He led our armies, so you see he was the warrior my father loved and proudly accepted. I, on the other hand, was nothing more than a bother, a mere scholar. My brother had been given many gifts during his honor ceremony. One gift he was given was women for him to enjoy."

Zephera laughed. "Fantastic."

Daegan scowled at her. "While my brother enjoyed his whores, I decided to take a bath. He'd beaten me to a bloody pulp right before his ceremony and I needed to wash the dried blood off of my body."

Zephera raised an eyebrow. "He beat you and made you attend the ceremony covered in your own blood?"

Daegan shrugged. "It was Tomic, what can I say? He liked to torture puppies."

Zephera shook her head, disgusted.

Daegan cleared his throat. "When I had just begun to relax and drift off, I heard screaming coming from my brother's rooms. They weren't screams of pleasure. I still don't know what made me dress and enter his room that day, but I'll never be the same. When I entered his rooms, what I saw, it shook me to my core. A bloodied husk of a body had been hung from the ceiling. My brother held a stick with blood covering it, and him. He wore a wicked grin. I remember asking him what he had done, why... why he had beaten some poor woman to death. His answer horrified me. 'I only wanted to see what rosy treats her body held.'

Daegan stared into the fire, his eyes full of the memory.

"He treated this poor innocent woman like a child's game, and he laughed. He thought it was humorous, Zephera. Now, my brother was evil, and I don't regret what I did. I do regret what it did to my family. His actions, his death... it tore my family apart. And you know who my father blamed? He blamed the King of Lucent. Not me, not Tomic, but the King of Lucent. My father was an idiot. He only saw the hatred of what the splitting of the realms had done to our people.

"What he didn't realize is there's always a choice. You choose who you become. What Tomic chose to be was a warped, evil human being. I have to remind myself of this often, to never become like him. If you surround yourself with darkness and filth, you become it. It's hard, for I remember the feeling that came when I dealt the killing blow to my brother." He let out a hollow laugh.

"Blood, there was blood everywhere. I had never taken a life before. I wasn't sure how it was supposed to feel, but it was freeing. I felt a strange sort of exhilaration. Tomic had been there, minutes ago, alive. And then, then he was nothing more than an empty body, all because of me and molded steel. Life is so fleeting.

"I could feel Death's strong grasp in the room as it embraced me and my newfound skill. I welcomed the warmth and acceptance I felt from my new master. For the first time in my life, I felt as if I belonged."

Daegan stared off into the distance, finished with his story. They sat in silence for a moment. Zephera wasn't sure he was telling her everything, but she knew better than to ask. She cleared her throat.

"Who else knows about you being a Dark One?" Zephera asked, wanting to change the uncomfortable subject.

"No one that is alive anymore," he whispered sadly.

"What have you been doing for five hundred years?"

"When I was sent here, I was but a mere scholar. Not a warrior. When the last Dark Age came to an end with the cycle still unbroken, I had no choice but to wait for the next one to begin. I failed my people because I wasn't strong enough. I vowed it wouldn't happen again. So, I trained. I became the apprentice of a great warlord. I fought for him in many wars. When it became noticeable that I wasn't aging, I faked my death. For five centuries, I've served countless masters, gaining knowledge and skills, biding my time until now."

"You haven't had any friends for five hundred years? No lovers, no place to call home? That sounds lonely."

"I've had a few friends. But it became too painful to watch them die. To outlive others, knowing you will live far beyond even their grandchildren's lives, makes it difficult to get close to people. As for lovers, I've had many—none that I cared to get to know any further than their beds. They were simply a means to an end, a way to satisfy a hunger, nothing more." He put a fist to his chin and stared at her expectantly. "Does that bother you?"

She stared at him intently before answering. "No. Sex is natural. I would be concerned if you hadn't partaken in the fruit of its splendor for five hundred years." She clucked her tongue.

Daegan threw his head back, his laughter filling the air. "There you go again with your perverted thoughts."

Smiling widely, she mused, "You already know I'm not a prude. I enjoy a roll in the hay as much as anyone."

Daegan's eyes danced with curiosity. "Oh? Aldon isn't the only lover you've taken?" he asked.

"That, Sir Knight, I'll leave for you to ponder, as it's none of your business," she replied.

"Very well. I'm certain you have more questions for me. It's much to take in. I'll answer what I can."

Zephera stared at him, her eyes narrowed in thought. "Everything in my training is telling me to kill you, but my gut is telling me you can be trusted. Can I trust you, Daegan? Or should I kill you?" She tapped her fingers together.

"I'm very hard to kill. And before you say I'm being an arrogant ass, I'll tell you I'm simply stating a fact. The magic that's halted my aging grants my body extra defenses. Believe me, I've tried to get past them, but it's nearly impossible."

She raised an eyebrow at him. "Then I'll trust you. But if you betray me or anyone I love, I'll do everything in my power to get past those defenses and put you down," she snarled half-playfully, raising her lip in a growl.

"I would expect nothing less of you, Zephera. You are a cruel mistress indeed when it comes to those who've earned your loyalty. I don't envy those who cross you."

She smirked. "Well then, you've been warned."

They sat near the fire, watching the flames slowly begin to wither. When only a few embers remained, Zephera stood, making her way to her bedroll. "If we want to make it to the path down the mountain by tomorrow evening, we should probably get some rest."

He nodded. "I'll take first watch."

Daegan gazed at Zephera as she drifted off to sleep, thinking how easily she had accepted his story. She didn't even blink when he told her that he came from the Darkness. Perhaps it was because she harbored a darkness of her own. He loved that piece of her, the darkness that she had. It was glorious and strong. It was what had caught his eye. He had known of her for quite some time. He had heard rumors of an assassin as cold and dark as himself. But her fierce loyalty would be her undoing. He needed to gain her trust, to push her in the right direction. If she was who he thought she was, she would be his greatest weapon. She would bring balance to their worlds.

When Zephera awoke, she sat up quickly. She had been dreaming about Gregour, the man she had seen in her vision. His eyes were so cold, so full of hate. They followed her whenever she closed her eyes. Would she ever again have peace?

She searched the clearing for Daegan. He was sitting against a tree, sleeping. He seemed so young, so different. He was from another realm, another time. She was taught to fear his kind, that they were consumed with darkness and evil. Yet, as much as she wanted to, she couldn't bring herself to fear him. He had said that everyone had a choice. She had understood that. She may have been born of the Light, but light she certainly was not.

She had always felt a pull between both, and she had never understood it. It was as though there were two creatures warring inside her, both struggling for dominance. It was exhausting. She stood, stretching her arms to the morning sky. She watched Daegan, giving him a few more moments of blissful slumber before she cleared her throat loudly. He awoke, wide-eyed and alert.

"Did you fall asleep on your watch?" she mused.

He stood, straightening his dark leathers. "Obviously. I apologize." His voice was filled with regret.

"We are both still alive, are we not? It happens. No harm done." She shrugged.

"Indeed. How did you sleep, Zephera?" he asked.

"Not well. The man from my vision—Gregour. I can't seem to shake him. His eyes, everything about him. I feel like he's trying to tell me something. It's maddening…" she paused. "But it isn't important right now. We still have so much to do. Damn it all to hell, it's going to be a while before we can put all of this insanity behind us, isn't it?" Zephera murmured.

"It's going to get a lot worse before it gets better," Daegan replied dryly.

"Well, here's to forging our way through the impossible. Shall we?" Zephera asked, waving her hand toward the stone path.

CHAPER 19

Zad spent the day wandering Watford. It was a quaint and charming place, resting alongside a beautiful harbor. He sat quietly in the market square, watching the shoppers flutter around from cart to cart. He closed his eyes, listening to their harmless, mundane chatter: a mother trying to calm her children as she shopped for their dinner, an older man haggling over the price of silk with a merchant. The merchant was cheating him, but the poor sod didn't have enough skill with numbers to see it.

Zad's memory peacefully drifted to the time when he and Zephera had gone to the shopping square near the Keep. It had been a particularly busy day as thousands of merchants from all over their world had flocked to the city for the annual Illuminae Festival. The city usually had many merchants, but this had been a special occasion, one Zephera had been talking about for weeks. She had saved her wages for months, resisting purchasing even those blasted cinnamon cakes, though it didn't stop her from begging Zad to buy her one every week. She had a particular item in mind—a curved sword, like the one she had seen the handmaiden of a Verasha foreign princess wielding.

She was so excited that she hardly slept the night before, pestering him to go with her. He hated going into the square during festival week. It was always overcrowded and filled with unknown dangers. It was hard to concentrate with all of the commotion and excitement. If there was a threat, he knew he wouldn't be able to detect it until it was too late. He liked to know his enemy, to see them clearly. If he had to kill, he needed to know that it was for a reason. In a bustling crowd like that, anyone could be hurt. One mistake, and he could kill an innocent. But Zephera was relentless and he refused to let her go out on her own. She wouldn't care who she killed if she sensed danger. He wanted to be there, not only to protect her, but anyone that she might deem a threat.

She had stormed into his bedroom at dawn that morning and jumped on his bed. "ZAD! ZAD! Wake up! C'mon, you old lunk. It's morning! The market's been open for nearly an hour."

"Getoffme!" he grumbled sleepily.

"ZADKIEL! If my blade's gone because you wouldn't get out of bed, gods help me..." She hit him with a pillow.

Groaning, he sat up groggily. "Okay, okay, I'm up," he said, his hands raised in mock surrender.

"I'll meet you in the courtyard in five minutes," she called as she rushed out of the room. She paused at the doorway. "If you aren't there in time, I'll leave without you," she threatened.

He smiled as she left the room, shaking his head. True, she was exhausting, but he still couldn't help but follow her.

He stayed close to her side as they made their way through the crowded streets. The air smelled of sweat mingled with salt from the sea. He followed her to the far end of the busy square to the only Verashan arms dealer's booth. Zad eyed the man carefully. The Verashan people were brutal and cruel. Living in a frozen tundra, they lived as barbarians. They produced the finest steel and arms, making them essential for trade in weaponry. Their women were seen as second class citizens—property.

Zad watched Zephera carefully, if the man disrespected her in any way, she might snap. He wasn't sure who would win that fight. They would both have their choice of weapon; there were hundreds of daggers and swords with many different carved hilts. Most were just ceremonial and couldn't do any real damage, but some were definitely capable of significant bloodshed.

Picking up an obsidian dagger with an ivory carved hilt, he turned it over in his hands, testing its weight on his fingers. It was beautiful, made of both Dark and Light.

"How much?" he asked the dealer. The man looked up from where he had been sitting, cleaning his fingernails with a small pick.

"Five gold," he barked, putting the pick between his yellow teeth and chewing on it.

Zephera, who had been listening to the exchange, laughed. "Five gold? It's odd that you would sell such a small, meaningless dagger for such a price. Do you have any idea who this man is?" She scoffed at the dealer in disgust. Shooting Zad a look of quiet death, Zephera warned him to stay silent. Seeing what she was about to do, he exhaled shallowly and shut his mouth.

"Don't know who he is, don't care," the man growled. "Either buy it or get the bloody hell out of my stall."

Zephera cocked her head in that way she always did when assessing her prey. "Speak like that again to His Royal Emissary and he'll have your tongue," she growled, glaring at the man as if she were about to devour him whole. To his credit, the man didn't back down easily, a feat that even Baleem found difficult. When Zephera set her mind to something, she got it, consequences be damned. Zad had learned the hard way to just move out of her way and try to deal with the aftermath later.

"Four gold then," the man had said, not taking his eyes off Zephera.

"Three gold, and that gorgeous curved scimitar, and I won't spill your guts on this table."

The curved blade—their whole reason for venturing out into the day's maddening crowd—was on a table in front of Zephera. The blade itself was made of Verashan metal, one of the lightest, strongest, and rarest metals in the world. It had a blue-black tint that complimented the hilt of the weapon, which was made of carved wood inlaid with mother of pearl. Black leather straps wrapped around it, completing the design. It looked like pretty rainbows and unicorn shit, and it was worth a pretty penny all on its own.

The man's eyes flashed in anger. Zephera had counted on that. She was asking an insultingly low price for the dagger on purpose. It was clear to Zad that she was looking for a fight.

"Emissary or no, I'll not have some bitch insulting me and making idle threats. Now, get out!" the merchant snarled.

Zad put his head in his hands. He almost felt sorry for what was about to happen, but the man had tried to cheat them. And he really hated that word, "bitch." He took a step back from the stall just as Zephera leapt over the wooden counter. The man jumped back in surprise.

Zephera landed in the space he had just vacated. She backed him against the stone wall, pressing a dagger to his throat.

"Apologize. You've hurt my feelings."

In answer, the man spat on her cheek. He gasped and sputtered in small breaths, but he didn't dare move beyond that. Zephera didn't even flinch as she leveled a stare at him with her wicked smile. "That wasn't very nice." She clucked her tongue and wagged a finger at him. "I think it's time this *bitch* taught you some manners."

She pressed the dagger to his throat, nicking his skin. Zephera was mesmerized by the small drop of blood that dripped onto the dagger. She brought it closer to her gaze, keeping the man pinned with her knee against his crotch.

Glaring down at the man, she didn't notice him reaching for his weapon, but Zad did. "Zephera! Look out!" he yelled as the man threw her off, pinning her to the table. He had snatched up the curved blade and held it now to her throat. Anger shone in his eyes as he glowered down at her. Zad held tightly to his own weapon, ready to spring.

Zephera smiled darkly up at the man, her eyes twinkling. Then she pushed her lips into a mocking pout. "Now that's not any way to treat a lady," she cooed. Swiftly, she kneed him between his legs and kicked him away from her. The man fell to the ground, clutching his crotch and gasping for air.

"Take it. Take it all! Just get out of here!" he rasped.

Zephera bent down to look at him. "That's a boy!" She laughed, patting him on the head like a dog. Grabbing the dagger and the scimitar, she leapt over the table and walked off.

Zadkiel shook his head in disgust as he followed after her, glancing at the merchant who was still groaning in pain and writhing on the ground. She was something else, his Zephera. The pleasure she took in the pain and torment of others was appalling. Even though the man had been trying to swindle him, he never would've taken such extreme action. She was dark, cruel, and cold. She was selfish and mean, determined to wallow in her self loathing and misery. Yet, when he looked at her, he couldn't help but want to save her. The woman he loved was still in there, and he wasn't going to give up on her. He would never stop trying to save her from herself.

He scrambled through the crowded streets in the direction she had gone. He was about to give up and head back to the Keep when he found her near the center of the square, sitting near the large ivory fountain. She was talking softly to a disheveled woman whose grateful eyes were trained on Zephera. Zad watched as Zephera handed the woman a small package wrapped in red silk. Tears in her eyes, the woman lunged forward and threw her arms around Zephera, thanking her profusely. Zad laughed as Zephera's whole body went taut, her eyes wide with surprise. Awkwardly, she patted the woman on the back and shrugged out of her grasp.

"He will never harm you again. I promise m'lady," she said to the woman as she stepped away from the embrace.

"Thank you! You've saved my life. How can I repay you, mistress?" the woman asked through her sobs.

"Go far away from this city, make a new life, and never return," Zephera said. "This place is full of poison. Get out while you still have a soul," she said before walking away from the woman.

Zad stood in stunned silence. He had never seen this kinder, more gentle side of Zephera. Before he could think better of it, he walked towards the woman. Still wiping tears of gratitude from her cheeks, she didn't look up as he sat beside her.

"Excuse me, madam. What did that girl do for you?" he asked curiously.

"She saved my life. My ex-husband, the arms dealer, was going to sell me and my son to the slavers." She paused and wiped her cheeks with a dusty cloth. "She just bought our freedom."

That was the moment when he knew Zephera could be so much more. She may have put on a prickly, uncaring facade, but inside beat a pure heart, one that would bleed for the innocents. And there was the proof of it, light as day. He decided right then that he would do everything he could to bring her out of that dark shell.

"Use your new freedom wisely." He left the woman to her thoughts.

Zad opened his eyes, smiling at the memory, the hubbub of the village market drawing him back to the present. He had never told her what he had witnessed that day. Even if he had, she would never admit to it. She was a living, breathing weapon, one that could destroy anything she touched. Or one that could protect and serve. But he still saw that girl at the ivory fountain—the one who could change the world, if she only dared. He needed to show her that she didn't have to hold the world on her shoulders all the time. He could hold it with her, and together they could do anything.

He turned his attention to the water. The sapphire ocean reached out endlessly toward the horizon, immense and tranquil under the cloudless sky. Its waves lapped gently against the shore. He missed his Beasty and wished she was there, enjoying the view with him. He would've taken her hand in his and shown her how such a powerful, potentially dangerous thing as the sea could gently soothe the troubles of life away.

He shook himself from his musings. He was about to head back to the inn when a hushed conversation nearby caught his attention.

"I hear a deadly sickness is spreading throughout the land. My sister said that trade's been cut off completely from the north, and she's been having a hard time finding anyone who is selling spices for a decent price. She thinks it has something to do with another Dark Plague," the woman said, speaking in hushed tones to her companion.

"Another plague?" her companion replied. "Pish posh! That's simply nonsense. Why do you listen to such idle gossip?"

"So you say, but I think there's truth to the rumors. After all, odd activity has been reported at the old ruins near the flour mill. I know it's just a legend, but I wouldn't go poking my head around there after sunset. That place has a dark energy to it. The local children can't seem to stay away. They return home every night with peculiar scrapes and bruises. Something dark lurks there, I just know it."

The woman's companion rolled her eyes. "You are ridiculous. It's just an old ruin. Children's tales—that's all they are. Now, let us go before we are late for supper."

Zad watched as the two women hurried off down the cobblestone path and disappeared. He walked back to the inn, determined to find out more about those old ruins. It might be their first lead.

CHAPER 20

Zephera contemplated Daegan's broad back silently. They had been walking for hours and hadn't spoken since they'd left the clearing. He was a difficult man to read: callous and distant, with a disturbing habit of making her feel small. His confident bearing demanded compliance, but she wasn't the type of person to submit to anyone. She was certain he would betray her and Zad if it meant he could save his people, yet there was something noble and kind in that steadfast loyalty to those he cared about. The loathsome things he had seen and done had hardened him. But beneath the strata of stone that had formed around his soul she saw a man who was just as frightened as she was. Darkness consumed him, and still he held it at bay. The conflict within him called to her. Every small victory he had gained over the blackness in his heart comforted her lonely and sometimes murderous soul.

Her eyes left Daegan to take in her surroundings. They had come to the edge of a steep ravine and would soon begin their descent down into the world below. In a few hours, they would reach the village of Watford. The thought of a warm bath and a delicious meal filled her with anticipation. She was ready to be done with gamey rabbit meat and charred snake. Her mouth watered as she recalled the savory spiced soup she had eaten at the castle before they left. Her stomach complained noisily at the memory and she growled in annoyance.

"Only a few more hours, Zephera. How do you make it through

your missions in one piece?" Daegan asked. "That stomach of yours is insatiable."

"Oh, shut it," she snapped. "You are probably just as hungry as I am."

Daegan snorted. "What was it you were daydreaming about? Zadkiel and cake?"

"You are mocking me, aren't you?" she replied, hands on her hips.

"For someone so proud, you seem to let me slide under that tough skin of yours quite easily," he smirked.

She glared at him. "You are just jealous that you can't be inside of this skin," she said, turning on her heel and leaving him behind.

She heard a growl behind her and then suddenly she was twisted around and down on the ground, pinned under Daegan's powerful legs. His hands were like iron bands as they held her arms against the earth. She sucked in a breath, scowling up at him. He brought his face down to hers, so close they were almost touching. She parted her lips and stared up into his eyes. They were light and playful.

"You and that filthy little mind of yours ought to control your tongue." He brought one finger to her chin and pushed her mouth closed. He stared at her for a moment longer before releasing her. Standing up, he ran his fingers through his hair. "It's going to get you into trouble one day," he said, before offering her a hand.

She smacked it away. "I hate you," she spat.

"No, you don't. You want to, but you can't. I intrigue you, Zephera. Admit it."

"Shove off, prick," she said, sticking her tongue out at him. "I need to eat. Let us get off this blasted mountain."

"After you, my lady," he said with a flourish and a bow.

She threw a petulant smile at him as she stomped past, which he returned with a rude gesture.

"My mouth has gotten me into trouble many times. It's never ended in anything but pleasure for me," she sneered as she made her way down the rocky escarpment.

Daegan followed behind her carefully. "I would imagine you either gutted some poor sod, or..." His voice trailed off as he made a crude gesture with his hips.

Zephera laughed so hard she almost slipped on the steep trail.

"You would be correct on both counts, sir," she said through her laughter. "We are quite the pair of perverted fools. Don't we have anything better to talk about?"

"We can speak of anything you like, Zephera," Daegan said, his tone softening.

"All right." She pursed her lips, allowing the playfulness of their banter to fade away. She knew what Daegan was doing, inviting her to speak her mind, while at the same time asking her to trust him with her thoughts. Finally, she spoke, choosing her words carefully in case he wasn't done teasing her.

"Why do you think I'm immune to the effects of the plague? I understand your immunity, but what of mine?"

Daegan didn't answer for a few minutes. She allowed him his silence, unsure of what to expect. When he answered, his voice was guarded. "I don't know, Zephera. Baleem only told me that you were immune, but I think he knows more than he is saying." Cautiously, he added, "But I would like to find out."

She didn't know how to respond. She knew that her master hadn't told her everything. That was why he had given her the letter. Her stomach tightened. She should've opened that letter when they first got to camp. She should have never gone to clean herself up and change first, leaving it unread and unprotected. And then her stupid pride had kept her from confiding in Zad about the letter when it had first gone missing. If she had just told him, he could've helped her search the area. Perhaps she would have that letter in her hands now, along with all the answers she needed.

Baleem would be furious with her when he found out. He was always nagging at her to focus on the mission above all else. Even on solo missions, she struggled to keep her emotions under control. But this time, she had been forced to work with a team of irritating people who continually got in her way. She had to check her temper constantly. It was taxing and distracting, and she wished she could leave them all behind and find the cure for the plague herself.

But then she remembered Brenner teaching her to communicate with her mind; Zad's familiar, reassuring presence calming her; Daegan's fingers tracing the stone pillar and interpreting the symbols; and Oriana—she wasn't sure what Oriana did, but Zephera had formed a kind of begrudging bond with her. Where would she be now if they hadn't come with her?

Baleem had tried so many times to get her to play nicely with others. Over time, she had gotten used to working with Zad on missions, though for some odd reason, his presence had never seemed to bother her too much anyway. But she ended up almost murdering anyone else she was assigned to work with. She had threatened so many of her fellow assassins that everyone refused to work with her, except Zad. For this failure, however, she had no one to blame but herself.

Perhaps she was immune because she was the plague itself. The darkness inside her consumed everyone she touched. That's why she kept others away, why she wouldn't let them get close to her. The light inside her battled to repulse the darkness, but the darkness was winning.

Daegan watched Zephera closely, taking note of her reserved silence in the wake of his reply. He knew that she often withdrew into herself when her thoughts took her away. He wondered what the world was like inside her mind. *What a fascinating place it must be,* he thought.

He let his own thoughts wander to the mission, giving Zephera the space she needed. He couldn't risk anything this time. Five hundred years ago, he had run at the first sign of danger. He had been the worst of cowards and had let his people down. It had taken him five hundred years to gather the training and knowledge needed to stop the cycle. This time, he wouldn't let anything get in his way—not fear and certainly not

Zephera. He would redeem himself. He would vanquish this constant, mocking weakness that resided within his psyche and stop the cursed blight on the world.

He needed Zephera, needed the power she didn't know was locked away inside her. Like pulling a sword from its sheath, he would draw that power out of her and wield it as he needed. He only hoped that he wouldn't break her in the process.

She was as magnificent and dangerous as the Darkness itself. He wanted to tell her everything—who she was, her powerful potential—but he was afraid of what she would do with her power if she knew. She could destroy the world and everything in it if that was what she wished. He had seen what could happen if she chose that path. It would bring nothing but destruction. But if she chose the other path, she could transform the world into a paradise. When the time came for her to make that choice, he could only hope she picked the path that would bring life. If she didn't, he would be the one who would have to put her down. For now, he would bide his time, gain her trust. He would wait to act. He just hoped that when that moment came, he wouldn't be too late.

CHAPER 21

"**L**et me get this straight. You want me to do this alone?" Zad asked in surprise.

"No, I don't want you to do it alone—I don't want you to do it at all! Zephera's going to be furious if you go after the second item without her. I won't have any part in it," Oriana fumed.

"Yes, but we don't even know if it's a tangible lead, Oriana," he argued. "It could turn out to be nothing. We don't have time to wait. We need to check out every lead."

"Zad, please?" she pleaded. "Just wait for Zephera and Daegan. They'll be back soon. It won't kill you to be patient, you know."

"No, I'm going. Zephera and Daegan are out there now, risking their lives for some damned item. I can't sit idly by and do nothing. We are in the bloody village. It's safe here. She would understand," Zad fumed.

"Well then, I'll let you tell her about your stupid quest when she gets back. Just go, Zad, and be careful. I don't fancy having to face her wrath if you disappear or die." She waved at him dismissively.

"Glad to have your blessing, Oriana," he said, rolling his eyes. "Tell Brenner where I've gone when he wakes up," he commanded as he left the room.

The old flour mill was a few minutes' walk south of the village. As he explored the mill, it began to rain. The sky blackened as a storm rolled in from the sea. The wind began to swirl around him, its strong breath causing the air around him to churn in anticipation. The world went silent with an eerie calm just before the clouds opened up and it began to pour. Zad swore under his breath.

He was about to turn back when a small ball of light caught his eye. It danced and swayed in the rain, illuminating the world around it. The orb moved slowly up into the churning sky just ahead of where he was standing. Mesmerized by its gentle movements, he followed it up a crumbling stone path to a small hill. The orb stopped and circled his head, as if asking him to dance with it. He reached out to touch it but it bounced out of reach, making its way up the hill. Zad trotted up the incline with an almost childlike playfulness, unaware of the mud that caked his boots. When he arrived at the top of the hill, he glanced around, searching for the orb. It had come to a stop and was bobbing gently over the ruins of an old house, the foundation and a single crumbling wall the only evidence that a building had once stood there.

Zad entered the ruins and jerked as the light disappeared. Then he noticed something odd. He extended his hand out into the air. There was no rain. He stepped out of the ruins, and the rain started lashing against his skin again. When he stepped back inside the house, the rain stopped, as if an invisible roof hung protectively over the house. His brow furrowed.

He hunted for anything out of the ordinary. He searched every nook and cranny the old ruins had.

"What exactly am I meant to find?" he asked the empty ruin. "Any sign would be great. Lightning," he asked, his hands in the air. "No? How about a rock falling?" Again, he looked around him, feeling quite silly.

Shaking his head, he plopped down on the ground. The light returned and began circling him fervently. He watched in puzzlement as it accelerated. Suddenly, hundreds of balls of light appeared, illuminating the ruins and transforming them. Before his eyes, the fallen walls arose and fit together. A ceiling formed overhead. Doors and windows flew into place. Before the darkness could overcome him, he thought he saw a shadow of a woman looming overhead. His head spun at the dizzying display and just as he heard the thunder, he lost consciousness.

"Wake up, boy," said a harsh voice. Zad blinked, struggling to clear his blurry vision. He lay on the floor of a cobblestone cottage. A woman with black hair and cold eyes stood over him. Her face was severe, yet had a serene beauty about it. The curve of her lips formed a perfect scowl that would put Zephera's to shame. "Up, up!" she called.

His body groaned with stiffness but he stood and looked at her curiously. "Where am I?"

The woman clucked her tongue. "Your location isn't a matter of where, as you are nowhere, yet everywhere," she said imperiously.

"What? That doesn't make any sense. Who are you?" he asked.

"I am no one. I am but a memory. You, however, are here for something important, boy. Do you know what it is?"

"Reina?" Zad gasped.

"I am Reina, or at least part of her. I am her mind—a piece of her consciousness left for only those of a pure heart to find."

Zad eyed the woman warily. "And my heart's pure?"

She shrugged a shoulder. "Pure enough."

He scoffed, growing irritated with the woman's tactics.

Growing impatient and wanting to get out of there, he asked, "What's the item I need? I assume that's why I'm here?"

With a flourish of her fingers, she twisted her hand, and a small vial containing a mysterious dark liquid appeared.

"What am I supposed to do with that?" he asked.

She handed him the vial. "Drink it and ignite the Decay from within."

His eyes widened. "The Decay? But, that would…"

"Kill you?" Reina interrupted. She smiled wickedly. "Those pure of heart do what's needed to defeat the darkness. You've gotten this far. Can you continue?"

Zad clenched his jaw. "The cure? Will I receive that?"

The woman laughed. It was a small, girlish laugh that didn't seem to fit her. "A true hero rushes into battle with little thought for his own life. I can see it in your eyes, dear boy. You fancy yourself a hero, a savior. When the time comes, will you falter?"

Zad stared at her. He shook his head slightly, pocketing the vial.

Reina smiled darkly. "Just as I thought. Take care, Zadkiel. The road ahead of you is grim. Goodbye." Laughing, she began to disappear. Her body became more and more transparent until Zad was alone in the room with nothing but her echoing laughter.

The house began to shake and a section of the ceiling fell. Zad dove out of the way before it could crush him. He got to his feet and ran to the door of the cottage just as the walls started to collapse. When he stepped outside, there was no ground for his feet to land on. He tumbled into an abyss, trying to grab onto something, anything, but there was nothing around him but darkness. He opened his mouth to scream, but before he could, the ground appeared. He hit it with a thud.

He groaned and sat up, his head spinning. "Bloody hell! What was that?" Looking around, he saw that he was back in the ruins. There was no sign he had ever left. Clutching the vial of dark liquid, he got to his feet and walked slowly out into the rain.

By the time he reached the old flour mill, he was soaked through. Mud covered his boots and leathers, and his head pounded from the fall. His world grew blurry. He needed to sit down for a moment and rest. He limped over to the wall of the flour mill, leaned his arms against it, and emptied the contents of his stomach. "Gods above," he swore. Closing his eyes tightly and shaking his head, he tried to combat the nausea. It was useless. He felt himself start to sway. He needed to lie down. He closed his eyes. He was so tired. He would rest, just for a moment. He put the vial in his pocket, slumped down to the ground, and drifted off.

When he woke, he was stripped bare, a fur blanket wrapped around him. He was back at the inn, and a fire roared beside him. He tried to sit up but noticed someone was lying next to him. Her dark hair was swept behind her ear. Zephera. She was safe. He watched as she slept, her pale skin glowing beneath the light of the fire. She was so beautiful. She was back, she was safe, she was his. As if feeling his stare, Zephera began to stir.

He placed his hand on her shoulder. "Zephera…" he breathed.

She opened her dark eyes, gold and blue dancing through them like the night sky itself. "Hi," she whispered, smiling sheepishly at him.

"You are safe," he mused, his face close to hers. She inched closer to him until their noses were almost touching. Zad stared at her, embarrassed by the intimacy. He tried to pull away.

"Don't," she whispered, drawing him close. She brought her mouth to his and kissed him hungrily, her tongue exploring every surface of his mouth.

"Zephera…" he moaned. She pressed her lips harder against his. He grabbed her head gently and entwined his legs with hers, feeling the heat of her nexus against his knee. His mind filled with her.

"I want to feel every inch of you," he growled and pushed her onto her back.

His lips brushed against her neck, making a tantalizing journey down to her collarbone. He watched her chest rise and fall. She was a goddess, the most gorgeous creature he had ever seen. And he loved her.

"I'm going to make love to you now, Zephera," he whispered.

She moaned, her body molding to his. His breath caught as she moved her hips against his. He slipped into her, and it was as if a hot summer night had embraced him, as if the gods had designed her only for him. She clenched herself around him, and his breath exploded. He pushed into her faster as they rushed to the peak together. He felt her pulsing around him as she released, and his body bucked as he found his own release. They lay together, panting, still joined. When their breath evened, he withdrew and collapsed down next to her.

"You have no idea how long I've wanted to do that, Zephera," he murmured as he kissed her neck tenderly.

"Me too," she replied. She turned to face him and looked at him with her familiar, beloved eyes. "I love you, Zad," she said sleepily.

"I love you too, Beasty," he whispered, kissing her forehead. His arms wrapped around her and they lay there, tangled between the sheets. They closed their eyes and were soon lost together to sleep.

He felt himself being shaken awake. "Zadkiel! Wake up, damn it! C'mon, Zad, please, wake up!" the voice called.

He opened his eyes. He wasn't at the inn. He was back at the flour mill, the rain pouring down onto him. He looked up into the worried eyes of Oriana. "Oriana?" he gasped.

"Yes, you idiot. Who did you expect?" she yelled. "I can't lift you, Zad. Can you sit up on your own?"

Blinking a few times to clear his vision, he sat up.

"What happened, Zad? You've been gone for hours. When you didn't return, we came out to search for you." She looked worried and her brow was furrowed into a scowl.

"I must've passed out. I'm sorry, Oriana," he said, standing.

She eyed him suspiciously as she hobbled to where Brenner was standing. His expression was inscrutable.

"Did you at least manage to find something out?" she barked at him.

He nodded. "Yes, actually, I did." He told them what had occurred at the ruins. They stared at him in disbelief. He reached into his pocket and pulled out the vial. "This is what she gave me. I'm not sure about the rest of it. We'll need to figure it out. Do either of you have any ideas?" he asked, pushing his hair back from his eyes.

Brenner only shook his head and motioned for them to follow him.

"We can talk about it more when we get back to the inn," Oriana said. "We need a change of clothes. Hopefully Daegan and Zephera will be back by now." She limped after Brenner.

Zad shook his head. How could he face Zephera after that incredibly forbidden dream? Sighing deeply, he followed after them, hoping he would have time to take a cold bath before Zephera and Daegan returned.

CHAPTER 22

Zephera almost cried with happiness when she saw the lights of the village below them. "Thank the gods! Look! We're almost there!" she squealed.

Daegan looked at her like she had sprouted horns. "Did you just squeal?" he asked.

She shrugged. "Food." Then she turned a dazzling smile on him. "And I can't wait to get out of these wet clothes."

He opened his mouth to reply, but she held up a hand. "Don't say it," she warned.

Daegan tried his best to look surprised. "Don't say what?" he asked innocently.

Rolling her eyes, she continued trudging through the mud and rain. Her hair was soaked and matted to her forehead. "What you told me about yourself—about everything—do you want me to keep that to myself?" she asked.

Daegan clenched his jaw like he always did when he was deep in thought. "I trust you, Zephera, and I trust that you'll do what you think is best. I've given you my secret. It's up to you to decide what you want to do with it."

She felt the weight of his trust settle on her. She almost wished he had forbidden her flat out, but she didn't comment on his answer. Instead she said, "Can I ask you something, Daegan?"

"Why ask permission? Even if I said no, you would just ask your question anyway. What you really should be concerned about is whether I'll actually answer your question."

"Ugh! You are insufferable. You did promise you would answer any question I asked. So, if you consider yourself an honorable man, then you must satisfy any and all curiosities I have."

"I've created a monster," he lamented. "You do know what they say about curiosity..."

"Yes, that poor cat. I, however, am not a cat."

"Ask away, my dear."

"Why do you torment Zadkiel?"

Daegan raised his dark eyebrows. "I find his presence infuriating. He is weak. His performance on the battlefield is underwhelming. He's a waste of my time. He chooses to spend his life doing things he hates because he thinks he can change the world. Yet he doesn't have the courage to foster that change. And it pleases me to watch him pine for you. I suppose most people would feel bad for him, but I'm not like other people. I find it perversely funny. He knows he can't have you, yet he doesn't seem to care. He keeps trying to win your heart. Any man who wears his feelings on his sleeve so adamantly makes himself fodder for mockery."

Zephera scoffed. "You've never seen him kill. His technique, his efficiency—it's a work of art. While I like to take my time, he's quick and merciful. He's stronger than you give him credit for. You have no idea the things he's done for me and for Nostorra."

"I can't comment on what I don't know, Zephera. I've never seen him fight or kill in such a way. I base my judgments on what I know, and what I know is that he's inferior to you and me."

"You can't pass judgment on someone you've known for only a little over a fortnight."

"I won't argue that you view him differently from me. You see Zadkiel as the cup half full while I see him as the cup half empty. But he's the same cup and has the same lack of wholeness. Setting that aside, how can you possibly be upset when my opinion of him is hardly any different from your own?"

Zephera's mouth fell open. "What are you talking about? You just said we saw him differently. You are the most idiotic, contradictory man I've ever met!"

Daegan laughed coolly. "I'm not referring to his character and skills—or lack thereof. I'm talking about the fact that he's in love with you."

Her mouth snapped shut. She threw her head back. "He... I'm not... he's not... ugh... I don't know what to do."

"Yes, you do. You just don't want to do it."

"No, it's not that. I'm just not sure how I feel about..." her voice trailed off.

"Him," Daegan finished for her. "You don't know how you feel about him."

Zephera nodded, biting her lip.

"He doesn't deserve you, Zephera. You are strong where he is weak, and you are in every way his superior. You are cold and calculating. You have a darkness about you that rivals the night sky, and you can't possibly give him what he craves."

"And what's that, Daegan?"

"Normalcy. He loves the parts of you that he wants to and despises the others. He wants to be your protector, your savior. He would sooner chain you to a life of peace and normalcy than have you fight and be the woman that you are."

"And what's so wrong with a nice, quiet life full of peace?" she asked.

"Nothing, for people like Zadkiel," he spat. "But for people like you and me, we could never be happy with such a life. We are killers. We enjoy the fear in the eyes of our prey. We love the dark crimson color of their blood, the way it leaks out of their wounds. We share a sickness, Zephera—one that can never be cured, and one that certainly can never be chained by a life of peace." His nostrils flared.

Zephera wondered what terrible things Daegan had done. His dark gaze petrified and annoyed her. "You know NOTHING about me, Daegan! Nothing. Stop trying to analyze me and diagnose my *disease*. You are wrong." She screamed in annoyance and marched ahead, leaving him to drown in his stupid assumptions.

As Daegan and Zephera made their way to the base of the mountain, the rain beat harder and visibility diminished. They arrived at the outskirts of the town and heard muffled voices ahead.

"You should've just listened to me! Imagine what would've happened if we hadn't come out in this storm to look for you, Zadkiel." There was a huff and a grunt of exasperation, and Oriana's soprano voice rattled on. "If you'd gotten hurt, Zephera would've gutted us and served us up on a platter."

Zad and Oriana's forms appeared ahead in the stormy mist. Brenner was a few steps ahead of them. Zephera grinned. Zad was hunched over, cowering before Oriana's impassioned lecture. Zephera decided to step in and save him. "And why is it that I would've gutted you?" she asked, running to catch up with the group.

Oriana stopped mid-sentence, her eyes wide. "Zephera! Daegan!" she yelled happily, reaching to hug her.

Zephera ducked out of the way. "I don't like hugs."

Oriana laughed. "I don't care," she said and grabbed Zephera tight.

"All right, all right, get off!" she barked.

Oriana smiled widely at them. "I'm so pleased you are safe!"

Zephera wiped the rain from her eyes as she glanced at Zad. He looked both pleased and mildly upset to see her. "What? Aren't you happy to see me?" she asked.

Zad smirked. "Get over here, Beasty," he growled. She didn't flinch away when his arms went around her.

He picked her up and twirled her around. "You are a sight for sore eyes. I missed you, Zephera," he said, setting her down.

"I missed you too, Zad. Gods above, don't ever leave me again," she scolded, hitting him playfully in the chest. Zad put his arm around her and guided her towards the inn. She slowed and let the others walk ahead so she could spend a few precious moments with him. She glared at Daegan. He gave her a warning look before stalking away to join Oriana and Brenner.

"You smell horrible, Zad," she laughed. "What was Oriana yelling at you about? Did you get drunk and toss up your liquor?"

Zad shook his head in annoyance. "No, Zephera, I didn't get drunk. But I did follow up on a lead for the second item."

Zephera stiffened under his arm. "Alone? Zad—"

"It's fine, Beasty. Trust me," he replied. "Look." He pulled the vial out of his pocket. He handed it to her and told her about his encounter with Reina.

Zephera didn't know if she should hug him or slap him—the idiot, going off by himself! Anything could've happened. She was glad that he'd found the item. She just wished they knew what it meant. Hopefully, they'd figure it out over the next few days while they recovered and waited for Baleem to contact them.

"And what of your journey? I see you and Daegan are both still in one piece."

"It wasn't as horrible as I thought it would be. I don't particularly like him, but I do think he has his uses."

Zad barked out a laugh. "Going from hated to useful is quite the transformation. What did you get yourselves into?"

She leaned her head on his shoulder. "I'm starving! And I need a bath and a good night's sleep. Can we talk less about Daegan and more about food?"

Zad laughed as he held open the door to the inn. Zephera exhaled in relief as they walked out of the storm into the warm, dry inn. Her eyes almost popped out of her skull when she saw what they were serving for dinner. Soaked clothes forgotten, she sat down at the nearest table and ordered just about every item on the menu. The innkeeper's daughter shot her a disapproving glare as she peeled off her wet boots and began to rub her sore feet. Zad shrugged at the woman and excused himself to go change before their food was brought out. When he returned, Zephera had a roasted turkey leg in one hand, a fork full of potatoes in the other, and a mouth so stuffed with food she looked like a chipmunk. She moaned when he sat down, her eyes glazed over in exhaustion.

"Mmmm… Thuh ith the motht dohlithous meh I ha eweh eathen," she attempted to say, bits of food hurling out across the table.

Zad chuckled. "What?"

She chewed a few seconds more and then swallowed loudly. "This is the most delicious meal I have ever eaten," she repeated, waving at the innkeeper's daughter, whose scowl turned into a smile of delight. Zad helped himself to a plate of creamed corn and rolls as he listened to Zephera rave on about the food.

When she was finished, she leaned back in her chair in a state of stupid satisfaction. She patted her bulging stomach. "I never want to leave this place. That was divine!" She smiled, closing her eyes. "If I eat one more bite, you're going to have to carry me to my bed."

Zad blushed, thinking of his dream. A piece of corn slipped down his throat and he coughed and beat at his chest. When he could breathe again, he said, "It's been a long day. I'm exhausted. I'm going to head to my room, all right? It's just down the hall from yours. Knock on my door if you need anything."

"Mmm hmm… since when did I need to knock?" Her words were slurred. She shrugged without opening her eyes. "Night, Zad." He arose and left her in her food-induced stupor.

The sound of dishes clattering on the table brought her out of her daze. The innkeeper's daughter was making a big show of cleaning up. "Thanks for the excellent grub," Zephera said. "What's your name?"

"Ella, miss." Zephera tipped her head at her in acknowledgement and then made her way to the room she shared with Oriana. Oriana didn't look up when she entered. She was cuddled up snugly beneath a sable blanket, reading a book. Zephera grabbed a fresh set of clothes and made her way to the communal washroom down the hall. She undressed quickly, stepping behind the curtain before turning on the bath water.

She sunk down into the bath and groaned as the warm water soothed her aching muscles. She scrubbed her filthy body with a pumice stone and used her favorite dusk-rose perfumed soap for her hair. She stayed in the water for over an hour, refilling the tub when the water began to cool.

Her thoughts wandered to Daegan's words from earlier. He'd said she could never be content with normalcy and peace. She'd been so angry with him, with what he'd said about Zad, how he'd compared himself to her. She didn't want to hear it. But deep down in a secret part of herself, she knew he was at least partially right, even if she refused to voice her acknowledgement. They may have been similar in their love of dealing death, but that was where their similarity ended. He acted as if he was above everyone, as if he alone could stop what was coming. She knew better, though. He needed her. She didn't know what for but she knew there was something he wasn't telling her. His need for her was evident when he extended kindness to her in her worst, most broken moments. Every time she had fallen, he had lifted her back up and made her feel strong. He was grooming her for something, and she was determined to find out what it was.

The door creaked, yanking her from her thoughts. She pulled the stop out of the drain and reached for her towel, wrapping it tightly around herself. Then she snatched the privacy curtain aside.

Her eyes bugged as she came face to face with a very tall, very naked Daegan. Her face flamed, and she shut her eyes tightly and turned her head to the side.

"What are you doing?" she yelled.

"I'm about to wash up," he replied nonchalantly, as if they were both fully clothed. "What are *you* doing in the men's washroom?"

"What? I didn't know there were two washrooms. Gods above," she squeaked, eyes still firmly closed. "Can you please turn around or put a towel on so I can get by?"

Daegan's bellow of laughter echoed off the golden-tiled walls. "And miss the Lady of Death squirming like a scared rabbit at the sight of my naked body? I think not."

She made a disgusted noise. "At least get out of my way!" She pushed past him, catching her hip on the wash basin as she attempted to get around him without making contact, her eyes looking at everything but him. She heard him laugh as he got into the bath and turned on the unheated water. As the cold spray filled the tub, Daegan let out a muffled curse. She smiled ruthlessly and then stomped out of the washroom, leaving her clothes behind. It was the second time that insufferable man had managed to make her walk in shame without her clothes. Oriana jumped as she barged into their room and slammed the door hard enough to make a picture frame fall from the wall to the floor.

"What happened to you?" she asked, her eyes wide as she took in her brooding roommate.

"Daegan." Zephera grimaced.

She grabbed her last set of clean clothes from her bag. Then she pulled her cotton tunic over her head and fell onto the bed next to Oriana, who was laughing so hard she had tears in her eyes.

"Why don't you just bed him already? You can't seem to keep your clothes on around him. Unless you did that already?" she asked curiously.

Zephera stared daggers at her. Oriana stifled another laugh. "You need to release some of that pent up stress, Zephera. If Daegan can't help you with it, I'm sure Zad wouldn't turn you down if you asked. I've been feeling a bit peckish myself…"

Zephera buried her head in her pillow. "Agh!" she screamed, kicking her legs. "I'm going to sleep. Get the light, will you?"

"I'm only trying to help. You'd feel so much better if you got some of that tension and anger out," Oriana muttered as she blew out the candle on the bedside table.

"Goodnight, Zephera," she cooed.

"Hmmphhh," was all Zephera could say before she was lost to her dreams.

CHAPTER 23

Zephera woke to a cold hand pressed against her mouth and a dagger at her throat. A pair of hateful eyes gazed down at her from above. Valessa's face bloomed into view from the darkness of the room around her.

I am not going to hurt you, girl, the Keeper's voice sounded in her head. *I need you to come with me quietly. Don't wake Oriana. Meet me outside, and keep your mouth shut. If you tell anyone where you are going, I will scramble their brains and serve them to you for breakfast.* Valessa swept out of the room soundlessly.

Zephera sat up slowly. The sun was just starting to peek over the horizon. Gray light filled the room. She glanced at Oriana who was sound asleep, blissfully unaware that a demoness had just infiltrated their room. She filled her lungs with the crisp morning air and then forced herself to exhale slowly, her hands trembling as she dressed. She pulled on her boots, which were still damp from the night before. Sheathing her weapons, she tiptoed quietly out of the room and down the wooden steps of the inn. The tavern was empty this early in the morning. Unsure of how long Valessa would need her, she picked the lock to the kitchen. She rifled through the cupboards and found some dried meat and a few apples, which she placed in a burlap sack. She crept out of the tavern, making sure to leave no trace of her burglary behind. Then she pulled her dark hood up over her ears and stalked off into the village.

Valessa was waiting for her with a stony face. She turned on her heel, motioning for Zephera to follow. Zephera trailed after her quickly. She followed her to the harbor, where a small fishing boat was waiting. "Get in, girl," Valessa ordered.

Shaking her head, Zephera glared at her. "No. I'm not going anywhere with you until you tell me what you want."

Valessa pursed her lips impatiently. "The village will be awake soon and we can't be seen together. We don't have time to dawdle. Now, get in, or I'll seize control of you and put you in the boat myself."

Zephera crossed her arms and Valessa tapped her foot impatiently.

Finally, the woman begged. "Please?"

"Tell me why!" Zephera barked.

Valessa shook her head in exasperation. "Baleem sent me to help you obtain the next item. It can only be you, Zephera. No one else can know."

At the mention of her master, Zephera bit her lip nervously. She eyed Valessa, who was looking around in agitation. Hoping she wouldn't regret it, she climbed into the boat.

Valessa followed, her weight causing the craft to pitch gently. "*Tractus,*" Valessa whispered, and the boat started to row itself out into the harbor. They rode in silence across the water. The village of Watford grew smaller and the shore turned into a distant smudge before disappearing altogether. They were now in the middle of the ocean, water surrounding them as far as the eye could see. She had never been this far from land. She squinted as the sun rose, illuminating the water in golden splendor. The others would be getting up soon. She wondered how long it would take for them to discover she was missing. She tried to reach out to Brenner but she felt nothing.

She pulled out an apple to munch on as Valessa stared at her in silence. "Since we're sitting here enjoying each other's company so spectacularly, would you care to elaborate on where the bloody hell you're taking me?"

Valessa let out a breath. "I suppose you're right. And you can't exactly run away now." She gestured at the vast expanse of water around them. "The third item you seek is in the crypt of one Sebastian Mirrarow. It's located underground in a maze of traps and tests. Once you're deemed worthy and have found his crypt, you are to retrieve his finger bone."

Zephera laughed. "Because, of course, why should any of this be even remotely easy? Bloody hell, the gods have a wicked sense of humor."

"Just Reina, I think."

Zephera swallowed a piece of apple. "Is there a particular reason that you wouldn't allow my companions and me to do this ourselves?"

Valessa smiled. "Because the only one that would be allowed to enter would be you. The others would have been deemed unworthy and killed the instant they stepped across the threshold. I figured I would save you the trouble of finding out that nasty bit and take you myself."

"Why should I believe you? How am I supposed to know this isn't some kind of trap?"

"Because I have the answers that you seek, if you care to know them."

Zephera clenched her jaw. "Tell me then, woman! Do you take joy in torturing me? You have the answers I seek because you stole Baleem's letter when you attacked me!"

Valessa's eyes widened in surprise. "I did no such thing. I mean you no ill will, Zephera. I know the answers to your questions because I was there when Baleem found you. I know what you are."

Zephera stared at her in shock and confusion.

"You are born of Light and Dark. Since the beginning, when the Realms were split thousands of years ago, you have died and been reborn time and time again. You are the key to stopping the cycles." Valessa spoke with such assurance that Zephera hadn't realized she had stopped breathing.

Zephera shook her head slowly. "That can't be true. I'm no one. I'm not—"

"You are. I can feel the energies inside of you warring with each other. I watched you die at the hands of the Cycle twice now, and I won't watch it happen again. This time you will break the curse that haunts my people and yours."

Zephera felt herself start to sway. "You are the Eighth, aren't you?"

"Yes, I am. How did you know?" Valessa asked quietly.

"Daegan. He was the ninth to be sent over. If you've watched the Cycle pass twice, that would make you the Eighth."

Valessa huffed. "I'm surprised Daegan told you who he is. He is a fool. He is trying to redeem himself from what he did last time."

"What did he do?" Zephera asked.

"We each have a duty to fulfill when we are sent to this realm: find the children who will restore balance and rescue our realm." She motioned to Zephera. "The King of Lucent seeks the children as well." Zephera made a small noise of exclamation.

Valessa smiled bitterly. "Yes, dear girl. The King of Lucent is still very much alive. I'm sure you have heard the story of how our realms were split in two?"

Zephera nodded, and Valessa continued. "When the King of Lucent cleansed the world of darkness, he didn't realize that he would be undoing the balance of nature itself. Separating Light and Dark was a grave error, for one can't exist without the other. Nature compensated for the imbalance by creating a loophole of sorts—the Cycles. But in doing so, it cursed the King of Lucent with everlasting life. The King of Somber is also cursed with life eternal. Neither can die until the world is whole again. Every five hundred years, one of us is sent here to end the cycle, and every five hundred years, we fail. Gregour, the King of Lucent, will stop at nothing to keep our realms separate. Though he was once a good man, grief and power have darkened his mind. He is as cruel and evil as the dark creatures themselves. I have spent my life studying his patterns and disguises. Every cycle, he continues to hunt you down and kill you. His refusal to end the Cycles is that of a man who wants to hold on to his power. He was once your father. Now he is nothing more than a monster."

Zephera felt like she had been kicked in the stomach. "Are you saying I'm the child of the King of Lucent and the Dark Priestess?"

"Yes."

Zephera looked down at her hands. Valessa had just shattered her world. How long had she seen herself as damaged and unwanted, a thing to be hated and discarded? She had always felt like there was something horribly wrong with her. But now she felt angry. How could her father murder her—not just once, but over and over again? Her mother had died for her, not once, but twice. Zephera had a twin who died within her mother's womb. She felt a keening sense of grief.

She bit her lip, trying to stifle a sob. "And Baleem? How does he fit into all of this?"

Sadness passed over Valessa's sharp features. "That isn't my story to tell. It is his. When we finish with all this nasty plague business, I'm sure he will tell you."

Zephera wasn't sure if she wanted to know who Baleem truly was. All these new revelations were smothering her like dirt thrown on a coffin, piling up and burying her whole. She was slowly suffocating. One more shovel-full and she would break. She closed her eyes and took a deep, steadying breath. She wouldn't let Valessa see her falter. If she was supposed to stop the Cycles and make the Realms whole, she needed to be strong. How was she going to do any of this? She was the Lady of Death, made to ruin and destroy, not save the world. Bile rose up in her throat, and she emptied her stomach over the side of the boat.

Valessa patted her back gently in an awkward attempt to comfort her. "I know it is overwhelming, love. You'll be all right." Zephera grunted and then retched again. Valessa cursed and scrambled out of the way.

Zephera splashed cold salt water on her face to clean off the vomit and then lay back in the boat, letting the rocking motion of the sea take her back to the lake. She imagined herself swimming freely, floating on her back in the cool water. The sun warmed her face, kissing her bare skin as she swam. She drifted peacefully, all her inhibitions and worries gone.

Her nerves calmed and her nausea passed. Once again feeling anchored, Zephera opened her eyes. She breathed slowly and deeply as she scanned the horizon. They had arrived at a small island and were only a few stones' throw away from the shore.

Valessa eyed her suspiciously, wondering if she would have another fit. "Are you sure you're all right, Zephera?"

"Would you be?" Zephera barked, glaring daggers at Valessa. "Baleem knows, doesn't he? He had every opportunity to tell me and he didn't. I had to find out who I am from a monster!"

Valessa looked hurt, but she quickly replaced the emotion with indifference. "A monster? I'm no angel, but a monster? Hmm… I suppose I have been called worse." Valessa frowned slightly. "Yes, Baleem knew. I am sure you have many questions. You will get your answers, Zephera, I can promise you that. Just know that he had his reasons. Your master is a good man."

Valessa tied the boat to a dilapidated dock. "Welcome to the Island of Infernos. You will find the entrance to the catacombs just up that path. Good luck, Zephera."

Zephera jumped onto the dock and took off down the path without so much as a glance at Valessa. She hadn't gone far when she came to a rusted iron gate that guarded the entry to a small cavern. Taking a deep breath, she opened the gate and stepped inside. The cavern was larger than it appeared to be from the outside. The floor descended into blackness. Zephera reached into her tunic and pulled out the smooth, blue, magicked stone that Brenner had given her. Reaching into her bag, she pulled out a ball of thick thread, pulled a long piece off, and cut it with her dagger. She attached the small stone to a large stick she had found outside on the path. "*Lux*," she whispered, and the stone lit up, illuminating the path before her. Her eyebrows disappeared into her hairline. The stone actually worked. She made a mental note to thank Brenner later. Zephera took in her surroundings and gasped at the sheer immensity of the cavern. She stood at the top of a stone staircase that led deep into the ground, peeked over the precipice and yelped. The staircase descended endlessly into a chasm far below. Stepping back, she pressed her body against the damp stone wall.

"Breathe, Zephera, breathe. It's nothing to be worried about. Just a deep, dark hole, that leads to almost certain death." She let out a nervous laugh, said a prayer to the gods, and began her descent into hell.

CHAPER 24

"**W**HERE IS SHE?" The angry scream woke Daegan immediately. He blinked, glancing around the room. His covers were gone. A pity. Zadkiel was quivering furiously in the doorway, blankets in hand. Apparently, the imbecile was going through some sort of crisis. As usual. The morning sun was practically burning a hole through the window, and, by default, Daegan's eyes. It was too bright and early for consciousness, let alone Zadkiel's nonsense. The idiot was lucky Daegan's blade was in his trousers on the far side of the room.

"Where is who?" Daegan asked, yawning.

"Zephera! Where is she?" Zad asked again.

Daegan stood up, pushing Zad aside like he was nothing more than a curtain. Ignoring him, Daegan pulled on his black tunic. He cracked his neck from side to side before he began to lace up his pants.

"Answer, you fool!" Zad shouted. Daegan grabbed a dagger from his boot, and began to examine his nails. Zad pushed Daegan hard, causing him to drop his dagger. Zad snatched it up and nicked Daegan's cheek in one sharp movement. Daegan stared at him, surprised by Zad's sudden act of violence. He wiped his cheek and looked at his finger, which was covered in deep red blood. He cocked his head, smiling at Zad, who looked ready to pounce, dagger in hand.

"I haven't seen her, Zadkiel. What makes you think that I've done something to her? She's her own person, perfectly capable of making her own choices."

"Oriana said that you had a run-in with Zephera in the washroom last night. She said Zephera was quite upset. When Oriana woke up this morning, Zephera was gone. We have been out looking for her for over an hour," Zad seethed, his eyes wild with anger.

Daegan raised an eyebrow in amusement. "Perhaps she was so shocked at what a real man looks like naked that she went to the local brothel to employ the services of one of the men. Those rather carnal desires of hers need to be satisfied in some way."

Daegan knew he had crossed a line. He was ready when Zad raised a fist to punch him. Daegan was quicker and caught it mid-air. Zad cried out as Daegan twisted his arm. "If you struggle, your arm will break. Listen to me very carefully, Zadkiel. I don't know where Zephera has gone. If you ask nicely, I'll help you look for her. But if you continue to accuse me, I won't hesitate to snap your arm. You are trying my patience, and it isn't even nine o'clock. Don't test me." He let go of Zad's arm and sat down to buckle his boots.

"What are they serving for breakfast?" Daegan asked, as if nothing had happened.

Zad stared at him in disbelief. "You're just like her," he scoffed before heading out of the room, slamming the door behind him.

Daegan smiled. It was true he and Zephera were similar. If Zad had meant it as an insult, Daegan didn't take it that way. To be compared to the Lady of Death was an honor. It amused him how easily he could get under Zad's skin. The boy had attacked him and even managed to cut him. Daegan was impressed. He was beginning to think that anything involving Zephera was Zadkiel's weakness.

He had to admit, however, he *was* a bit worried about her abrupt disappearance. It wasn't like to her to leave without eating breakfast first. He grabbed his weapons and bag and made his way to the tavern.

The room was full of patrons.

Daegan sat down next to a disheveled Oriana, who was deep in conversation with Zad. They ignored him. Brenner was the only one who offered him a greeting, nodding slightly.

Any leads on our missing Zephera? Daegan sent his voice over to Brenner telepathically. The mage almost fell off his stool. Daegan chuckled coolly. Don't be so surprised. *Did you really think no one would notice your silent conversations with Zephera?*

Brenner's jaw tightened. *I was not concerned with anyone noticing. What does alarm me is that you share the same skill and did not think it was important to tell either of us about it.*

Dagean smiled over his poached eggs and cider. *It isn't something I share with people whom I've just met. However, time is of the essence, dear Brenner, and for some reason Zephera's gone missing. I figured now would be an opportune time to reveal this useful skill to you.*

Brenner nodded slightly in a way only Daegan could see. *I cannot feel her. I have tried to reach out. This morning she sent something down our link, but it was weak. She must be out of range.*

Daegan stared at the mage, eyes narrowed. Zephera wouldn't go that far away without telling someone where she was going. Something was off.

"No one's seen her," Zad murmured to Oriana, shaking his head. "She must've left before sunrise this morning. I asked around town, but no one's seen anyone matching her description."

"She'll turn up, Zad. She wouldn't just leave without telling anyone, especially after just getting back. She's probably just exploring the village, looking for something sweet to eat," Oriana said kindly, taking his hand.

Brenner shook his head. *She did not just wander off. I felt her presence leave. Either she planned on going somewhere far from here, or she was taken—I would guess the latter. A strange energy lingered in her room this morning, one that does not feel like hers or Oriana's.*

Daegan let out a breath. "Do you really think she would just wander off, Oriana? After talking about nothing but *him* for two days," –he jerked his head in Zad's direction– "I don't think she would let him out of her sight, especially with his little accident at the ruins."

Zad cleared his throat loudly. "So, what are you suggesting, Daegan—that she was taken, without Oriana noticing, and with no signs of a struggle?"

"Unless she went willingly," Daegan replied, crossing his legs and leaning back in his chair. "Whoever took her must have something she wants, or perhaps they threatened to hurt you?"

"Her weapons are gone," Oriana noted. "Who would take her and allow her to bring her weapons?"

Someone who needs her services. Whoever took her needs her for something, Brenner mused, his brow furrowed.

That mage who attacked her in the woods—did you know her, Brenner? Daegan asked suddenly, his heart beating quickly in his chest.

Brenner's face went pale and he nodded. *Valessa. I knew that third energy I felt was familiar. She tried to cover her scent, but it was her. It was the same scent from the woods where Zephera was attacked.* He stood quickly, knocking over the stool.

Oriana jumped at the commotion. "What did you do to poor Brenner, Daegan?" she asked accusingly.

Daegan arose and looked down at her. "I believe he's just determined where Zephera went, and, by the looks of it, it isn't good."

"It looks like there was a boat tied here," Oriana remarked.

Zad examined the rope carefully. "It isn't a very large rope, so it couldn't have been a very big boat. It would have been large enough for two people to fit comfortably, which means she couldn't have gone very far."

Daegan turned to a nearby fisherman. "Sir, is there an island near here that a small fishing boat could reach in a few hours?" he asked as kindly as he could muster.

Despite softening his voice, the man still looked frightened. Daegan rolled his eyes, and tried his best to smile at the man. "Y-y-yes, sir," the man squeaked, "but 'tisn't a place you'd want to journey to. 'Tis haunted and full of evil." The man shook Daegan off before tottering away.

"Just the place where a batty old wench would hide an item," Daegan said coolly.

"I'll find us a boat," Oriana called cheerfully, countering Daegan's gloominess.

Daegan clenched his fists, trying not to punch something. If something happened to Zephera... he closed his eyes, breathing deeply. "We need to get to her quickly. That third item won't be easy to find. I fear that her quest is a dangerous one."

Zad looked at him, quiet despair in his eyes. He too, was clenching his fists, his knuckles white.

Oriana returned and led them to a small boat which could only hold four people. "I can stay here. You'll need the extra seat for Zephera if—I mean when—you find her. I wouldn't be much use anyway, with my leg," she whispered sadly. "You need to hurry. I didn't exactly ask if we could borrow this boat." She let out a small giggle.

Zad and Brenner looked at her in shock and she shrugged. "I'll wait at the inn. Hurry back, all right? And stay safe," she said as she gestured hurriedly for the trio to get into the boat.

Daegan, Brenner, and Zad clambered into the small boat and began to row away just as an irate fisherman came pounding down the dock, fist raised high.

Daegan smiled to himself. "I've got to admit, that girl is one of a kind." He laughed as Oriana kneed the man between the legs and ran off, Dorjan running at her heels.

Brenner smiled nervously, but Zad ignored the show altogether, anxiety etched across his face like rivulets of rain on a muddy hill.

"We'll find her, Zadkiel. She's a strong woman. She knows what she's doing. She won't let anything defeat her," Daegan said.

"That's exactly what I'm afraid of," Zad replied, staring steadfastly at the horizon.

CHAPTER 25

Zephera stopped to catch her breath as she finally reached the bottom of the staircase. She wasn't sure how long she had been walking, but she guessed it had taken her at least two hours, maybe more. She shook her head as she thought of Zadkiel. He was probably tearing apart every inch of that village searching for her. She smiled at the thought of it. Though she didn't need saving, the thought of him scouring the earth to find her made her heart flutter, a feeling she wasn't sure about. She made herself a promise. She didn't care what happened. If he somehow found her, she was going to kiss him. She bit her lip nervously, shaking back the silly thought, and peered ahead.

The passageway was made of stone walls and wooden archways. Cobwebs hung from the corners and a layer of thick dust coated the ground, untouched by human footprints. It looked like no one had been in the tunnel for centuries. Stepping forward, one hand on her scimitar, the other holding the stone torch, she proceeded with extreme caution. She hoped that Reina would've had the decency to at least place her traps further down the path. A fork in the tunnels loomed up to meet her. *Which way... which way...* she thought. Closing her eyes, she listened, hoping to tune into any helpful energies that might lead her where she was supposed to go.

Nothing. "All right then, I'll take the left tunnel. Hear that, Reina? I'm going down the left path!" Only the echo of her own voice answered.

As soon as she stepped into the tunnel, she knew she had picked the wrong one. Her world flipped upside down as a rope snatched her by the ankles and yanked her feet up to the ceiling. Her weapon and torch clattered uselessly to the floor below.

"Damn it!" she swore. She tried reaching for her sheathed dagger but just as her fingers touched the hilt, it too fell to the ground below. "No weapons? Seriously, Reina?" Zephera yelled. She growled angrily, arms crossed as she hung there. "Fine. You want me to prove myself to you? Watch and learn, you old hag!"

She rocked back and forth, coaxing a little movement from the rope that held her. She continued to swing like a pendulum, using her stomach muscles to increase the oscillation. Her body protested and her head spun as she continued to work but she didn't give up. When she finally got high enough, she used her momentum to reach for the rope that held her. Her hands grappled for the rope, but her grasp was too weak. The rope slid, burning her skin. Zephera growled angrily. She tried again, pushing herself as hard as she could and using all her strength to swing upward and grab the rope. This time, her fingers gripped the rope tightly as she pulled herself upright. She squinted at the knot that held her. It was a double fisherman's knot, practically impossible to loosen. She almost let go of the rope in anger. Her arms were beginning to shake as she held her weight awkwardly. She was going to lose her grip if she didn't act fast. Just as she was about to let go, she heard a grinding noise. Looking around wildly, Zephera groaned in dismay as the walls began to move.

Thinking quickly, she took one hand off the rope and began to loosen her boots. The walls were almost touching her. She had maybe one more minute before they crushed her like wheat in a millstone. Her foot slipped out of the boot, causing her to drop the rope. She screamed in frustration. She wasn't going to make it. She didn't have time to try to get her body back to the proper position to grab the rope again. Cursing Reina loudly, she tried desperately to loosen her other boot. After a few agonizing, desperate seconds, she managed to pull her foot free.

She braced herself as she fell, rock and soil crashing down on top of her as the ceiling gave way. She didn't have time to think about the pain from the fall. She reached for her weapons and pushed through the pile of rubble. Dust and dirt filled her lungs, cutting off her air supply. Grit burned her eyes.

Just as she was about to surrender to suffocation, she breached the surface. She sucked in a breath, coughing out dust and black phlegm. She crawled towards the entrance of the tunnel and rolled out just as the walls slammed together, erasing all traces of the path.

Zephera sprawled on her back and groaned. Sitting up slowly, she took a deep breath. It hurt like hell. Pressing lightly on her stomach, she grimaced. One of her ribs was broken. Her body creaked and cracked, pain flashing everywhere. Wiping her face, she felt something warm and sticky on her forehead. *Marvelous,* she thought. She was bleeding, too. Hoping the gash wasn't too deep, she grimaced, standing up as carefully as she could. She felt the wall where the tunnel had been and moved her hands along it, feeling for the tunnel on the right.

"Happy, Reina? The other tunnel it is, you crafty witch," Zephera barked, her voice cracking. As if to answer her question, a small light flickered ahead of her.

"Thank you, I think," she muttered as she limped down the tunnel towards the light. When she reached the end of the tunnel, she sat down to rest. The room the tunnel opened into was cavernous. She squinted at the shadowy walls and gasped. Thousands of skulls lined the walls, in varying states of decay. Some were cracked, as if whatever force had caused their deaths had been heavy and powerful. Others were tinged with black ash, as if their owners had been burnt alive. Others still had no visible signs of wear or decay. The skull walls were macabrely beautiful. Death itself was the most alluring of all things in this world. To see it used so brazenly was breathtaking. Perhaps she and Reina would get along after all.

She pulled out the remainder of the small meal she had stashed away and nibbled on the dried meat. Zad was going to kill her if she ever made it out of this. She smiled sadly at the way her stomach tingled at the thought of him.

What would he think of her once he found out who she was? What would any of them think? Would they expect her to embrace her past and take on her new role? Or would they laugh at the idea of her, Zephera, being the key to reuniting the realms? Standing slowly, Zephera grabbed the torch that lit the room and limped toward the only other exit.

As she stood at the new tunnel's entrance, she closed her eyes and slowed her rapidly beating heart. Then she peeked into the darkness. The tunnel rose on a slight incline, which she hoped meant she was getting closer to the surface. She trekked up the shadowy passageway, the torch illuminating her path. After several minutes, the ground began to even out. The tunnel dead-ended at a tall statue of a fox with nine burning tails. There was nothing else in the tunnel except the statue. She let out a bitter scoff and sat down, releasing the torch.

The warmth of fire begin to kiss the air around her. She opened her eyes, startled. The torch she had dropped at the base of the statue had illuminated a ring of old magic, making the statue glow with life.

She inhaled sharply as the statue began to melt, revealing the creature it was modeled after, a nine tailed fox.

"Hello, Zephera," the creature cooed, its head cocked playfully. Zephera's jaw dropped.

The creature spoke, her voice as smooth as silk, "I am Vulle. I am the guardian of this path. Should you wish to continue, you must answer a question."

"Like… a riddle?" Zephera asked, still too shocked to do anything but stare.

Vulle uttered a small, sweet laugh, her mouth opening to reveal two perfect rows of sharp, white teeth. "No, dear girl, I am not a Sphinx. They are tricky, fickle creatures. I am something far more dangerous. I am the judge of your heart, your soul. All I'll ask is one question. Choose your answer wisely, dear girl, for if I find you to be deceptive in any way, I'll devour you," Vulle purred. Noting the look of horror on Zephera's face, she added, "You can turn back now. Abandon your task, and I'll let you leave. I don't think, however, that is what you will choose to do, is it?" she asked, her wide amber eyes blinking slowly.

Zephera bit her lip. "If you must judge my heart and soul, so be it. Ask me your question," she told the creature.

Vulle bowed, her tails of fire making the shadows dance darkly around them. "Are you innocent, Zephera?"

Zephera's features scrunched up in confusion. "Am I innocent of what?"

Vulle cocked her head and smiled. "Are you innocent?" she repeated. Zephera opened her mouth to reply, but Vulle interrupted her. "Choose your next words carefully, Zephera, for they could be your last."

Zephera nodded, her mind racing. *Innocent? Innocent of what? I'm a bloody assassin, and I take great pleasure in my kills. Am I innocent of dealing death? Have I ever cared if a mark was truly guilty before bringing their life to an end? It isn't for me to deliver judgment. I deliver death and I'm very, very good at it. Am I innocent? I don't take pleasure in the pain or suffering of those who can't help themselves. I do what I can to help those who need it. Yet, I could do more. Am I too lazy, or too tired? Am I selfish? There's always more that could be done to stop the corruption and hypocrisy that plagues our realm.*

Zephera was strong and powerful. She knew that only she could make the world whole again. Did her world even deserve to be saved? Did the Realm of Darkness deserve to be saved? She hated herself for it, but no, they didn't. She wasn't about to risk her life and the lives of her friends for a world that deserved to burn. Yet, for five thousand years her father had been casting his shadow upon this realm, twisting it and turning it to fit his needs. She shuddered to think what the Lands of Sorrow were like, the innocent lives that would be lost if she refused to act. She hated that she had to think about this, that she alone had to make the choice. She knew what Zad would do. He wouldn't hesitate to give his life if it meant saving their world. Even Daegan wouldn't hesitate. So, why was she? She was born of both worlds. She was Balance and yet she couldn't make the choice. *Am I innocent?*

"No," she heard herself say. "No, Vulle, I'm not innocent." She bowed her head and waited for the creature to attack. When the attack didn't come, she looked up.

Vulle was smiling. "You may pass, Zephera. No one is innocent, no matter how much darkness or light they may have inside of them. Go forth, child. Remember that whatever choice you make, it must be your own. Don't let others influence you to fit their needs." The fox guardian jumped down off the stone slab she had been sitting on, revealing a small tunnel just big enough for Zephera to crawl through.

Zephera turned to thank the creature but found that she had disappeared, leaving the torch to illuminate the room around her.

Zephera grabbed the torch and carefully began to crawl through the tunnel. When she reached the other side, she stepped out into a large stone room. Pillars held up a glass ceiling. Zephera could make out the blue tint of the water above her. Nothing but the glass was keeping her from certain drowning.

The room itself was an obsidian crypt. It matched the altar in the mountains perfectly. It was surrounded by seven small slabs of stone that held blue flames. This had to be the resting place of Sebastian. She walked cautiously toward the casket, trying to avoid disturbing the room. The air was thick with a feeling of reverence about it. She didn't like the idea of disturbing the grave of a man who was nothing but a ploy in Reina's game. He didn't deserve to be used as a pawn in her maze of horrors. She sucked in a breath when she saw what was carved into the top of the obsidian coffin.

Here Lies
SEBASTIAN MIRRAROW
Lover, Husband, and Friend
The Light to my Dark

Zephera pushed on the obsidian lid, expecting it be heavy, but it moved easily. She crinkled her nose in surprise when she saw the body of Sebastian. It wasn't a skeleton; it was a magically preserved corpse. He looked as if he was only sleeping. His silver hair hung perfectly against his shoulders as if it had just been brushed. He was wearing an embroidered black and gold tunic which Zephera thought must've been from his wedding.

She gasped as she ran her fingers over his hand. It was warm to the touch. She cocked her head and unsheathed her dagger, bringing it to her left hand. "I'm sorry, Sebastian," she whispered as she snapped his finger, breaking it. Warm blood spilled over her hands as she sliced through his skin. The magic that kept his body warm had also kept his blood from coagulating. Gritting her teeth tightly she continued to saw through the bone. She shuddered in disgust as she pocketed the freshly cut finger. "Again, my deepest apologies." she murmured. Then she pushed the lid of the coffin back into place.

She kissed two fingers and touched them to the coffin in a sign of respect for the dead. Letting out an audible sigh, she brushed her fingers through her matted hair. "Well Reina, I look forward to meeting you soon," she said aloud.

She had taken only a few steps when the room started to shake. Before she could reach the exit, the glass ceiling shattered into a thousand pieces, dropping water down into the burial chamber. The water hit Zephera like a tsunami, sending her tumbling toward the wall and dousing her in ice cold water. She took an involuntary breath and choked. Her lungs seized up and her body locked. She couldn't open her eyes, couldn't try to find the surface. Panic flooded through her. She wanted to kick, to scream, to curse, but she was caught in the water's lethal grip. She could do nothing to expel it. Every muscle began to tighten. She was dying and there was nothing she could do about it. It hurt, and she was so tired. She gave up and floated towards whatever was pulling her, suddenly tranquil. She was willing to greet Death. It would be easy, peaceful—no more struggle, no more choice, no more sorrow. She smiled as her world ended.

CHAPER 26

D aegan shivered. The air around him was cold. They had been sitting in silence for hours. He looked to Brenner.

Anything? he asked.

I can feel her. Our link was getting stronger, but I cannot reach her. I am not sure why. Brenner's mental voice was full of worry, and his eyes were narrowed in confusion.

What do you mean you can't reach her? Daegan asked cooly, his face a mask of calm.

We are so close but she is not responding to me. I felt fear pulsating from her. It was so strong and overwhelming, I almost had to break our connection. But then it stopped, and the connection went dark. I can still feel her, barely.

Daegan's eyes narrowed as he gripped the sides of the boat tightly. There was an island in the distance. A small rowboat was tied to a large rock on the shore. Zadkiel and Brenner rowed in silence as Daegan searched the horizon for any sight of Zephera or Valessa.

Suddenly, they heard a large crash as something under the surface of the water began pulling their boat forcefully towards the island.

"Bloody hell!" Zad cried, as the boat began to spin quickly.

"HOLD ON!" Daegan yelled over the crashing waves as the sea around them formed a powerful vortex. Daegan closed his eyes tightly. *What have you done, Zephera? Gods, please be safe.* Then, as quickly as it had started, the waves calmed, and the swirling eddy straightened and faded away, leaving only froth and foam.

"What in the name of all that is holy was that?" Zad breathed heavily, wiping briny water from his face.

"I don't know, but it couldn't have been good," Daegan replied, his eyes scanning the island once again.

Squinting, Daegan thought he saw a hooded figure in a red dress running towards the boat on the shore. Daegan sucked in his breath. "Valessa," he murmured. Brenner and Zad turned to look at her. She stood on the shore, staring at them intently before snapping her fingers and disappearing.

Brenner's cool laughter filled Daegan's head. *She is smart, porting away like that. 'Tis a shame, for I would have liked to have greeted my old Keeper.*

"Where did she go?" Zad yelled out in surprise.

"She ported. Meaning she used her magic to get elsewhere," Daegan replied.

"What? Where's Zephera?" he bellowed, standing up.

"Sit down before you fall out, Zadkiel. She didn't have Zephera with her." Daegan ordered.

Zadkiel was about to reply when Brenner grabbed Daegan's shoulder urgently and pointed to the water.

She is under there! She is dying! We need to move NOW! Follow the lights! Brenner jabbed his finger down in the direction of the strange blue lights that hovered near the ocean floor.

Without a second thought, Daegan unbuckled his weapon belt and dove into the dark unknown.

The brisk water stung his face as he swam swiftly toward the lights. He searched frantically for any sign of Zephera, seeing nothing but debris and an old obsidian crypt. *Zephera! C'mon, buttercup, where are you?* He could hear his heart beating loudly in his chest.

He squinted his eyes. Zephera was floating near an old crypt, her shirt pinned beneath a large rock which was holding her fast to the floor. His eyes widened in fear as he realized she wasn't conscious. Cursing the gods, he grabbed the dagger that was strapped to his leg and began to cut the back of Zephera's tunic. The dagger sliced through the linen quickly and he pulled her loose. If she knew he was holding her in his arms while she was shirtless she would tear out his eyes with her bare hands. He shook his head, thinking he must be getting oxygen-deprived to think of such a thing when she could be dying. He kicked off of the sandy floor, towing Zephera's unconscious body with him as he swam upward.

He sucked in a deep breath after breaching the water's surface, filling his lungs with air. He pulled Zephera onto his chest, holding her tightly with one arm, and swam backwards towards the boat. Zad and Brenner reached into the cool water, pulling an exposed Zephera into the safety of the boat.

Zadkiel laid her down on the middle bench and pressed his ear to her chest. "I can't hear her heartbeat!" he keened, his voice cracking.

"You need to get her heart pumping again," Dagean said, sounding calmer than he felt. "Press firmly on her chest, with your elbows locked. You might break a rib or two, but that'll heal."

Zad looked at him, horror in his eyes.

Daegan stared. "Now Zadkiel! You must work quickly."

Zad shook his head. "I... I can't," he whispered, his voice cracking. In all his fantasies, he had never imagined touching her in this nightmarish way. Fear seized his body and he froze.

"Please, Daegan, I can't," he panted.

Daegan growled with anger, pushing him out of the way. "Cowardly fool!" he yelled. He straddled Zephera and began to press down on her chest. He began to count. He leaned her head back and opened her mouth. He breathed into her heavily. One. Two. Three. "Again. One-Two-Three-Four-Five."

Zad whimpered, his voice hoarse with desperation. Tears streamed down his face.

Daegan repeated this process three more times, each time growing more and more frenzied. He didn't stop until Brenner put a hand on his shoulder and shook his head sadly, tears falling from his eyes.

Daegan looked away and forced himself to focus on the waves as Zad let out the most soul-crushing sound he had ever heard. It was the sound of a heart shattering. Daegan employed every ounce of his will to hold onto his composure. He was so angry. She was the first person that he had deemed worthy enough to call a friend in centuries. She was supposed to be his savior. She was supposed to free him and his people from their curse. She was so strong and ruthless.

To see her small body lying there, bare and exposed, nearly broke him. Getting off of her, he grabbed his cloak and placed it over her, giving her a befitting semblance of decency.

Zad gently picked her up by the shoulders and cradled her in his arms, his tears falling onto her face. He rocked her back and forth. "You can't leave me, damn it. Please. Don't leave me, Beasty. I love you. Please…" he begged her lifeless body. He shook her violently. "Wake up Zephera! WAKE UP!"

"Zadkiel," Daegan warned. "It is no use. She is gone."

Zad ignored him and continued to shake her. Daegan was about to punch him, to get him to stop the useless action and let Zephera rest, when she let out a small cough, expelling water onto Zadkiel's chest.

Zad let her go in surprise. "Zephera! Zephera, look at me. I'm right here," Zad cried.

Zephera let out another cough. She opened her eyes and tried to sit up. She let out a small moan. "The finger. Check my pocket. The finger," was all she said before she rested her head against Zad's chest and closed her eyes.

Daegan smiled in relief and shook his head. "Damned girl. A finger? What is it, a memento from one of her kills or something?" He chuckled.

She's going to be okay. She just needs rest. Let us get back to the inn. If we leave now, we should reach it by nightfall, Brenner spoke, his mental voice steady.

Daegan nodded. "Zadkiel, keep her warm while Brenner and I row us back to the inn."

CHAPER 27

Zephera felt a dark abyss of shadows swirling inside of her. She had died, she had reached the end of life. She had been so ready to greet death. He was ready for her, too. Death pulled on her lifeline, trying to get her back. But the darkness that surrounded her held true and steady. It fought off death and held Zephera in its grasp. The darkness was strong, powerful. It carried her back to the world of the living, and when she woke, it didn't let go.

Zephera could feel a change start to take place. She could feel it in her bones, her muscles, and in her very core. She tried to fight it, but the power it gave her… it felt like home. It had a familiar feeling to her soul, one that she had known before. Zephera ached for it to stay, and her heart smiled as it did. She wasn't going to let it go, so she breathed in the darkness as it circled her soul. It had awakened her.

Her limbs grew heavy as she began to feel the world assemble around her. She could feel strong arms around her as she was carried up the stairs to her room. She tried to open her eyes. Someone stripped her down and wrapped her in a tunic as she lay still on the bed.

"Thank you, Oriana," she heard Zad whisper.

"She does need some privacy. I'm glad you asked me to dress her instead of just doing it yourself," Oriana replied quietly.

Zad let out a tired laugh. "Brenner, can you heal her? She has at least a few broken ribs and quite a few nasty gashes that could require stitches."

Zephera heard someone shuffle over to her. She felt warm, smooth hands on her belly.

This may sting a bit, Zephera. I have you in a magical slumber. I pray it will not hurt as bad this way.

She tried to reach out to Brenner, to tell him she could handle it, but her body tensed under the mage's spell. She wanted to cry out as her bones fused back into place. The pain was excruciating but she could do nothing except scream in her mind. It felt as though hot, piercing metal was melting her bones back together. She tried to inhale, but heat scorched her lungs. She felt like she was drowning all over again, this time in molten rock.

Almost there, Zephera. Hang on.

Just when she thought she couldn't possibly endure the agony anymore, the pain stopped. She took a deep breath and filled her lungs. She could breathe fully again.

There we go. Get some rest now. Let your body do the rest of the work. You might be a little sore in the morning, but I'm sure you have had worse pains.

Zephera relaxed as the voices around her grew hazy.

"Thank you, Brenner," Zad smiled, patting the mage on the back.

"I can stay with her and get you when she wakes if you would like," Oriana told Zad.

"No. I'll stay. I'm not leaving her side ever again." Oriana left the room, shutting the door behind her. Zad brought a chair to the side of the bed and sat down, taking Zephera's hand in his. "I'll be here when you wake up, Zephera. I'm not going anywhere," he promised softly, pushing her hair behind her ear and kissing her forehead gently. "I almost lost you today. You swore to me you would never leave me. You almost broke that promise."

He watched her as she slept. There was a serene beauty about her that she didn't have when she was killing things and saving the world. Her round lips were parted slightly as she breathed in life. She had never looked as perfect as she did lying there. He had almost lost her and there had been nothing he could do about it. He had never felt as much pain as he did when Daegan couldn't get her to breathe, couldn't get her heart to beat. He had lost a piece of himself in those few strenuous minutes, a piece he would never get back. The guilt he felt when he had let Daegan save her was overwhelming. For a split second, he had almost been relieved by her death. She could no longer hurt herself or anyone else. In those few minutes, she had just been Zephera. Not the Lady of Death, not a deadly assassin, just Zephera, the woman he loved. She had broken his heart and he hated her for it. He realized in those brief moments that he loved her more than life itself.

She had always loved the water. Even as kids, when he had just begun learning how to swim, she would jump right in and splash around, disappearing under the water and popping back up several yards away. She was so at home there. How terrified and betrayed she must've felt when her one place of safety had turned into her tomb.

She let out a small groan and closed her mouth. He laid his head down beside her, clinging to her hand and closing his eyes. Her breath was a lullaby.

Zad didn't know how long they slept. Feeling her watching him, he sat up and looked down at her. She was smiling sleepily up at him. "Hi, Beasty," he said.

"Hi," she replied.

"I almost lost you," he whispered, taking her head in his hands when she leaned against his chest.

She nodded softly. "I'm so sorry, Zad," she cried softly, looking up at him with tears shining in her dark eyes. He wiped her cheek as a single tear fell.

"Shh, don't cry, Beasty. I'm here. I'm not going anywhere. Unless you want food?" he said, trying to coax a smile from her.

She shook her head. "For once in my life, Zad, I'm not hungry. Just tired. So tired," she breathed.

"Okay. Do you want me to get Oriana? I'll wait outside the door if you want. Or I can sleep in my room," Zad said, standing up.

"Please stay with me," she said quietly. Zad nodded and grabbed a pillow off the bed and set it on the floor to make a bed.

"No, up here, with me. I want you to hold me." Zad didn't respond. He just stared at her.

Hurt flashed across her features. "Unless you don't want to. It's okay. I shouldn't have—"

He grinned lazily and got into the double bed beside her. She snuggled up to him, laying her head on his chest. He wrapped his arms around her and held her tightly. He could feel her heart beat against his.

"Zad?" she whispered.

"Yes, Beasty?" he murmured. She moved closer to him, her lips meeting his in ferocious hunger. She tasted just as he imagined she would. Her lips were soft against his as she deepened the kiss. They explored each other's mouths and bodies, the moonlight from the window making her skin glow like she was a goddess of the night. When she pulled away, she took his breath with her, leaving him staring at her swollen lips lustfully. She cocked her head, her midnight hair falling over her shoulders.

"I love you, Zadkiel Gethine. I had to taste death to realize just how much. I'm sorry that it took me so long," she said, her eyes glowing brightly.

He smiled sheepishly. "Last I heard, you wanted to save the world without any pesky little distractions like love." He laughed softly, touching the ends of her hair.

"Yes, well, death does tend to bring a person to their senses."

He raised his eyebrows at her. "You're so precious, Zephera. I have loved you for so long and I'll never stop."

Zephera felt a pang of annoyance at the word precious, but Zad was trying, so she would, too. She flashed him a shy smile. "I don't want you to," she said conspiratorially as she lay back down. He stared at her as he rested his head on the pillow.

She bit her lip. "We have much to do now that we have found all three items. I don't want to think about what's going to come next."

"Tonight, let's just be here, you and me. Let me keep you safe, Zephera. Just give us tonight. Tomorrow we can worry about saving the world." Nodding, she curled up next to him and closed her eyes. "Goodnight, Beasty," he said, kissing her head.

Zad stared at the ceiling as he held her, not wanting to sleep, fearing he would wake to discover that this was just another one of his dreams. He wanted to savor every second he had with her. He smiled, imagining infinite nights like this one, making love as the stars kept watch. A world where she was safe and happy. A world where she looked at him as she had tonight. He didn't want morning to come.

CHAPTER 28

Zephera woke to a knock at the door. She looked over at Zad, who was sleeping deeply, and crept carefully out of bed so as not to wake him. Pulling the fur blanket tightly around her shoulders, she tiptoed to the door and opened it slowly.

Daegan was standing there. He swallowed hard as he took in her appearance. He looked around her to see Zad sleeping on the bed and frowned slightly. "I see you are well. Did you have a good night?" He tried to use a teasing tone, but it came out forced.

"The best," she replied. "What do you need, Daegan?" she asked.

"Nothing. I just wanted to make sure you were all right. I brought you something to eat. And you need new boots," he said, holding up a plate of eggs and pastries in one hand and a wrapped parcel in the other. "But I see that you are busy." He turned to leave.

"Wait!" she called after him. "Leave the food."

Something flashed across his features, but it disappeared as soon as she blinked. Jealousy? She shook her head as she took the plate and closed the door in his face without so much as a thank you.

She sank down next to Zad, a strawberry pastry with sugar sprinkled on top in her hand. She put it under Zad's nose like it was a smelling salt and kissed his cheek.

"Mmmm," he groaned, not opening his eyes.

"Open your mouth," she enticed. His lips parted, and she put the pastry against his tongue. He took a small bite, smiling as he chewed.

"Either I'm incredibly famished or that's the most delicious strawberry pastry that I've ever tasted," he said as he sat up. "Ahh, and I even get served by a lovely vixen." He kissed her. "If I'd known that all I had to do was watch you die to get you into my bed, I would've killed you ages ago," he joked.

Zephera's mouth fell open. She punched him in the shoulder. "You are despicable." She giggled as she took another bite of food.

"But you love it," he said playfully.

They ate the plate of food and spent the morning in bed, kissing and reminiscing. It was the first time she had ever felt true happiness. Sure, she had experienced moments of joy throughout her life. But this—this was unlike anything she had ever felt before. For the first time in her life, she had hope. Hope for her world, for her future. Now that she had glimpsed a small sliver of what her life could be like, she would do any-thing to keep that hope and happiness alive. How delightfully dangerous to finally have something worth losing.

She got out of bed and walked over to her bag to put on some pants. She smiled at Zad, who frowned and folded his arms in protest as she laced them up.

"Come on, naughty boy. We need to get back to the real world now. The others will wonder where we've gone."

He groaned as he pulled his own shirt on. "No, they won't. They know I've been keeping you all to myself this morning." He growled as he threw her onto the bed and kissed her.

She pushed him off. "As much as I want to stay in bed and kiss you for the rest of the day, we need to get back to the mission."

"Once we find Reina and get that blasted cure, I'm going to make love to you, Zephera. All night and all day," he said, kissing her hand.

Her stomach did a flip. Last night she had thought about how it would feel to be with him in that way—to give him all of herself. She had also thought about it that morning, and she was thinking about it now. She bit her lip and threw her head back. If he kept looking at her like that, she wouldn't be strong enough to resist him. She wanted to wait, at least a little while. It had to be different with him. He wasn't like the others. She hadn't cared about them, at least not in the way she cared about Zad. She pecked him on the cheek and grabbed her things. Sending him her most flirtatious smile, she opened the door and left him behind in the room.

Zephera walked to the tavern where Oriana and Brenner sat finishing up their breakfast. She sat down, beaming. Oriana let out a squeak.

"Did you do it? Did you? You did, didn't you? You are glowing from ear to ear."

Zephera pursed her lips. "Hello to you too, Oriana. And no, we didn't, not that it's any of your business."

Ignoring her, Oriana squealed. "I just knew it! Didn't I say that, Brenner? I mean, especially after Daegan stormed down. I don't think I've ever seen him so angry. But never mind him. You and Zad! AHHH! The babies you will make!" She squeaked excitedly, clapping her hands. "Wait. Did you say you *did not*?"

"Who's making babies?" Zad asked as he sat down.

"Don't get her started," Zephera said. She snuggled into the arm Zad threw around her as Oriana gushed over them.

Zephera looked at Brenner, who smiled. *I am pleased to see you alive,* he projected. She smiled, bowing her head.

I'm still a little sore. But I'll manage. Zad told me everything you and Daegan did yesterday. Thank you. You saved my life.

He waved a hand at her. *You would have done the same for me.*

She felt Zad staring at her and she turned to smile at him. "What?" she asked coyly.

He touched her left cheek, where the wound from her battle with the Shasakar had begun to scar. "I do wish you'd be more careful. You have such a beautiful face. I don't want you to have any more scars," he whispered softly.

She cocked her head to the side. "I rather like it. It makes me look tough."

"You don't need to be tough. Let me take care of you, my love."

She didn't answer as Daegan appeared, broody as usual, and dropped all three items onto the table. They stopped talking, the severed finger a gruesome reminder of their mission. They all turned their heads toward Daegan and gave him their attention. "We need to figure out what to do with that vial of liquid," he said abruptly. He glared at Zephera and Zad tightened his arm around her protectively.

"Reina—or her memory—said that I need to use this," Zad said, picking up the vial, "to unlock the Decay from within."

Zephera took the vial from his hands and stared at it, turning it between her fingers. The liquid was a dark, murky substance that swirled around like smoke. "We've got the horse, which was a rather anticlimactic search."

"And the finger," Oriana offered.

"So, what does this mean? What are we supposed to do with it?" she asked, holding up the vial.

"Blood," Zad answered. "I think I need to drink that and mix it with my blood."

Zephera shifted uncomfortably. "What makes you say that?"

He stared at the vial. "I don't know. Just a feeling."

"No, you can't do that. We don't even know what's in there," she argued, gesturing to the vial.

He turned to look at her. "Zephera—"

"NO! Absolutely not. It's too risky!" Her voice rose.

Daegan slammed his fist on the table, causing them all to jump. "We all knew there would be risks! Just because you're screwing him doesn't exclude him from what must be done." Zephera's eye twitched; Daegan was on her last nerve. He had poked at Zad one time too many and this time he had brought their relationship into it. After everything they had been through, how could he think that Zad would ever consider being excluded? How dare he! Her blood began to boil. She heard Zad call her name just before she launched herself over the table, tackling Daegan to the ground.

She straddled him, screaming and punching him over and over. He pushed her off with ease, pinning her to the ground. "If I'd known sleeping with you was all it would take to become exempt from the dangers of this mission, I would've taken you to bed that first night," he snarled.

She squirmed underneath him, trying to flip their positions, but her shoulders were immobilized by his massive hands and her thighs were fastened to the floor by the weight of his powerful knees. Daegan's hatred was like a spear, piercing her to her core. She spat at him, her saliva landing on his cheek. He laughed bitterly.

Zad pressed his sword into Daegan's back. "GET. OFF. OF. HER," he growled.

Daegan stared down at her, his expression softening slightly. He held his hands up in surrender and stood up, walking towards the tavern door. He paused before he opened it and turned to her. "Mark my words, Zephera. He will ruin you." And with that, he stalked off into the busy village.

Zad offered Zephera a hand and pulled her up. The entire tavern had gone quiet and was staring at their group with questioning glares.

Oriana clapped her hands loudly. "Nothing to see here, folks! Just a wee bit of jealousy, a lovers' quarrel. Nothing too exciting." She smiled sweetly at the onlookers. She heard people scoff and mutter under their breaths at the annoying disturbance. Oriana turned to face the group. "Our boat back to Illuminas leaves in a few hours. We should gather our things."

Brenner nodded and followed Oriana out of the tavern to their rooms.

"Zephera, look at me," Zad said gently after the tavern's patrons had returned to their murmured conversations. She stared intently at the table. Zad touched her chin with his index finger, turning her face toward him. Reluctantly, she met his eye. "It's going to be all right. I need to do this. If drinking the contents of that vial means we can find Reina and stop this plague, I have to do it. I would gladly do it a thousand times over if it would keep you safe."

She held onto his hands tightly. "I just got you. I can't, I WILL NOT, lose you," she choked. Zad smiled.

"I already told you, Beasty, I'm not going anywhere. Even if you wanted me to, I wouldn't leave. You're stuck with me."

She groaned. This was why she had distanced herself, why she had fought her feelings and buried them deep. To have tasted what life could be like only to have it taken away was the purest, most exquisite form of torture. "If that vial kills you, I'm going to be so pissed," she grumbled.

"There's my girl." Zad laughed, kissing the tip of her nose. "C'mon Beasty, we've got a world to save," he said, grabbing her hand and leading her up the stairs.

CHAPTER 29

They waited at the docks for the ship that was to take them on a two-day journey through the Ballah Sea to Illuminas. There, they would meet with Baleem and the king and track down Reina. They were so close to the end of their journey. Zephera smiled. Reina could stop this. Even if Zephera was the Balance, it didn't matter. Reina had the cure. They would be able to heal the land without some broken savior who failed time and time again to unite the Realms.

The sun had begun to set when they boarded the large ship. The whole village seemed to have come out to gawk at the famous vessel. It was a passenger ship, one of the finest in all of Nostorra, shimmering white and carved from the oldest and strongest widowmaker trees. It was spelled with magic to preserve its pristine gleam. The brilliant orange and purple sunset cast a spectacular glow over the ship.

Zephera climbed onto the main deck, which had been constructed from the redwood of the almost extinct sequoia tree. The large round steam stacks were carved from ivory. Although it was beautiful, Zephera hated to think how many animals had been killed for the beautiful pillars.

"I have a surprise for you," Zad whispered in her ear. "C'mon, I'll show you."

Zad wrapped his arm around her shoulder and steered her below deck. Her heart flipped when he opened a door and led her inside a small, private cabin. A large bed dominated the room. It was covered with black fur blankets and silken sheets and was big enough to fit their entire party.

A small nightstand was squished into the corner of the room. Atop it sat a wash basin and mirror.

"This is our room, Zephera. We'll make great use of that bed," Zad growled at her, tickling her sides and making her squirm.

"Oh, my goddess!" Oriana exclaimed from the doorway. "I guess we won't be seeing much of you two for the next couple of days." She giggled. "My room only has bunk beds which I get to share with a mute mage and the ever-so-lovely Daegan. Speaking of which, I haven't seen him since he stormed out of the inn, have you?"

Zephera didn't care where he was. If he got too close, she might bite him. She grunted in amusement, thinking of the rude remark Daegan would've given.

"Well, I'll see you two later. Have fun, and don't do anything I wouldn't do! Actually... err... nevermind. Be safe!" Oriana quipped before leaving Zad and Zephera alone to their room—or bed.

"Is it too much?" Zad asked her quietly.

She shook her head. "No, not at all. I just—how did you manage this?" she asked, forcing a smile. She didn't want him to think she was ungrateful. But, she wasn't ready to be with Zad yet. She was confused by that fact, not sure how to feel.

Shutting the door behind him, he smiled wickedly. "I can be VERY persuasive when I need to be." He started unbuttoning his shirt. Zephera's eyes widened.

"I thought you wanted to wait! It hasn't even been a day, and you've already skipped the wooing to take me straight to your bed?" Sucking in her breath, she bit her lip. She couldn't deny the reaction her body had to him as he stripped bare, and crawled towards her on the bed, pinning her. He kissed her neck softly. She closed her eyes and brought her lips to his, kissing him passionately.

They were interrupted by a knock at the door. "Leave it," Zad growled as Zephera moved to answer it.

Zephera laughed. "They know we are in here," she said, her eyes wide.

Zad smirked, "Then let them listen as I make you scream." Zephera pushed him off.

"Zad! We have two days. You can wait," she said, answering the door, relieved by the interruption.

A man in a stark white staff uniform was waiting on the other side, his face red with embarrassment. He cleared his throat before speaking. "I'm very sorry if I interrupted anything. But there appears to have been some sort of mix-up with this room. I fear we may have mistakenly booked two couples for this suite."

Zephera stepped out of the room, closing the door behind her. A nervous young couple with a baby in tow was standing behind him.

"You see, I misplaced this family's booking card, and when your husband—"

Zephera interrupted him. "He's not my husband. He's just… go on."

The man nodded, his face turning an even deeper shade of scarlet. "Well, they booked the cabin first, and we don't have any other private cabins available. And they have a child."

Zephera nodded. "It's quite all right. Let them have the room. We can bunk with our group down below."

The man's shoulders sagged in relief. "Thank you, miss. I can offer you a full refund if that pleases you."

Zephera smiled. "Yes, I'll send my… companion to collect it. Just give us a few minutes to gather our things."

Zephera breathed a sigh of relief even as her traitorous body seethed at her. She just wasn't quite ready to go there with Zad yet. She smiled at him sheepishly as he lay buck-naked on the bed, waiting for her to return. "All right, lover-boy, get dressed. They double booked our cabin. We need to gather our things and join Brenner and Oriana."

Zad sat up, anger in his eyes. "What? No! Zephera—" he protested.

"It's done, Zad. It's all right. We'll have all the time in the world after we find Reina. I want to take things slow with you, at least about this. Believe me, I want to—I really, *really* want to. But I don't want to ruin what we have by jumping in too soon."

She watched Zad carefully.

He nodded. "You're right. I'm sorry. I just..." he trailed off.

"You are just a horny bastard." She laughed and kissed him. "I'll meet you down below, all right? Don't get lost."

Zephera found Oriana and Brenner playing a game of chess on a small table in the middle of the cabin. The room was about the same size as the one she had just been in but instead of one large bed, there were two bunk beds on each side of the room. There was no way that two people could fit on one of those together. They were just too small.

"Hey, you guys. Looks like we'll all be sharing a cabin," Zephera said, throwing her belongings onto one of the beds and laying down.

"What? Why?" Oriana screeched so loudly that Brenner made an annoyed face and rubbed his ear. "Sorry, Brenner," she muttered. He waved her off.

"They double booked our room. Any sign of Daegan yet?" she asked.

They both shook their heads. "No, still no sign. I do hope he's all right. But he was so horrible earlier, he can sleep on the floor," Oriana said, folding her arms.

"Ugh, two days stuck in a cabin with Zad and Daegan together? If he's smart, he'll run back to the city," Zephera said, pretending to vomit.

Zad arrived with his bags and a sour look on his face. He sat down next to Zephera and rested his head on her shoulder. "We should be leaving port in just a few minutes," he yawned. "I think I'm going to take a nap. I'm exhausted," he said, winking at Zephera. She rolled her eyes and pushed him down onto the bed.

"I think I'll go see if I can find Daegan. Oriana? Care to join me?" she asked.

Oriana's eyes grew as wide as saucers. "Are you sure you don't want to ask Brenner?" She pointed to the mage next to her, who looked up innocently.

"I think you've grown on me, Oriana," Zephera said slyly. Oriana jumped up excitedly.

"Don't get too comfortable, now," Zephera cautioned. "I meant that you've grown on me like a case of the pig warts." Zad chuckled from the bed and Brenner looked amused.

"I'll take it!" she said, pulling Zephera into a hug.

"Pig warts," she murmured affectionately, patting Oriana on the back.

Oriana chattered on about the deck party that was to be thrown the following evening before they reached Illuminas. Zephera bit her lip. She was going to be trapped on this vessel for almost two days with a bunch of nosy strangers, a horny Zad, a brooding Daegan, and Oriana. The only one she didn't mind was Brenner. Lovely. The party did sound nice, though. It was going to be a feast, with dancing and music and free-flowing drinks. Zephera wished she had access to her closet back home. Her lips turned up in pleasure as she thought of her favorite fitted black silk dress. It had a delightful red-dyed border along the bottom hem that made the garment look like it had been dipped in blood. Baleem had given it to her to wear to the king's Autumn Ball in the coming months. She supposed the ball would still be held if they could get the damned cure.

"Where did you go?" Oriana asked, waving her hand in front of Zephera's face.

"Hmm?" she mused. "Far away, to the land of fancy clothes and delicious food," she replied, smiling dreamily.

Oriana's jaw dropped. "The Lady of Death pines for fancy dresses? How curious."

Zephera glared at her. "Why? Just because I love the feel of death along my fingertips doesn't mean I'm not a lady."

Oriana laughed. "My apologies, mistress," she said with a mock curtsy.

They looked out at the night sky, the moon beaming brightly down on the water. The stars stretched like a glittering scarf across the vast expanse. Weeks ago she had killed the Shasakar under a moon such as this.

"It's beautiful, isn' it?" Zephera remarked. "I feel so safe in the dark. So at home. It gives me strength and hope, like I could conquer the world."

The ship creaked and drifted away from the dock as a horn sounded three times, signaling their departure.

A man wearing a uniform similar to the attendant she had spoken with earlier tapped her on the shoulder. "Excuse me, miss. Are you Zephera Travelle?" he asked.

"I am," she replied.

"This was left for you earlier today by a rather surly man." Oriana let out a laugh but Zephera didn't smile. She felt her heart drop. She took the brown paper package and began to unwrap it. Inside she found a single apple and a dagger—Daegan's dagger. A note written in sprawled handwriting was included.

Buttercup,

You know that I'm not the type to beg forgiveness from anyone. Neither are you. But I feel the need to apologize for my behavior earlier. You didn't deserve it. I just know that he wants to protect you, to change you, to keep you from reaching your full potential. Don't let anyone, especially him, tell you that your darkness is a thing to be hated and purged, Zephera, because it isn't. It's magnificent.

I'm sorry to say that I can't join you on your journey back to Illuminas. However, we will meet again. There are many things I wish to tell you, that I wish I could have told you sooner. But the reasons will become clear soon enough. I know that you want Reina to be the answer to all of this madness so that you can be free of all of this. But I fear this is only just beginning. Fret not. You will make it out of this, though I'm not so sure about the rest of us.

Trust your gut and you will be fine, my friend.

Until we meet again,

Your Arrogant Ass

PS) I have Dorjan. Pups don't belong on ships.

Zephera clenched her jaw tight and sank down against the wall.

Oriana looked at her curiously. "What is it, Zephera? You look like you're going to be sick."

"Daegan won't be joining us. He left," she said, her voice small. She folded up the letter and put it into her pocket. Then she picked up the dagger. It was cool in her hand. Daegan had somehow wrapped a chain around the hilt and fashioned it into a necklace. She could just imagine what he would say: *A Lady of Death with such perverse desires ought to never leave her breasts unprotected.* She threw the apple at Oriana and stood up.

"I'm going to bed," she muttered and left Oriana. Who shrugged and bit into the apple with a crunch.

When Zephera returned to their cabin, Zad was snoring and Brenner was sleeping peacefully on the bed above him. She wrapped the chain around the dagger, pulled the letter from her tunic pocket, and exhaled. She placed the necklace into the letter and folded it up, putting it at the bottom of her bag. Daegan was infuriating. She hated him and his sour moods. But that didn't mean she wanted him gone. He had trusted her with his secrets. She loved their ridiculous, dirty banter and she hated to admit it, but she felt safer when he was with them. She resented how he caused her to lose control of her temper, but his darkness matched her own. He understood her as no one else did. With him, she could take pleasure in a kill without feeling like he was disgusted with her. It was refreshing. She sent a prayer to the Dark gods. *Did they even exist?* She hoped that wherever Daegan was, he was safe.

CHAPER 30

Zephera woke around noon and found the cabin empty except for Oriana, who was still sound asleep. She wondered when the willowy girl had crept in last night. *Must've been after I fell asleep.* She glanced at Oriana, who was sleeping with her mouth wide open, drool pooling on her pillow. Her golden hair was pulled into a knot on her head and her arms and legs were sprawled behind her in what looked to be a rather uncomfortable position. Even in that awkward position, drool dripping down her chin, Oriana managed to look beautiful. Disgusting.

Zephera made her way to the main deck to search for Zad. There were people scattered about the deck. Closing her eyes, a crisp, delicious smell filled her nose. *Food...* Following her nose, she came to the Great Hall where the ship's galley crew was serving lemon roasted chicken and dumplings. Smiling at the vast, open room, she waved down a server. They exchanged pleasantries and Zephera made her way to an empty table near the entrance of the hall.

Stretching her arms high above her head, Zephera took a seat. The chair creaked beneath her. Looking out the numerous windows, she smiled at the lovely view of the open sea.

The server returned with a large tray of food. Zephera had ordered enough for three. Rubbing her hands together greedily, she helped herself to a large ladle-full. Zephera scarfed down one plate and started on the other. She moaned in ecstasy. The chicken was so tender and juicy, it melted in her mouth. She washed it down with a pint of pumpkin mead.

She grinned as the liquor filled her belly, making her feel warm and relaxed. She was just about to get up and leave when Oriana wandered in. She sat down next to Zephera, who offered her a sip of the mead. Oriana gagged, laying her head down on the table.

"Rough night?" Zephera teased.

"Bugger off," Oriana breathed, flipping Zephera a rude gesture.

Oriana raised her head to glare at Zephera. Unknowingly, she had rested her head in spilled gravy. Zephera began to laugh so hard her stomach began to hurt. She fell off her chair at the sight of Oriana's beautiful face covered in gravy and dumpling crumbs. Clutching her sides, Zephera howled uncontrollably until she had tears in her eyes. Oriana stuck her bottom lip out in mock sadness.

"Oh, gods!" Zephera gasped, still struggling against the convulsions. "Thank you, Oriana, for proving that you, too, can be human."

"Glad this blasted hangover could amuse you," she muttered under her breath.

"Where did you get off to last night, anyway? I fell asleep before you returned. When did you get back to the cabin?" Zephera handed her a napkin, stifling another hysterical giggle.

"I was gambling with the crew. I was winning, too, until the first mate bet double or nothing. The loser had to drink their weight in some goddess-awful concoction of everyone's drinks mixed together. I lost. I should've backed out while I was ahead, but it was such an intriguing offer, I couldn't refuse." Oriana waved a weak hand in the air.

"So, I guess you won't be joining me in getting blasted drunk tonight and dancing till dawn?" Zephera laughed.

"Oh no, you underestimate my abilities, dear Zephera. I will most definitely be joining you tonight." Oriana smiled, her eyes half closed.

Zephera cleared her throat. "What are we going to do about our mission? I feel mildly guilty for not putting any work into it. I mean, we have three days of sailing. The least we could do is devise a plan."

Oriana rolled her eyes. "We are relaxing. Go find Zad if you want to talk about the mission. I'm enjoying the calm before the storm."

Zephera shrugged. "You're probably right… I'll see you back in the cabin. I'm going to find Zad."

Wandering the decks of the ship, she found many different types of people. Some spoke in Verashan. Others wore revealing swimwear that barely covered anything. *Wearing that will get you a lot of sun. Daft idiots. And they look ridiculous.* She smiled to herself when she saw a mother pulling along her screaming child. Zephera pulled a face at the child, which made him cry even harder. Her eyes widened when the mother glared at her as they passed.

Climbing the stairs to the top deck, she found Zad leaning against the mast, reading a book. His golden hair blew in the wind.

He looked up when she arrived. "Good morning, gorgeous. You look lovely today." He smiled, kissing her cheek as she sat down next to him.

She leaned her head on his shoulder. "What are you reading?" she asked. Zad shut his book and held it out to her. She read the title:

The Shasakar and Other Legendary Creatures
By Amous Roderik

She raised her eyebrows in surprise. "As in King Amous, the one who defeated the Rot?" she asked.

Zad nodded. "The very same."

She handed the book back to Zad. "Hmm. Find out anything interesting?"

"No, not really. Most of it's just fictitious tales of a handsome prince rescuing damsels from the clutches of monsters."

Zephera laughed. "I didn't know you liked to read fairy tales, Zad. You learn something new every day, I suppose."

"Oh yes! I'm quite fond of tales where the handsome hero rescues a beautiful maiden from almost certain death." He laughed, tickling her. She shrieked and made a feeble attempt to push him off. He tickled her more, causing her to fall on her back. Then he started in on her sides.

"STOP, ZAD!" she hooted. "STOP." Finally, he relented and grabbed her hands. As he pulled her up, he planted a tender kiss on her brow. She smiled. "Are you excited for the celebration tonight?"

Zad put his arm around her. "Am I excited to spend the evening dancing with the most alluring girl in all of Nostorra? Absolutely."

"Well, then, it's a date. I'm going to find Oriana and get ready. We'll meet you and Brenner on the main deck tonight," Zephera said, getting to her feet. "Enjoy your fairytales." He obediently picked up his book and buried his nose in it, though she saw his eyes ogling her as she walked away.

On her way back to their cabin, Zephera hummed to herself, excited about the evening ahead. They all deserved a night of fun. After all, they were about to save the world. Zephera was determined to forget about all of it, just for the night—Daegan, Reina, her father Gregour, Baleem. If all of them had such an interest in her and her future, then the least they could do was give her the night off.

She met Oriana by the door to their room. Her companion looked cheery and bright despite her blood-shot eyes. She was chatting away excitedly with a couple of Elite women.

"Zephera! Come here!" she called when she saw her. "This is Charolette and Eviee. They are traveling across the Ballah Sea from Sarilo."

Zephera smiled politely. "It's a pleasure," she said as she stuck out a hand in greeting. "I've been to Sarilo a few times. The rose fields there are lovely."

The tall brunette—Charolette—smiled, her teeth white and perfectly straight. "Yes, zey are. Vhat brought you to Sarilo?" she asked in her native Sarilan accent.

"Business, unfortunately," Zephera replied.

The small blonde, who rivaled Oriana with her beauty, clucked her tongue. "Oh, zat is a pity. You vill 'ave to visit sometime. Perhaps a vedding holiday? Oriana here 'az told us so much avout you and your lover, Zadkiel."

Zephera opened her mouth to respond but then promptly shut it again and smiled tightly, shooting Oriana a daggered glance.

"Love ez such a beautiful zing, don't you think? And zere is no better place to celebrate et zan Sarilo," Eviee cooed.

"Indeed. Sarilo is the country of love," Zephera agreed.

"I was just telling them that we had nothing to wear tonight. Our bags were lost so we are stuck with our traveling clothes." Oriana pouted, motioning to her outfit.

Zephera pursed her lips. She knew exactly where her bag was. What kind of game was Oriana playing?

Charolette looked sympathetic. "Such a pity! Please, you both look avout our sizes. You can't go to ze celebration looking like zat. Let us show you how women from Sarilo prepare for a party."

Oriana looked so excited that Zephera was afraid she might jump on the two women. "Oh, that would be just lovely. Right, Zephera?" she asked hopefully.

Zephera had to admit dressing up did sound delightful. It had been ages since her last ball. Contrary to popular belief, she didn't enjoy being all grimy. "Oh, all right. Charolette, Eviee, how can we thank you?"

The two women glanced at each other and laughed. "Zer is no need. Ve simply enjoy beauty and you Nostorran woman rarely 'ave a chance to show off yours."

Zephera let out a hollow laugh. Floozies. But she wouldn't turn down an offer to wear a beautiful gown, especially one from Sarilo.

"Come now, ve 'ave a lot of verk to do if ve vant to 'ave you both ready for tonight," Eviee said, grabbing Zephera's hand. Charolette seized Oriana's hand and the two women led them to their spacious, luxurious suite.

Zephera gasped at the size of their cabin. The walls, the ceiling, even the floor were all white. There were two double beds with golden frames and more pillows on the bed than there was a mattress. Intricate lace fabric draped from the pristine ceiling, making the room feel like it was resting in a cloud. They had their own private washroom with a golden washing tub and more perfumed oils and soaps than Zephera had ever seen in one place. A golden chamber pot sat by the water basin. One wall was lined entirely with mirrors. It was breathtaking.

"Zis is ze king's suite. Our father vanted to make sure ve vere comfortable on zhe long journey across the sea," Eviee informed them. "Come, ve vill call a servant to fill ze tub." She scrunched her nose at Zephera.

A half hour later, the tub was filled to the brim with steaming hot water by a small, mousy servant. Since there would only be time for one of them to bathe, Oriana insisted Zephera be the one.

"I'll go and wash these and have them returned to you in the morning, miss." The servant bowed, addressing Zephera.

"Thank you." Zephera nodded as she stepped into the bath. She let out a moan as the hot water tingled along her skin. She leaned back, closing her eyes. If this wasn't heaven, Zephera didn't know what was.

She looked at all the beautiful crystal bottles full of soaps and perfumes. She took one that contained pink-tinted liquid and pried the lid off. It smelled just like her rose perfume at home. She measured a small amount into the lid and poured it into the water, soaking her aching muscles.

She was so excited to eat the delicious food and dance the night away. Her thoughts were interrupted by a knock at the door. "Come in," she called.

Charolette made her way into the washroom with a large, fluffy towel. "Come, Zephera, you must pick your dress," she said eagerly.

Zephera groaned and disappeared under the water, rinsing her raven hair. When she was finished, she stood up and took the towel from Charolette. "Do you enjoy this sort of thing? Sharing your life and your belongings with strange women?" Zephera asked.

Charolette tittered. "Strange? No, you are a fellow voman. Et ez our duty as ze fairer sex to take care of one another. We take great pleasure en et."

"Well, then, you're kinder than me," Zephera replied. Charolette moved behind her and grabbed her shoulder.

"Come, ve ave much to do!" The Sarilan sister steered the assassin out of the room.

Oriana was sitting on a striped bench in her undergarments while Eviee brushed her hair. She shot Zephera a toothy grin.

"Sit," Charolette demanded. Zephera sat. She watched as Charolette pulled out a case full of powders, kohl, rouge, and varying sizes of brushes. "You 'ave such beautiful, porcelain skin. But I would like to add some rouge to your cheeks if zat es all right?" she asked, holding up a light, rose-colored powder.

Zephera nodded excitedly. Charolette worked with pursed lips, running a brush over Zephera's cheeks. When she was finished, she opened a small vial of black powder. She sucked on a thin brush to moisten it and dipped the brush into the vial, covering the bristles in dark kohl. She worked silently, using gentle strokes to apply the kohl to the top of Zephera's eyelid.

She grabbed another brush, one that was ridged. "For your lashes," she explained. Dipping the strange brush into the kohl, she brushed Zephera's lashes carefully. "Oooh, la! Exotic!" Charolette sat back, admiring her handy work.

"Eviee, let us switch. You are much better at hair zen I," she said, standing.

"Oh! Vhy, Zephera, you look lovely!" Eviee gushed. Zephera smiled to herself as Eviee began to brush her long hair. "Vatch, as I verk my magic," she commanded, pulling Zephera's ebony locks back. She dipped her hands into a clear, sticky substance, slicking Zephera's hair against her head. Eviee's motions yanked Zephera's head back. "Keep your head straight," she scolded, smacking the back of Zephera's head with her hand. Zephera grimaced. Oriana whooped musically, causing Charolette to trail a squiggly line of kohl onto her cheek, which sent Oriana to the floor from laughing so hard. The sisters smiled widely at Oriana's comical reaction. Zephera shook her head, rolling her eyes, fighting the urge to laugh herself.

After Zephera's hair was finished, she stood in front of the walled mirror. Her breath caught when she saw her reflection. The kohl had sharpened and accentuated her natural, dark beauty. Her long hair was parted down the middle, slicked back tightly and held together with a black velvet tie. Charolette brought in a knee-length scarlet gown. It was made of the finest silk and had a plunging neckline. Zephera stepped into the dress, and Charolette laced the straps around her neck. Zephera smiled wickedly at her finished appearance. She followed Charolette into the main room of the cabin.

Oriana's mouth fell open. "Oh, Zephera! Your beauty could rival the goddess herself!" Zephera grinned as she spun around.

"You aren't so bad yourself, Oriana."

Oriana was in a dusty-rose-colored floor-length dress of tulle and lace, golden hair pinned to one side of her face. Eviee handed them both silk slippers that matched their corresponding dresses. Three horns sounded from somewhere on the boat as violin music tinkled through the air.

"Our vork es complete," Eviee said with satisfaction, leaning her head on her sister's shoulder and beaming at the girls' transformations. "Now, go! Enjoy your evening. Ve vill meet you for breakfast in ze morning."

"You aren't joining us?" Zephera asked.

They laughed. "Ve 'ave attended many parties in our life, and ve are tired. They are all zey same. But, please, go meet your lover and dance zey night away," Charolette said brightly. She walked toward the cabin door. "Go on, shoo!" she ordered, shoving the pair out into the hallway.

Zephera turned, her heart beating quickly. "Thank you both so much. Really," she said to Charolette. The woman beamed and bowed her head before shutting the door.

"Wait, I want to grab one thing from my bag before we go," Zephera called to Oriana, who was already three steps ahead of her. They talked excitedly as they made their way to their cabin. Zephera shuffled in and rummaged through her bag. Finding the dagger necklace, she pulled it over her head. An angel of death should never be without her weapon. Now she felt complete.

Oriana raised an eyebrow when she saw the necklace.

"Don't," Zephera warned, walking past her to the staircase. Oriana merely shrugged and followed closely behind her. When they reached the main deck, they both gasped. It had been transformed into a dance floor. Fairy lights entwined the pillars and spread like dewy cobwebs through the air above the deck. Passengers dressed in varying styles—from plain tunics to silken finery—milled around the small round tables that dotted the deck. The air was festive and filled with mirth. Zephera spun around, taking it all in, her face lit with joy.

Oriana squealed and pointed to some of the crew who were filling in as the ball's musicians. Zephera let out a surprised laugh as she spied Brenner among them, playing the cello. He was smiling and tapping his foot in time to the music. She glanced around the crowd of boisterous people, searching for Zad. He was chatting with a tall, thin man who was dressed in a crisp, navy blue suit decorated with gleaming medals.

"Ooh, Zad's made friends with the captain," Oriana murmured appreciatively. "I think I'll go say hello to Brenner." Zephera nodded, her eyes never leaving Zad.

He glanced up as she arrived, his mouth going slack with shock. She glanced at him sinfully and then hooked her index finger under his chin and pushed up, closing his mouth. "Are you going to stand there all bug-eyed the rest of the night, or are you going to ask me to dance?" she said playfully, running her finger along his ear and jaw and sending shivers through his body.

The captain gave a short bow and excused himself. Zad growled and pulled her close, kissing her deeply.

"You look divine, Zephera. Dance with me?" he asked. Zephera pointed to her chest.

"Me? Why, I'd love to," she cooed. He grabbed her hand and led her to the dance floor.

CHAPER 31

He almost hadn't recognized her when he had first caught sight of her in that titillating, blood-red dress. She looked radiant, though he could do without that dagger around her neck. Her normally scowling face was replaced with a playful smile. This was the Zephera he knew and loved—the Zephera that rarely showed the world her soft and flirtatiously feminine side, the woman he knew she could be. It was all he could do to not take her right there on the dance floor. Had she gone to all the trouble of dressing up for him? His heart filled almost to bursting, and in that moment, he loved her more than he ever had before. They danced in time to the quick melody. Zephera laughed as she threw her arms to the sky, spinning in time to the beat.

Zad shook his head and smiled. Wild joy rolled off of her like waves from the sea. She deserved this night after everything she had gone through. She deserved her happiness. They all did.

When the song ended, Zephera leaned into him, her voice breathless and ecstatic. "Oh Zad, isn't this amazing?"

Wrapping his arms around her tightly he whispered, "It sure is, Zephera. It sure is."

Oriana joined them with drinks in her hand. She handed the delicate fluted glasses to them.

"I propose a toast," she said, raising her glass. "To surprising friendships, Sarilo women, and this delicious champagne." She giggled.

"Here, here," Zephera added. Their glasses chimed musically as they tapped them against each other. Zephera and Oriana tipped their heads back, emptying their glasses. Zad merely took a sip.

"Let's go get more alcohol." Zephera grabbed Oriana's arm.

Zad chuckled. "All right, you two. I'll be over there," he said, pointing to a table nearby. He was glad Zephera was finally connecting with Oriana. The golden-haired girl seemed to share Zephera's love for fine things and it pleased him to see her bringing out that side of Zephera so perfectly. She would never admit it, but Zephera needed another woman who could hold her own against her. It was refreshing to see them dancing and giggling together.

When Zephera looked like she was well taken care of, Zad silently slipped away from the main deck and made his way down the staircase to their cabin, hands in his pockets. He had to be quick. Zephera would notice his absence soon and come looking for him. He opened Zephera's bag and searched through it for the vial of dark liquid, careful not to disturb anything. He felt a twinge of guilt, but he needed that vial. His hand touched a letter that was addressed to Zephera. He sucked in his breath and looked over his shoulder at the door.

He pulled the letter out and unfolded it. His fists tightened as he read it. He snarled viciously and shoved it back into her bag. Daegan was a fool. He knew nothing of him or Zephera. He was a murderer and wanted Zephera to follow him down his own twisted, dark path, to join him in his loneliness. Zad would never allow that. If they ever met again he would make sure that bastard left her alone. The coward was so jealous of what he and Zephera had that he had slithered off like a scared snake. Disgusting.

He rummaged again through her bag, finally finding a small parcel wrapped in cloth. "There you are," he whispered. He unwrapped it carefully and grabbed the vial. He pulled an identical one from his pocket and held it up, comparing them. He had acquired the fake vial from some of the ship's supplies. It had been a simple thing to create a liquid that looked like Reina's concoction. He wrapped the cloth around the fake vial and then placed the package back in her bag, careful to put everything back as it was. He sighed in relief and leaned his head against the wall.

"All right, Reina. Let us see what you are made of." He opened the vial and wrinkled his nose at the smell of rot that met the air. He took a deep breath and brought the vial to his lips, swallowing the putrid liquid in one gulp. He stifled a gag. Shaking his head with disgust, he stood up and made his way to the door. "That's it? That's all you wanted from me?" he asked the air around him. He didn't feel any different. Perhaps it was Reina's idea of a cruel joke.

He made his way back to Zephera and Oriana who were now joined by Brenner. They were all laughing and dancing jubilantly. He reached them just as the song came to an end.

"Where did you go off to?" Zephera called over the music as it started up again.

"Nature called," he replied, giving her a wink.

"You know, I've never understood that expression: *nature calls*. Like, is there a tree calling you? Or perhaps a flower? No, what you really should say is, 'I've got to piss,' or something like that." Zephera was spouting off words and slurring them together, drunker than a drowned kitten.

Oriana giggled loudly, her arm slung around Zephera. "A talking tree! Ha!" she said before tripping over her own feet and pulling Zephera down with her. They sat on the ground, laughing deliriously. Zad looked at Brenner, who grinned.

"Come on, you two. We have a big day tomorrow. Let's get you to bed," he commanded, helping the two inebriated girls up. He took Zephera under his arm and motioned with his head for Brenner to grab Oriana.

"Mmmm... you are no fun, Zaddy." Her alcohol-laced breath tickled his ear.

"I know, I know," he replied, his lips pressed together but turned up.

"Carry me," she said, leaning against him and closing her eyes. He bent down and scooped her up in his arms.

"You smell good," she murmured, her head resting against his chest. "What do I smell like?"

"You smell like liquor and roses, Beasty," he replied and kissed her head. She giggled, softly closing her eyes.

He carried her in silence down to their cabin and opened the door. Then he put her on the lower bunk and tucked her under the cotton blanket.

"Sleep well, Zephera. Dream of this night, for tomorrow will be trying indeed." She began to snore softly. Zad smiled. "Good night, Beasty."

CHAPER 32

Zephera groaned as she sat up, rubbing her eyes and smearing kohl onto her fingers. *Ugh.* It wasn't the first time she had fallen asleep with makeup on. This always tended to be the aftermath of her festivities.

She glanced around the darkened room. Oriana was sitting in the middle of the floor, still in her dress, mouth open, eyes half-closed and staring at the ceiling. Zephera stood, feeling slightly dizzy.

Oriana turned to look at her. "Remind me to never drink with you like that again, especially while we are at sea."

Zephera nodded, collapsing down next to her. "How much did we drink last night, and what was in it?"

"Rum, mead, everything." Oriana moaned, poking her face with her index finger. "My face is numb."

Zephera giggled. "For the first time in my life, I actually look better than you. You look deplorable."

Oriana merely pointed to the wash basin. "Is that so? Why don't you take a look?"

Zephera crawled over to the basin and pulled herself up to the mirror. She laughed. "I take it back. You still look better than me." Her eyes were shot through with scarlet lightning, and the kohl had smudged, leaving huge black circles under her eyes and bruise-like marks all over her face. Remnants of her lipstick stained the skin around her mouth like she had been smashed with red berries, and her lovely, slick-backed hair had lost its velvet bow and now looked like a bird's nest.

She filled the basin with water from a jug and dipped her hands in it, scrubbing her face. The chilly water cooled her skin and constricted her blood vessels, making her headache dissipate slightly.

"That's better," she said, drying her face on a small hand towel. "I'm not sure what to do about this, though." She pointed to her hair.

"Shave it off," Oriana mumbled, rising to join her. Zephera handed her the towel so Oriana could clean off her face.

"How does your hair still manage to look so perfect?" she asked, running her fingers through Oriana's soft curls.

Oriana shrugged, stepping toward her bag. "Here," she said as she threw a brush at her.

Zephera mumbled a thanks. She grimaced as she pulled the brush through the tangles. Twenty minutes later her hair had cooperated enough to be pulled into a knot on the top of her head. She slipped off the dress and pulled on her freshly cleaned tunic from the day before. Oriana waited by the door for her until they stumbled up the stairs to get something to eat.

They found Brenner and Zad in the dining hall, dressed in full armor and reviewing a notebook together. "Good morning, ladies! Or should I say good afternoon? We are about to dock," Zad teased, amusement in his voice.

"What? Seriously?" Zephera pouted. She sat next to Zad who handed her a bowl of oats and an apple. She ate quickly, satisfying her growling stomach.

Brenner handed her a glass filled with a green, chunky liquid. *It will help clear your head, though it does not taste pretty.* She made a face at him.

"Thanks," she said, giving him a small smile. She glared down at the beastly concoction and pursed her lips. Oriana had a glass, too. They raised their glasses in unison and choked down the mess.

"Ick," Oriana grimaced.

"Oh, no," groaned Zephera as Charolette and Eviee glided into the room. What would the sisters think of her haggard appearance?

"Vell, hello, my lovelies," Charolette purred. "I take it your night vas satisfactory?" Her eyes twinkled knowingly.

"Perfectly peachy," Zephera replied.

"Thank you again for your kindness," Oriana said, getting up to hug the two women.

Eviee waved her off. "Et vas nothing, our pleasure. If you are ever in Sarilo, please look us up."

Zephera smiled. "We will. You'll have to show us how a real Sarilan lives."

"Yes, it vill be delightful." Charolette smiled. "Farewell, my friends, until we meet again." She bowed and she and Eviee turned to leave.

"Wait! Your dresses! Where should we have them sent?" Zephera called after them.

"Keep zem," Eviee answered from the doorway before flashing them one last smile.

A horn sounded three times, signaling that they were about to dock. Zephera sucked in her breath.

"Well, back to reality, I suppose. Meet you on the docks?" she asked Zad and Brenner, who already had their belongings piled at their feet. The two men nodded and turned their attention back to the parchment. Zephera and Oriana returned to the cabin to dress in their leathers and gather their belongings.

Oriana looked to Zephera nervously as they packed.

"What is it Oriana?" Zephera asked.

Oriana bit her lip. "Are you ready for this?"

Zephera slung her bag over her shoulder. "Not particularly. However, I'm anxious for it all to be over."

Oriana nodded in silent agreement.

A few minutes later, Zephera felt her stomach begin to knot as they walked off the ship onto the docks. She bit the inside of her cheek as she stared up at the castle across the harbor. The diamond towers glittered in the sunlight, making the edifice glow with crystalline fire. She caught up with Zad, who was talking to a carriage driver about a ride back to the Keep.

Zephera felt a familiar, unpleasant presence. Brenner felt it too. He grabbed Zephera's hand tightly.

"Hello," said a sinuous voice. "I don't believe we've had the pleasure of meeting before." Zephera whirled around. Valessa was holding out a hand to Zadkiel. Though he looked shocked, he at least had the sense to shake her hand. Valessa smiled, her lips curling around her teeth like a feral animal.

Zephera unsheathed her curved blade. "You left me to die!" she hissed walking towards Valessa.

Oriana put a hand on Zephera's shoulder. "Zephera…" she warned.

Valessa cocked her head, her red hair falling perfectly onto her shoulder. "I had no way of getting to you, Zephera. When I saw that your party had found us, I made a judgment call. They were perfectly capable of rescuing you. I needed to be back in the city to prepare for Reina's summoning spell, so I ported. You cannot fault me for doing what needed to be done."

Zephera shook Oriana's grasp off and growled. "You could've at least brought one of them along with us!" She gestured to the others. "I almost died!"

Valessa laughed, pushing her hair behind her ear. "Such is the nature of your chosen lifestyle. You deal in death. Do you think it won't come for you?"

Zad growled, stepping in front of Zephera protectively. "What is it you need, woman? Speak and be gone."

Valessa laughed. "Oh, you have spirit. I like you."

"What do you want, Valessa?" Zephera asked coldly, stepping from behind Zad.

"So hostile," she laughed. "Baleem sent me. You are to come with me so I can perform the summoning spell."

Zephera narrowed her eyes suspiciously. *She is the only one who is capable of performing the spell. We need her.* Brenner's voice said inside her head.

Zephera felt the warm hum of Brenner's presence in her mind. She nodded, groaning. "Very well, let's get to it. Lead the way, Valessa."

Valessa looked surprised. "And here I thought you did not trust me."

"I don't," Zephera replied.

Valessa laughed. "Very wise, dear girl." She turned, pointing to the carriage. "Get in. I'll pay the driver to take us to The Tower of Light."

Zephera nodded at Zad, who eyed Valessa with distaste. "You are in charge, Zephera. We'll do whatever you tell us," he said.

"Come on, let's get this over with. We'll be rid of her as soon as we find Reina," Zephera said, getting into the carriage.

The others followed, taking their seats. Brenner sat between Oriana and Zad, leaving the seat next to Zephera open for Valessa.

"Where is Daegan?" the woman asked curiously, as if she had only just noticed his absence.

The others looked at Zephera. "He was needed elsewhere," she barked, turning abruptly to look out the window at the passing roads. They rode in awkward silence for twenty minutes before the carriage pulled up in front of a large tower near the edge of the city. The tower itself was made of carved white wood. Amethyst embellishments lined the sides. Zephera blinked at the blinding purple light reflecting off the gems.

The driver opened the carriage door and took Valessa's hand, helping her down. She smiled coquettishly at the driver, who looked embarrassed by the attention. Then she strode off toward the front door, beckoning the others to follow her. Not looking at the others, Zephera pulled her bag onto her shoulder and followed the woman into the tower.

CHAPER 33

Zephera gasped at the tall, vaulted ceilings. The walls were made of a light wood with gold outlining in spirals. *It is beautiful! This…this was your home?* she asked Brenner.

He frowned. *This was the part they showed people like you.*

Valessa led them through a long corridor and up a cobblestone staircase. They came to an ornate door at the top of the landing. Valessa ushered them inside.

Zephera stifled a laugh when she saw the plain interior of Valessa's rooms. The walls were painted a stark white. They were undecorated and spare. A faded wooden writing desk sat in a corner of the small living room, buried in papers. There was a small armchair by the fireplace with a linen blanket and a book on it. *This was it? The lair of the monster?*

As if reading her thoughts, Valessa curled her lips, revealing the sharp glint of her teeth. "What did you expect? Torture chambers and a coffin?"

Zephera shrugged. "Well…"

"This is my study, Zephera. Not the dungeons." She leered at Brenner, causing him to shudder. Zephera snarled, stepping in front of him protectively.

Valessa crowed and clapped her hands. "Such a touchy bunch. Shall we begin?" Not waiting for an answer, she turned and led them to a smaller room, filled with candles.

Chalk markings covered the floor. In the center of the room, there was a wooden stand with a large ceramic bowl on it. Valessa walked to one of the shelves that lined the room and grabbed an old book.

"My grimoire," she explained. "The only thing I brought with me from the Lands of Sorrow." She stroked the spine sadly.

Oriana sucked in her breath. "I'm sorry, did I hear you correctly? The Lands of Sorrow?"

Valessa beamed cruelly at Zephera. "Oh, this is too good! You didn't tell them, did you?"

"Valessa, don't…" Zephera warned.

"What's she talking about, Zephera?" Zad asked cautiously.

Zephera glared at Valessa, who shuddered mockingly. "That expression of yours is positively glacial, Zephera."

"Can someone PLEASE tell us what the bloody hell is going on here?" Oriana yelled, her normally long fuse cut short by Valessa's taunting.

"I can."

Zephera's heart almost jumped out of her chest as Daegan walked through the door.

"What're *you* doing here?" she asked, her voice cracking.

"He missed me," Valessa said fondly, standing to meet him. Daegan greeted her with a deep kiss.

Ignoring the icy spear that shot through her at the sight of their kiss, Zephera scoffed. "Didn't you just ask me where he was?"

Valessa shrugged. "I can be such a nasty liar sometimes. My apologies."

Zad unsheathed his sword. "What's going on here? No more games, you bitch!" He strode menacingly towards Valessa.

Before Zephera could utter a laugh at Zad's word for Valessa, he fell to the floor, clutching his throat. His eyes widened as he struggled to fill his lungs with air.

"Let him go, Valessa," Zephera said, kneeling beside Zad.

Daegan stood in front of Oriana and Brenner, blocking their path. "I wouldn't," he said as they tried to push past him.

"*Bitch* is such a rude word. After everything I have done for you all, you dare to insult me in my quarters?" Valessa looked down at Zad, who was turning purple.

"Valessa, please!" Zephera sobbed.

"Ugh. Fine," Valessa said, taking a seat on a leather armchair.

The woman's invisible grip on Zad's throat loosened. He coughed, sucking in as much air as he could. Zephera helped him sit up.

Valessa pursed her lips. "You are no fun this time," she pouted.

Zephera threw her hands in the air. "What the hell does that mean?"

Valessa smiled. "I can show you a memory if you would like. If you really wish for everyone to witness this, that is your prerogative, but don't say that I didn't warn you."

Zephera closed her eyes, bowing her head. She wasn't sure what was to come of the memory. Baleem had shown her memories before, when he trained her in certain techniques. It was an odd magic that played out for everyone to see. They only showed what was, what had been. It was impossible to lie in a memory. This magic was frightening; it could show anyone anything that you had ever experienced. If Valessa had access to this memory, that would mean she and Valessa had been together in a past life. Whatever it showed, it couldn't be good. "Show us," Zephera ordered.

"*Ostende Memoriae*," Valessa whispered.

The room around her faded away, and a room made of stone took its place. She watched as Valessa walked in, followed by herself—or someone who looked like her. This version of Zephera had darker eyes and a foreign, cruel smile.

"What is it, Tatia?" Valessa asked.

"I'll show you," said the other Zephera—or Tatia. She turned away from her, swinging her hips suggestively.

A naked, gagged man hung in the middle of the room, his limbs stretched out by chains anchored to the ceiling and floor. She gave his face a condescending pat and he whimpered piteously. With a wicked grin, she reached into her robes and drew out a small dagger. "Now, if you need to scream, do it loudly. The more you struggle, the greater the pain, and the easier this will be for me. A soul taken from great pain is the most powerful."

She stepped behind him, peering around at Valessa, who stared curiously at the man.

Tatia drove the dagger directly into the man's spine, pulling it downwards and ripping his skin apart. A resounding scream filled the air. Tatia whispered something into the man's ear and he let out a sob. She laughed as she peeled his skin back, blood streaming from his wounds. The dagger fell to the floor as Tatia reached inside the man, bending each rib as far as it would go before snapping it. He never stopped screaming.

"Please! Please kill me," he begged.

"Patience," she scolded. "I'll kill you. Just not yet."

Burying her wrist deep in his back, she pulled the final rib and broke it with a snap.

"Delightful," she mused.

Wiping her hands on her robes, she tilted her head and stared at the man. "You are doing beautifully. You should be very proud," she purred. "Now for the fun part. Valessa? Care to join me, my love?"

Valessa smiled and stepped up to Tatia. Together, they studied the man's filleted back.

"See how his lungs are exposed?"

Valessa nodded.

"The lungs are the very essence of life. The goddess Therae will bless this ritual with her guiding hand." Tatia closed her eyes in silent prayer. "Now, you grab one lobe, and I'll grab the other. Gently lift it out and place it on his ribs."

Valessa nodded. Excitement shone in her eyes.

"Now," Tatia commanded.

They slowly lifted the man's lungs onto his ribs. He struggled and flailed, causing Valessa to drop her half of the organ. It fell sloppily onto the man's broken ribs, like a broken wing.

Valessa smiled apologetically at Tatia.

"Don't worry, my darling. You did very well," Tatia smiled, bringing Valessa in for a kiss.

The man's screaming quieted as he struggled to breathe. "It is time," Tatia whispered, breaking away. She pulled an amulet from her neck and stood in front of the man. Tatia looked up at him, her head cocked.

"*Trasenea, Nimaa.*" Thrusting her hand into his chest, she pulled out a dark, willowy ball. She stared at it, transfixed. "The human soul. Tainted by pain and evil," she paused. "*Tibacivv.*" The soul twisted and danced through the air, landing in the amulet.

Tatia grinned as she snapped the amulet closed, the soul trapped inside.

The man had stopped breathing. His face was now frozen forever in fear.

"Thank you for your sacrifice," she said with a mocking lilt.

Valessa smiled affectionately. "You do love to show off."

Tatia shrugged. "When I'm gone, you'll need to continue this work. I'm sure that you can find a cleaner way to take their souls," she said as she wiped her bloodied hands on a towel. "Perhaps eventually you won't have to kill them in the process. Such a waste of magic." Tatia shook her head. She held up the amulet with a clasp upon its dark design. "Fill this, and if we collect enough souls we will have the power needed to stop Gregour and return home. Then we can do whatever we want. We'll have enough power to rule both realms if we wish, and no one will be able to stop us."

The women's voices rose in a duet of savage mirth. "Oh, I do wish you did not have to go. You might not be as fun next time." Valessa pouted.

"Yes, well, my *father* is waiting. I can't let him think I know what I am, can I? It's a shame I have to die so soon. I rather liked the feel of the darkness," she said, kissing Valessa. "And darling, don't tell me about any of this until you are sure that I am ready."

Valessa nodded. "I do wish you didn't have to forget me, Tatia. I'll be lonely without you."

She smiled sadly at Valessa. "It will be worth it to rule this world with you, my love," she said before walking out the door.

The memory began to fade and Zephera was brought back to the present.

"So you see, Zephera, even if you want to deny it, it was *you* who chose this path," Valessa said, holding the amulet between her fingers.

Bile rose in Zephera's throat. *She* had done this. *She* had been the malicious, evil woman who had created this plan.

Oriana rubbed Zephera's back, trying to comfort her. "I still don't understand; someone please explain what we just witnessed," she asked.

Zephera coughed, glaring at Daegan. "Just get on with it so we can go," she spat.

He met her gaze boldly, no remorse in his cold eyes. The dagger necklace suddenly felt heavy against her chest.

"Where to begin…" he mused. Taking a seat next to Valessa, he pulled her up and over onto his lap.

Zephera closed her eyes. He was about to tell them everything. She folded her arms over her chest and looked at the floor, afraid to meet her companion's eyes. They were going to hate her after this. They would think she was one of *them*, a creature from the darkness.

Daegan cleared his throat and began to tell the room of his and Valessa's past. He spoke of the Lands of Somber, of the wicked kings who tore their world apart. He had known all along who she was, who Gregour and the Dark Priestess were. But he had never told her. Tears pooled in her eyes as she buried her head in her hands. When he got to the part about her true identity, she heard Oriana whisper, "No. There must be some mistake."

"There is no mistake," Valessa explained. "Do you see that mark on her arm? She did not always have that mark. She had to be awakened. Which is what we did when she was Tatia. She must die from unnatural causes and be brought back. It is quite tedious. Drowning usually does the trick." Valessa winked. "I awakened Tatia and ever since she has carried that mark, meaning she has been awakened. I have now watched her live three lifetimes. Each cycle I have awakened her."

"Why?" Zephera asked, staring at Valessa. She wanted to look at Zad but couldn't bring herself to risk it, to see the disappointment in his eyes. He'd been strangely quiet throughout Daegan's story.

"Because you and I are meant for each other. We are meant to rule over a cruel and wicked world. You know this, Zephera. You enjoy killing. You crave it. Yet for some reason you still harbor a piece of your humanity. Your heart longs for normalcy, which is why I assume you have taken to bedding him." Valessa nodded in Zad's direction.

"Why must you say such things?" Zad spat. Zephera finally glanced at him but he wouldn't look at her.

"What does Zephera's being born of both realms have to do with ending the cycles?" Oriana squeaked.

"For thousands of years, her father has taken many forms; always a form of power. The splitting of the realms gave him an immense reservoir of magic and he has become obsessed with holding on to that power. If it were not for Zephera, her twin and her mother's spell, the cycles would never have existed. Our realms would have been cut off from one another forever. Zephera's mother Malina was a gifted Dark Priestess whose magic came from nature. When she died bringing Zephera into the world, her magic returned to the earth but her spirit couldn't rest. When she realized what her husband had done, she searched for a way to make it right somehow. Gathering her magic back from the earth, she came back to life. Malina took the living child and created the cycles. She was killed again by Gregour at her altar in the Mountains of Dreer after she performed the final ritual. She sacrificed her renewed life so Zephera could live and undo what her father had done."

"If all you needed was the amulet of stolen souls to bring down the barrier, then why haven't you done it before now?" Zad demanded.

"Because I still need her. She is my dark queen. Only her immortal soul and that of her twin can bring down the barrier completely. Without them, I only have enough power to bring it down temporarily," Valessa said quietly.

Zad cleared his throat. "Let me get this straight, you want to unleash unspeakable darkness on the world and rule it with Zephera? A tad bit dramatic, don't you think?"

"Is that why you tortured mages and stole their souls? Why you rendered them mute? So you could be queen with some past version of me?" Zephera yelled.

"Partially, but I did what had to be done, Zephera. So did you. It was your idea, after all. You were a much darker version of yourself then, but still you, nonetheless."

"NO!" Zephera cried, "No," she echoed uselessly. She looked at Brenner. "Brenner I wouldn't... I never..." She watched him shy away from her and curl into himself.

She glanced at Oriana. She saw the pained expression on her friend's face. "Oriana, I swear. It might've been my soul that did those things, but it wasn't my hands."

Oriana bit her lip nervously and looked at the floor. "I don't know what to believe right now," she whispered.

"Believe me! Oriana, PLEASE!" Zephera cried.

Oriana shook her head. "I'm sorry, Zephera. I need time to process all of this madness."

Zephera sighed. "Brenner?" she said quietly. The mage looked at her sadly.

"I'm so sorry Brenner," she whispered.

He nodded slightly. *You are not that person Zephera. There is no need for apologies.*

She gave him a small smile.

"Zadkiel?" she asked, walking towards him. She put her arms around him. "Please, you have to believe me. I didn't know, I swear it. I would never—"

He pushed her away. "But you did." Tears were falling from his eyes. "I don't know who you are, but I do know that you aren't someone I can love."

Zephera's heart ripped apart at his words. She fell to the floor, devastated. "Why are you doing this, Valessa?"

The woman scoffed. "Because I can, love."

Zephera looked at Daegan through tears. He looked away stonily, avoiding her gaze. She breathed raggedly and bit her fist to deaden her agony. Every dream she had hoped for—a future with Zad, her friends—had been stripped away.

No, she had betrayed her friends all on her own. She was a demon disguised as an angel. She was a monster.

CHAPTER 34

Daegan stood up, seemingly irked. "Enough. Zephera, get up. The rest of you, prepare for the spell."

Zephera stood, looking at the floor, tears falling from her eyes.

"Yes, let's get this over with so we can be done here," Zad said. Zephera sensed he meant to say, 'be done with her.'

"The items, Zephera," Valessa commanded, holding out her hand.

Zephera nodded and grabbed her bag. She rummaged around inside, pulling out the carefully wrapped items. "Here." She handed them to Valessa.

Valessa unwrapped the cloth. Her right eyebrow rose slightly at the contents. She held up the finger. "Reina certainly has a morbid sense of humor."

She placed the finger and the wooden horse in the bowl on the altar. Then she picked up the vial and stared at it curiously. "And what is this?"

Zad stepped forward. "It's for me. I need to drink it, and then you need to use my blood."

Valessa snorted. "Oh, this is just too good!"

"Zad, please. Don't drink it," Zephera pled. "We can find Reina a different way." She cried out as Zad opened the vial.

Zephera darted forward, tackling Zad. The vial fell from his hands. Zephera grabbed it quickly before it hit the ground. She stood, backing away from Zad. She locked eyes with him as she drank the dark liquid. He simply stared at her, his expression unreadable.

Valessa clapped her hands. "What a show! Your hand Zephera, I think we would need your blood now. Though, as you are immune to the Decay's effects, I'm not so sure the spell will work. Never mind that for now, give me your hand."

Zephera held her hand out to Valessa who sliced it in a single movement. Valessa stared at the bloody dagger and smiled. "Beautiful, my dear," she whispered.

Valessa was about to place a drop of Zephera's blood into the bowl when Zad spoke up. "It won't work," he muttered.

Valessa spun around to face him, a wicked smile on her face. "Why is that?"

Zad let out a hollow laugh. "You ask stupid questions, Valessa. You know her blood won't work. Why bother slicing her hand? You know that the only one who can merge with the liquid properly is me. Fortunately for all of you, I had a plan. I knew Zephera would try and stop me. She's maddeningly stubborn. I swapped the vials while we were on the ship. I already drank the liquid within."

Zephera gasped. "Zad! What have you done?" she screamed.

Zad ignored her and pulled out a small dagger, slicing his hand. Holding it over the bowl, he let his blood fall. The liquid in the bowl began to simmer and smoke.

"Hmm." Valessa chuckled. "You have gotten rather predictable in your many lives, Tatia. What a shame." Valessa shrugged. "Pity I had to scar such beautiful skin," she gestured at Zephera's sliced hand. "Though I may have use for your blood yet." Valessa walked over to a shelf and pulled out an empty vial. She let a single drop of Zephera's blood fall in, then she corked and pocketed it.

"What use is my blood to you?" Zephera asked.

Valessa smiled. "Oh my dear Tatia, a single drop has a thousand uses. One of them being..."

She was cut off by Daegan, who had grown seemingly annoyed. "She wants to bring your past life back, a love potion more or less," he yawned. "Can we get on with this please? I don't have time for petty relationship squabbles, Valessa. If you want to get Zephera to love you by force, do it on your own time, but don't waste mine."

Valessa pouted. "Fine. But when she is mine again, you will be wishing I had more time for you."

Zephera laughed coldly. "I'll never be yours, Valessa. I'll fight you, even if it kills me."

Daegan cleared his throat and pulled his cloak tighter. "Yes, Zephera, we know… blah blah blah you love Zadkiel, you hate darkness, you want to have a normal life. No one cares."

Zad shook his head. "Zephera, normal? I've spent my entire life trying to protect her and make her see that she can be good. I've watched her kill, maim and steal for pleasure. She's sick and it can't be cured, I can't tame darkness." He let out an exasperated breath. "Zephera can never have a normal life. It isn't in her blood. Let's get on with this," he said, motioning to Valessa.

"It is ready," Valessa said. She cupped her hand and placed it in the liquid. Then she brought the liquid to her lips and sipped it. "*Loriaga, Ostednde, Reina*," she said. Her eyes rolled back in her head until only the whites showed. She began to chant loudly, her arms raised in the air. There was a large crack and a flash of light as smoke began to fill the room.

Zephera pulled her tunic up over her mouth, coughing. Waving her hand in front of her face, she tried to clear away the smoke. A gruff female voice spoke, "*Eripitay!*" The smoke began to clear.

In the center of the room stood a woman with long black hair that fell to her waist. She wore an emerald dress with a black cloak. "Hello," she said. "I believe you've been searching for me."

"Reina?" Zephera asked.

The woman turned to Zephera and gave a small bow. "Hello, my dear. You go by Zephera this time, correct? It's been such a long time since I last saw you. I believe it was during the third cycle? You were much different then. You went by the name Lilly."

"I don't care what I went by, or who I was then. I don't care about any of it," Zephera spat.

Reina raised an eyebrow. "Ah, I see. That is a pity. You were so good, so pure then. I see that has changed."

"So I've been told," Zephera replied.

"Well, child, don't look so glum. We can break the curse now and go home. You will love our Realm, though I haven't been back in over five thousand years. I would assume much has changed."

Zephera gasped. "You are the First."

Reina gave a small bow. "I am."

"How do you know that I can break the curse and reunite our realms?" Zephera asked.

Reina smiled. "Because you passed the tests and summoned me. Darkness radiates off of you. Now, all we need to do is find your twin. Though I don't suppose it'll be too hard, you are like two sides of a coin. Dark and Light. You usually find one another each cycle. Your friend Zadkiel over there almost ruined it this time, though. He would rather see you dead than dark. I do wonder what he will think of your sister."

"Me?" Zad asked. "What do I have to do with this mess?"

"Mess? Dear boy, this is no mess. This is chaos. Beautiful, dark chaos."

"It's evil and despicable and I want no part in whatever you're planning. I've had enough of this darkness. I refuse to take part any longer."

Reina raised an eyebrow. "You think it's darkness that is evil and disgusting, boy?"

"I don't *think* it is, I *know* it is. I've seen what it's capable of when it entangles you in its grasp. It curses and destroys everything it touches."

Reina let out a mad cackle. "Darkness isn't the only evil in this world. Light can be just as deadly. What of your actions, dear boy? You would have let Zephera drown rather than see her dark. You are the evil one here, Zadkiel."

"Yet any dark thing" —he spat at Zephera— "always turns out to be monstrous."

"Zadkiel!" Oriana scolded, shocked by his statement. "How can you say such a thing?"

He turned to respond, but before he could, he fell to the floor coughing. Black liquid oozed from his mouth.

"ZAD!" Zephera yelled, running towards him.

"Get away from me!" he snarled.

Zephera stepped back in shock, helpless as Zad continued to cough up black blood. "Reina, please, help him!"

Reina shook her head, "I can't. He ingested the liquid willingly. The sickness has already taken hold, though I didn't intend for it to work this quickly."

"I took it yesterday." Zad coughed. He stood, his chin covered in black blood.

"Ah, well, that was your mistake then, Zadkiel. If you had waited, perhaps you could have lived. Pity. It is rather fitting, though, for one who hates the Darkness so much to be consumed by it from the inside out."

"NO! NO! Please, Reina, the cure! Please, give him the cure. I beg you! I'll do anything. Please save him," Zephera cried, throwing herself at Reina's feet.

Reina glowered down at her. "Get up, girl. Don't beg at my feet for the life of someone so unworthy."

Zephera stood slowly. "He is worthy, I swear it. Please, the cure," Zephera whispered.

Reina smiled. "Cure? The only cure is blood of both darkness and light. But it needs to be pure, and purity is impossible to find."

Zephera felt like she had been slapped. "Wh—What?" She glanced around the room. Daegan merely shrugged. Valessa smirked. She looked at Zad, who stared at her with venom in his eyes.

"Did you know?" she snarled at Valessa. "Was all of this for nothing?"

"Of course I knew. Don't be stupid, Zephera. Daegan assembled this team for me. You were all meant to take the journey together so that we could be sure that you were ready. And, I am pleased to say, you are. Poor Zad here followed you to his own demise."

"Why? What's he got to do with anything?" Zephera asked angrily.

"Because he loves you—well, parts of you," Reina explained. "He hates your dark side. If only he didn't harbor such hatred for it in his heart, perhaps he could have been spared. But alas, then it wouldn't be so beautifully tragic. He never deserved you, Zephera. He would have betrayed you the first chance he got if it meant that he could shut out the Darkness."

"He would never betray me," Zephera said.

"Are you sure about that, Zephera?" Daegan asked. "Look at him now, how quickly his love turns to hate. I told you once that your loyalty and blind trust would be your undoing."

"You're wrong," she said, peering up at him.

"I'm sorry, Zephera, but this is for your own good," Daegan whispered in her ear. "Valessa!" he commanded.

Valessa held Zad's bag. He sucked in his breath as Valessa dumped the contents out at Zephera's feet. Clothes, coins and parchment littered the cold floor. In the middle of the parchment, was a small bundle of folded papers with her name scrawled across it. It was written in Baleem's handwriting. It was the letter.

Zephera reached down to get it but just as she was about to, Zad tackled her to the floor, grabbed the letter from her and tossed it into the fire.

"NO!" Zephera yelled, sickened. "Zad! What have you done?"

He looked at her, unfeeling. "You were supposed to let me protect you, Zephera. You were supposed to let me in, let me share your burdens. When you came back from hunting that stag, I knew something was different. You had a new darkness about you. I tried to get you to talk to me, but you wouldn't. So I took the letter. I hoped that when you had returned from the altar with Daegan you would explain what happened. I knew he had told you what he was. But you still didn't tell me. You put all of us in danger. By trusting them, you have endangered Nostorra and the entire world. You let their evil pull you in. Now it seems that you're the worst of them all."

Zad—her Zad—had betrayed her. He had known how badly she needed that letter. He had even known who she was and what needed to be done. He had been so caught up in playing the hero that he had kept it from her in some insane ploy to keep her "safe." Betrayal filled her chest. Her lip curled up in anger. She realized in that moment that he had never truly loved her, for if he had, he would've accepted her as she was, darkness and all.

"I'm not someone you can save, Zad. I don't want to be saved. You can throw a drowning sailor a lifeline as many times as you want, but he has to want to grab it." She stared at him, her heart breaking. "I'll never forgive you for this." The leaden words dropped from her like doves falling dead from the sky.

"I don't care," he replied coolly.

Reina began to laugh. "Oh, Zephera, come now. You didn't honestly think that he was worthy of you?"

Zephera turned to glare at Reina. "So all of this was just a test?"

Reina shrugged. "Is that so bad, Zephera? Without it, you wouldn't have known who you are and what you are capable of. You would have never known of his betrayal until it was too late. Now you are free, Zephera. Free to claim what is rightfully yours. Free to find your sister and reunite our realms. Nothing is holding you back."

Zephera growled at the horrible woman in front of her. They had all been using her. She was nothing more than a pawn to them. The darkness in them had been warped into cruelty by their evil designs. She looked up at Daegan, who stared at her deeply. *You always have a choice,* his eyes seemed to say.

Zephera smiled. She knew what she wanted to do. She made a choice. She lunged at Reina, pulling the dagger necklace from her neck and stabbing it directly into the woman's chest. She brought the blade down over and over, letting her anger and grief guide her hand. Blood sprayed Zephera's face at the force of her blows. Her teeth were bared as the life left Reina's startled eyes. She kept stabbing until she was pulled off by Daegan.

"She's dead, Zephera," he said softly, trying to calm her. She growled at him, dagger raised and feral rage in her eyes.

He held his hands up. "Easy there," he warned.

She turned from Daegan and walked towards Zad, Reina's blood dripping into her eyes. She wiped it with her forearm. Her vision cleared and she looked into Zad's eyes. They had always been so affectionate and carefree, but now they were full of arrogant contempt. The boy she had grown up with—the boy who knew her inside and out—was gone. In his place was a deceitful, hardened man. She answered his scowl with one of her own and pulled out her curved blade, bringing it to his throat as she pressed the point of the tainted dagger against his side and backed him into the wall. Brenner's magic crackled around her but Zad waved him off.

"Let her do it," he challenged.

Zephera laughed as the magic faded. "You would give up so easily on the woman you love, Zadkiel?"

"No, I wouldn't. But the Zephera that I knew and loved disappeared when she left to hunt that stag. She is dead. You... you aren't her. You're a sickness, a disease. My Zephera could have been redeemed. You are an abomination," he spat.

Zephera shook her head, her jaw clenched. "This is who I've always been, Zad. You just refused to see it. The only one who's fundamentally changed is you." She brought her arm to his throat, keeping him pinned to the wall. Then she brought her lips to his, giving him one final kiss. She released him and cast her weapons on the ground. Zad scoffed and spit on her feet, then wiped his mouth.

She smiled at him. "Hold on to that kiss and give it to my Zad for me. Let me know when he returns."

She turned away. "We need to get rid of that body," she said, pointing to Reina.

"Allow me." Valessa snapped her fingers. The body disappeared, leaving behind a pool of dark, crimson blood. "I sent it to my crypt. I want to study its magical properties."

"Of course you do." Zephera shook her head.

"Our task is done. We need to get to the castle," Zad said, leaving the room. Oriana had the decency to look thoroughly torn about what to do.

Zephera waved her off.

"I'm sorry, Zephera," she said before following Zad.

Brenner remained.

What was the purpose of all of this? It was pointless, utterly pointless, she voiced.

Brenner stared at her before answering, *Nothing is pointless, Zephera. Everyone and everything has its purpose.*

Then what is mine? I have caused nothing but harm and destruction. I have hurt everyone I care about. I'm a monster.

That is not who you are now Zephera, and monster is a matter of perspective.

Zephera smiled sadly. His kindness made her want to cry.

As if sensing her emotions, Brenner bowed, excusing himself.

As he left, so did Zephera's anger at Zad's betrayal. In its place came a sadness that cut so deep, she feared it would never heal. A sob tore out of her, and she fell to her knees, not caring that Daegan and Valessa could see.

Daegan coughed loudly and motioned for Valessa to follow the others. The woman nodded once and left. He approached Zephera cautiously and crouched down next to her, lifting her chin.

"He isn't worth your tears, Zephera. Don't let him take too many. I understand the need to feel the pain. Allow it now and then think on it no longer," he whispered quietly.

After a few moments, when she didn't answer, he gave up and left. Wrapping her arms around her knees she rested her head. Her tears mingled with the blood on her face and fell like rusty raindrops on her arms. She laughed softly. It wasn't quite a bath, but it would do for now.

Zephera was furious with Daegan and his deceit, but their quest was over. She didn't know what was going to happen next. But whatever it was, everything would be different. She could no longer trust anyone. Baleem had lied to her, and Zad... well, Zad wanted nothing to do with her. A vile sickness was engulfing the land, and there was no hope of finding a cure. The imbalance between the realms was tearing the world apart, and only she—the most feared woman in all of Nostorra—could bring the balance needed for it to heal. And what a sorry piece of work she was, spilling tears over a simple man. All she wanted right now was to give up and let the Darkness consume everyone. If she was destined to be their savior, they were all doomed.

She let herself cry a moment longer before taking a deep breath and getting to her feet. Then she grabbed her weapons from the ground and sheathed them. Walking slowly down the darkened halls, she willed her heart to steady. As she stepped out onto the darkened street, she was met by the Royal Guard. Zad, Brenner, and Oriana were standing nearby. Daegan and Valessa were on their knees, their hands tied behind their backs. Before Zephera could call out, she was shoved to the ground and tied up, too.

"Zephera Travelle," said the captain of the guard. "By order of His Royal Highness, the King of Nostorra, you are under arrest."

Zephera sucked in her breath and looked up at Zad, who appeared just as shocked as she was. "Under what charge?" he asked.

"For conspiring with the Dark Ones and plotting against the king. Do you have anything to say in their defense?" the Guard asked Zad.

He met Zephera's eye, and for a moment they stared at each other. She thought she saw a glimmer of sadness. In that moment, Zephera knew that although Zad had loved her, he blamed her for everything that was happening. After all, he'd told her once that being dead is better than being dark. She lowered her head, knowing his answer.

"I…I can't," he said and turned his back on them, leaving them to their fates.

"They can't do this! Zadkiel, you have to do something," Oriana pleaded desperately as Zad and Brenner pulled her along with them.

Zephera closed her eyes and reached out to Brenner. *Please, you must cure Zad,* she begged. As the three figures rounded a corner, she struggled against her restraints. The guard watching her grunted with impatience before bringing the hilt of his sword down on her head. Her world went dark.

CHAPER 35

Zephera sat up as footsteps scuffled outside her cell. She went to the small, barred window that was built into the top of the cell's massive wooden door.

"Zephera, my girl," Baleem said sadly.

"Baleem! What is happening? You've got to get me out of here!" she begged.

He looked at her sadly, his dark eyes narrowed. He shook his head. "I can't, Zephera. After listening to your charges and speaking with your team and Zadkiel, I've realized there is nothing that I can do. I apologize, Zephera. If I had just told you of your heritage earlier, perhaps the outcome would've been different. I'm sorry, I just didn't know how."

Zephera sunk to the floor. "I'm not entirely innocent of what they say. But it wasn't me who did those awful things. Sacrificing innocent mages for their souls? I would never do something so cruel, not this version of me, anyway."

Baleem sighed. "I know, dear girl. I know."

"Have you come to tell me what they're going to do to me?" she asked quietly.

"I came to tell you that it's okay to give in, Zephera. Our world may be Light, but it's just as cruel and just as twisted as the Darkness. If you want to give in to your dark side, let it reign; that is just fine. It's up to you to choose who you are."

"Why are you saying this?"

Baleem bowed his head in shame. "You and the others are to be executed at dawn."

Zephera nodded, taking in her master's words. She stood to face him, putting her fingers through the bars of the small window.

Baleem wrapped his hand around them and met her eyes. "Whoever you decide to be, Zephera, I'll be proud of you. You have grown into such an amazing young woman. I'm honored that you let me be a part of your life. And I'm so sorry for not telling you everything sooner."

"Thank you, Baleem," she said softly. "Take care of Zad, will you? There has to be a cure. And tell him I'm sorry."

Baleem nodded. "Goodbye, Zephera," he said, and then he was gone, leaving her to await her fate.

She didn't particularly want to die, but she was resigned to it. She couldn't stop the cycles, after all. Perhaps she could next time. Whoever she became, she hoped it was someone who had the strength to put an end to this madness.

She didn't sleep the rest of the night. Instead, she paced the floor, thinking of all that had occurred and all that she had lost.

When the dawn came, she stood as her cell door opened and held her hands up to be cuffed by the guards. Holding her head high, she felt no fear, for she was the Lady of Death, and she was ready to meet him.

She was led to a large stone room with three wooden blocks in the center. The guard took her to the center block. "Kneel," he ordered.

They were soon joined by four other guards, who shoved a scared looking Valessa to her knees on Zephera's left. Daegan knelt to her right, his face tight and ready to face his end.

The door opened and the king strutted in, followed by his personal masked guards, Baleem, and the executioner. Zephera looked at the king, defiance in her eyes.

"So, you decided to work with filth and evil, Zephera? Such a pity. I'd hoped this reincarnation of you would show more promise."

Zephera's eyes widened in surprise.

The king laughed loudly, his boisterous demeanor filling the small room. "Yes, Zephera, I'm your father. I'm surprised you are just now realizing it. This time, you seemed so intelligent. I'd hoped that you would help me this cycle, to rid this world of the black taint that seeks to consume it. But I guess I was wrong. Such a pity you have to die yet again." He smiled at her cruelly.

"You are a dark stain on this world, father." She spat at his feet.

He bent down and lifted her chin with his hand. "You're just like your mother. So spirited, even as you face death's door." He punched her, and she tasted the familiar coppery taste of blood.

Zephera smiled. "I would gladly die time and time again if it meant that you suffered."

He hit her again and then patted her face. "One day, my dear daughter. One day you'll understand. Until next time, my dear."

He walked to a chair near the wall and took a seat, motioning for Baleem and the executioner to start.

Baleem stood over a sobbing Valessa. She was bound in an extra layer of black magicked ropes to keep her from porting or using her magic. He pulled the dark amulet from her neck. She cried out as he did. "Please! Please, Baleem!"

"Stop your whining, woman," Baleem hissed. "Any last words?"

Valessa only cried.

Baleem nodded slightly, "Very well, then. You are hereby sentenced to death for aiding and abetting darkness and working to overthrow the King of Lucent, Gregour. May your gods have mercy on your tainted soul." He waved his hand, and the executioner swung a large axe.

Zephera watched as Valessa's head was severed from her body and fell to the ground with a thud. She looked at her hand on the floor. The cool tile drank in the warmth of the blood now pooling around her body.

Valessa's blood slowly seeped between her fingers.

Baleem stood in front of her next. "Zephera Travelle, you have betrayed me, your master, head of the Guild. You are also guilty of treason against your country and king. You have been sentenced to die for your crimes. Any last words?"

She met his eyes and smiled sadly. "I didn't mean to hurt you, sir, but as for the other charges—betraying a mad king? I would gladly do it again if it meant that he was kept from ruling this cruel world."

Baleem bowed. "Farewell, Zephera. Show no mercy," he said coldly to the executioner, his eyes boring into Zephera's.

She felt the light kiss of the axe against her neck and the rush as the executioner raised it above his head. She braced herself for the final blow. But it didn't come.

She heard a thud as Baleem tackled the executioner to the ground. "NOW, Morwynn!" he yelled. Zephera sat up at looked around as the room descended into chaos.

One of the king's guards ripped their mask from her face. "Morwynn?" Zephera gasped, bewildered. It was her old tutor.

Baleem threw the amulet to her and Morwynn opened it. She spoke quickly in a language Zephera didn't recognize and a bright light shot from the amulet to reveal an opening between worlds.

Morwynn bowed to Baleem. "Goodbye, my old friend." she said as she stepped through the portal and motioned for Zephera and Daegan to follow her.

"Run, Zephera! Quickly!" Baleem called as he slit a guard's throat while fending off another. She was frozen in fear. There he was, her master, giving his life for her. She didn't want to leave him.

"Baleem?" was all she could say.

He smiled at her as he slit a guard's throat. "I, too, am filled with Darkness." He grimaced as a sword went through his shoulder. "Go now, my girl! GO!"

Zephera ran to the portal, looking at Baleem one last time before she stepped through. The thud of an axe filled her ears as the door between realms slammed shut. Falling to the ground, she struggled to breathe. Her choked sobs filled the silent air as the world as she had known it came to an end.

She felt a warm hand on her shoulder and she looked up into Morwynn's familiar face. "Welcome to my home: the Dark Realm."

Zephera's jaw dropped. "Who are you?"

Morwynn smiled. "I'm Morwynn Sorrowhand, and I was the Seventh. Baleem was the Second. He was a great man. He sacrificed himself for our worlds so they could be whole once more. When Gregour revealed himself this time, Baleem had a plan. He acted as if he wanted to bring an end to the cycles and joined with Gregour, who forced him to hunt down our brothers and sisters of darkness and kill them to prove his loyalty. He told me of his plan and told me to disappear. I tracked down Daegan, the only one of us Gregour wasn't aware of, and together we decided that he would infiltrate the King of Lucent's court and gain his trust. It worked perfectly. We were so close to victory, but Valessa, that damned woman, was working with Gregour under false pretenses. He thought she was harvesting souls to give him more power. In reality, she just wanted the power for herself, for the person she hoped you would be. She deserved what she got. As for you, you have a choice to make. You can join us and help build an army of Darkness to fight in the war that your father is sure to bring. Or you can die." She pointed her blade at Zephera.

"Morwynn, she's on our side," Daegan warned.

"Are you, Zephera? Because if you are, you must let the darkness that lives inside of you out. We will reunite our realms and bring balance to the world—with or without you." Morwynn held the amulet between her long fingers.

Zephera looked at Daegan. "And you, what do you think?" she asked him.

Daegan stared at her in silent determination. "I told you that Darkness isn't always bad. Just like Light isn't always good. It's up to you, Zephera, to choose who you want to be. Good or bad, you always have a choice."

Zephera let Daegan's words sink in. She smiled as she remembered a poem that Baleem had always recited: *The Raven's Prophecy.*

> *An angel of midnight, with raven's wings*
> *Swept silently over the land.*
> *His eyes like an onyx and starless sky,*

He held her in ebony hands.
His Darkness wrapped her in warm embrace,
To whisper of all that he knows.
"Fear not the shadows, sweet child," he said.
"For the ink drip of night's in your soul."

She finally understood. She was Zephera Travelle, born of Dark and Light. She had a choice, a destiny—one that her mother had created for her. It wasn't until this moment that she felt like she truly belonged, that she alone mattered. She took the amulet from Morwynn's hand. The power of both worlds pulsed from within. She closed her hand around it tightly and looked up at the dark night sky. It wasn't much different from the sky back home. The stars shone brighter here, making her feel alive.

Her lips curved devilishly as she closed her eyes, letting her dark soul expand throughout her body. She felt power unlike any she had ever tasted before. She laughed at the sensation and put the amulet over her head. Her whole life, she had tried to conceal this side of herself, letting it out only to hunt and kill. Zadkiel had worked tirelessly to squash this power within her. She smiled at Morwynn and Daegan and took a breath of new life. They wanted darkness? She would give it to them. She let out a harsh burst of laughter as the Darkness enveloped her heart, devouring the last bit of Light she had left.

Darkness she became.

The End of Book 1 of the Age of Endings Series

ACKNOWLEDGMENTS

First and foremost thank you to my husband Callan. Thank you for listen to me ramble at 3am about the crazy ideas in my brain. You are the light to my dark. Thank you to our son Archer, without whom I would have finished this book ages ago.

Amy Carpenter: The best critique partner and friend a girl could ever have. You helped make Zephera into the badass she is today. You have been a fantastic friend who has gone above and beyond for Secret of Souls. Thank you!

Alyssa Kelso: My beautiful friend and critique partner, and fellow author. Girl, thank you for your constant inspiration and love. You were there for me when I needed it the most. You are always there to pick me up when I need it, and shake me when I am being an idiot. You are my rockstar!

To the Bookish Babes Book Club: What would I do without your support? You have all been there for me since day one. Cheering me on, buying my book and writing reviews. Thank you all! You have managed to make this cold heart beat. Now stop it, feelings are hard.

To Quill15: Gosh darn it you guys…I am so grateful for your critique and guidance. We have shared many laughs, cries, accomplishments, and failures. I love you all so very much. Thank you!

Kristen Lane and Diana Ault: Now if there were ever 2 people who I could call best friends, you two would be it. You have been there for me in my darkest moments. You managed to stay friends with me, even when all I talked about were my characters and their story. I am sure I got to be really annoying, but you listened to me ramble nonetheless. Thank you ladies for helping me create such a powerful and beautiful world. Seriously, the long drives, the SOS calls, the 3 hour one sided conversations we had. I owe you one!

Aunt Camille: You have been with me every step of the way. You were there when Zephera was just an idea in my head. When she was a character in a few chapters of some crazy story I was going to finish one day… Thank you for seeing Zephera as the fierce, beautiful assassin she is and supporting my dream.

To my editor John Dixon: I am pretty sure you summon demons in your spare time. You are blunt, scary and made my dark soul cry. But you made *Secret of Souls* into a masterpiece. You took it at its worst, and molded it into a fantastic novel. I adore you! I still think you are possessed sometimes, but with what you had to work with I suppose it couldn't be helped. Thank you for all of your hard work!

To my team at Shadow Wolf Press: Awww shucks, you guys! I am so grateful for the day I found you. You all have gone above and beyond to make *Secret of Souls* what it is. I am so grateful for your hands on approach. I am sure I got a little annoying with all of my questions, but thank you Arleen and Wendy for being so kind and patient with me. I love all of you guys!

Sarah J. Maas: Not only are you my favorite author, but you also saved my life. I was going through a rough patch a few years ago. When I read the words one of your characters said to herself, it not only saved my life, but I repeat it to myself daily. "My name is Aubrie Nixon, and I will not be afraid." Your words have inspired me to go after my dreams! Thank you!

Acknowledgments

Mom and Dad: You two are the cutest parents in existence. Thank you mom, for quite literally being my vessel into this world. I couldn't have written *Secret of Souls* without you. Thank you for the sweet packages, and sweet letters of inspiration you sent me. They made me ugly cry. My cry face would put Kim K's to shame. Thank you for always supporting my reading habits (aka by moonlight after it was time for bed) and not getting too upset when I was exhausted the next day. Thank you dad, for supporting me in my dreams, and always telling me to reach for the stars.

Last but not least, thank you to my readers. I am so grateful you decided to pick up a copy of Secret of Souls. I would not be a success story without your support and interest in this story.

I hope you enjoyed the ride, and hang on for more!

AUBRIE NIXON plays mom to the cutest demon topside and believes she is married to the hottest man in the Air Force.

When she isn't writing, she is daydreaming about hot brooding anti-heroes and sassy heroines. She loves *Dragon Age*, *Game of Thrones*, and reading all things fantasy.

She runs a local YA/NA book club with 3 chapters and over 200 members. Her favorite thing to do is eat, and her thighs thank her graciously for it. If she could have dinner with anyone living or dead it would be Alan Rickman because she thinks his voice is the sexiest sound on earth. He could read the dictionary and she would be enthralled.

Her current mission in life is to collect creepy taxidermy animals because she finds them cute and hilarious. She resides just outside of Washington DC.

Shadow Wolf Press

We hope you have enjoyed *Secret of Souls* by Aubrie Nixon.

CPSIA information can be obtained
at www.ICGtesting.com
Printed in the USA
FFOW02n0533110418
46197044-47455FF